# THE TYGER STRIPED BOY

## ELIZABETH COOKE

1

REBECCA

Eden begins to burn at four in the morning.

I run from the house in the half-light, following the child who's been sent to find me. Long Acre is silent, as if the whole of London holds its breath. In my panic I realise I haven't even put on my shoes.

When I finally see the flames at Drury Lane, up comes the old fear.

'Where's Mr Eliot?' I shout, grabbing the first man who runs past.

'In there,' he says. 'Saving his paradise.'

The men from the water cart are stamping on the flaming pile of fabric. One of the actresses is crying by the door.

'Give me your boots!'

'What?'

'Your boots, your shoes!'

In fright, she hands them to me. They almost fit.

The noise when I get inside is monstrous. I look up and see the ceiling of the old theatre crack. People run out carrying seats, cushions, scenery. The Tree Of Knowledge goes past me. A maid, squalling, staggers down the stairs with acres of costume, yards of silk that trip her up. An outspread fan lands at my feet, the big one from Naples, the one that covers Eve until the last moment, decorated with The Serpent.

I'm nearly knocked over by Hemp, our helper. 'Where is he? Where's the master?' I shout.

Hemp is black with soot. 'It weren't my fault. The burner went over. The behemoth kicked it. The curtains caught a'fire.'

'Weren't you watching her?'

'She moved in the night,' he protests.

I want to floor him. 'Where's the master?'

'In the wings. Trying to get the animals out.'

There's a team inside: Sheridan's men. Stagehands. I recognise most of them.

*Lord Jesus, where is he?*

They're struggling with the birdcages: the macaws flutter inside like multi-coloured snow. Yellow and green bodies beat the bars. One of the team of men has Gimcrack on his back: our monkey, a capuchin, little ruff-framed face staring, who now clings for dear life and bares her teeth. We named her for the horse of the Earl Grosvenor who won so many races, because Gimcrack was quick, and this monkey is quick like lightning. But I can't prise her from the man's collar.

'Take her out,' I tell him. 'Where's the other?'

We have her mate, Jem. They do tricks: thieving, counting.

'I don't know,' he says, sweat running into his eyes. The team staggers onwards.

I can hardly see. Joseph once told me he feared for the theatre roof; that it couldn't stand even the weight of the walls. Will it stand this? I look towards the stage and it's a charred mouth, paint peeling in strips. They're pumping water from the barrels and a black river is flowing on the floor. Smoke billows to the darkness of the roof.

There's a deafening crash on the stage. I run as fast as I can, choking on the smoke. I'm soaked with water as I pass. The floor is a slithering lake. Shouts come from the wings. I clamber up the steps where the great velvet curtains hang in tatters. The tree ferns from the New World that cost Joseph so much are charred stalks twenty feet high.

I see him then behind the stage shutters, the ones that pull out like doors. He and three others – these I don't recognise, perhaps he has just called the biggest men off the street, for they look mighty disturbed by their job – have our rhinoceros, Molly, by her chain. The sight of Joseph Eliot, great ringmaster, the great showman himself, trying to pour beer down the throat of our beast to keep her calm makes me want to laugh in the face of all the destruction. He looks up and catches sight of me, and I see the man is covered in muck: soil, straw, water, grime. There's a moment while he stares at me, the flagon up-ended in the behemoth's mouth. And then he starts to laugh too.

'It'll take me a week to clean off your linen,' I tell him. 'Do you think I've nothing better to do?'

The rhinoceros snorts and finishes. Her eyes, like ours, stream water.

'We won't worry about the theatre,' Joseph says. 'Just your struggle in the laundry.' He holds out his hand. I pick my way across trampled angels' wings, raising an eyebrow at the ruined costumes.

'They fled,' he tells me. 'Apparently.'

'Angels are known for it.'

He takes hold of my hand and places it on the chain, and I press my face to the armour of the animal, the loose flaps of leather, the nicked and mottled horn, and the smarting eye. She's got no teeth left to speak of, and her horn is blunted. I breathe into her mouth. 'There now, there now.' I pull the chain gently, she moves, and I back her down the slippery ramp. The men push her from behind, squawking like children.

'Hush your noise,' I say. 'There's no need of it.'

Joseph has gone to the floor of the theatre, and walks away, clapping his hands, bawling orders. We get Molly down and through the theatre and manage her out of the entrance. A great sighing shout goes up from those gathered on the street, but they keep away for fear of her. Hemp runs towards us and throws his arms around Molly's neck, and the beast's eyes flicker.

'I'm to take her to the 'Change,' he tells me.

I let her go. She's as docile as a baby now. On the ground is a playbill, such as those Hemp has been giving out.

*New Theatre Royal, Covent Garden, this present Wednesday June 16th, will perform a NEW COMEDY... and afterwards Harlequin's Museum with new machinery and TRICKS...*

*And to be enacted A FOX CHACE with hounds and horses, and FINALLY to the wonder of the AGE, PARADISE itself with a company of ANGELS and the GREAT BEHEMOTH and wondrous other BEASTS and FIRE...*

An omen, perhaps. A warning. Fire.

I'm soaked to the skin, and now the rhinoceros is not near me, nor am I needed, the nearest in the crowd begin to laugh.

'You, missus!' says the man closest to me. 'I know why that thing follows you.'

'Oh yes?' I take a step towards him. The sun's coming out; it's warm on my neck. 'And why is that?'

He starts to snigger. 'You look the same.' He turns to the other men around him. 'Got the same face.' He can hardly speak for laughing. 'You got shrivelled up in fire?'

He drops the bottle he's holding when I smack him in the mouth. Wheeling arm, full-handed. I look at them all. I haven't been Joe Eliot's right hand for these twelve years without learning to keep order. Two women at the back begin to whoop and holler. Hands on my hips, I wait for the hissing and murmuring and the back-row yelling to subside, and for the jesting man who thinks himself such a clown to slink away holding his face. 'Any more?' I ask them. 'Any more?'

There is no more.

I walk back to Long Acre, thinking there'll be no paradise tonight, and no Mrs Bartholomew singing, nor the Italian operetta, nor the leaps and japes of the boy Grimaldi, or any other entertainment. But we will rise again, like Christ on the third day. The heretical thought I shall keep to myself, but it's true. Joe and I have risen a dozen times from the ashes.

Joe comes home late in the evening. So tired he can hardly put one foot in front of the other. I place the food on the table in front of him, and sit to one side by the hearth.

When he puts down his knife, he and I hold each other's gaze. 'Just a small burner, to keep the beasts warm,' he says. 'And so much damage.'

'To keep Hemp warm, more like. To light his pipe.'

'Aye.' Joe looks past me.

I wonder at him being able to stay there at all, when the memories must have been licking at his sight, just as flames were licking at the edges of the theatre steps. Putting other faces in the place of those this morning.

'I thought of...' I begin. But he holds up his hand to silence me. He knows.

Eventually he begins to murmur about the animals and the actors. He has other trades as well as being a paradise maker for the theatres: there are the animal menagerie cages at Tottenham Fields and the Harlequin public house, and the stage at Greenwich Fair where he is showing *The Death of Orsina and the Appearance of the Accusing Spirit* this month. He doesn't keep track of the costs that well. But I hear it all, remember it all. He keeps my mind like a kind of notebook. He will say, 'What did I contract that actor for, a shilling, or three shillings? And for how long?'

I don't read and write. I remember.

I remember the reliable ones and the ones who can't be trusted. Like Fallow, who was supposed to give extracts as Shylock and was found, instead, dead drunk in a ditch on the first night, lying with a sailor and singing sea shanties at the top of his precious voice.

Joe regards me. 'What shall I do with Hemp?' he says.

'Whatever you want.'

'Molly might have died, and there would have been five thousand guineas lost. And Sheridan is after me for the cost of the fire.'

'Sheridan?' I tell him. 'The building's falling down. He means to raise another anyway.'

'Does he indeed,' Joseph murmurs. 'Where did you hear that?'

'About.' I stretch out my legs, and cross my feet.

'That's useful to know, Rebecca.'

I watch him as he starts to fall asleep with his head on the table, and then I take the plate away. *Yes, I'm useful to you*, I think. 'Go to bed,' I tell him. 'You never came home last night, so you must need your sleep.'

He doesn't stir. 'There's worse,' he murmurs. 'Look here.'

He's wearing the greatcoat of winter. Out of one of its inner pockets he takes something: something loose wrapped in a piece of cotton twill. Something small. He lays it on the table, and carefully opens the fabric piece by slow piece, and there contained within it is the body of Jem, the other capuchin monkey. 'He was found in the stage curtains when they pulled them down,' he says.

I sit next to him and together, in the candlelight, we look at this little body. So human in form, especially still dressed in the clothes the master had made for him: a velvet waistcoat with a black velvet ribbon around it. The capuchin seems very peaceful, as if asleep, though his fur is brittle from the heat, and the hair is completely gone from his small hands.

'He must have tried to climb,' I murmur.

'Yes, to climb,' Joe says. He puts his face in his hands, rests his elbows on the table, the very picture of sorrow.

'Joseph,' I say, quiet as I can. I reach out and touch his shoulder. I wonder if, this once – only this once – I should take this man in my arms. Would it hurt him so much to be taken in my arms? It would be dark; he need not look at me. But in a moment he wipes his face, shrugs away my hand and picks up Jem, wrapping him again in the cloth. He carries the little bundle with him and I hear him climb the stairs.

I listen. I look at what I've made for him here. The house that I keep so neatly, so carefully, so fiercely, for him. It's my pride. When we first arrived in London we had nothing at all. Nothing. We both lived with Blakestone's menagerie, sleeping under the cages out in the fields. Rain, snow, shine. Two refugees from something we could not name but which kept us both richly in nightmares. The place we had come from. Neither of us with shoes. We ate what we peeled from the animals' food: vegetable shavings, fat from the meat. I was only nine years old, and he seventeen.

Look at us now. I still follow him like a shadow – a roaring shadow, mind – but we are here in the Long Acre house. Frontage on the street, but a large yard behind, a smokehouse and a washhouse. A gate with a lock. Large windows, three floors, a cellar. We're respectable personages. We sleep no more in the mud and, if you please, we have a passageway upstairs that separates the rooms. I sleep in the kitchen, but Eliot sleeps in a bed. A fine carved bed, mahogany. It has a straw mattress below and a feather one above. With linen sheets that I make sure are white and pressed. And both of the mattresses are punched and turned and aired and shook by me twice a week to keep them fresh. Which means I've got the strength to strike any man who makes remarks about me in the street.

Joe took me with him as he made his way in the world. So I pray now for the man standing at the top of the stairs holding poor little Jem and weeping to himself, thinking I cannot hear.

This is the man they say has no heart because he keeps animals and makes them prance and perform, and insults God by building a paradise.

But I know different.

# 2

## JOSEPH

I came to London as a boy, but quickly became a man.

Of all the changes that came upon me in this city, Sophia Baddeley was the first. Her shoes I see still. Of yellow brocade and an arched sole like the curve of a bridge so impossibly high; a very pointed toe, and black ribbon lacing. The decoration over this shoe was of the gaudiest and most brilliant embroidered design: bright purple flowers and green vines and leaves, and white birds delicately sown.

I looked up the wooden stair at the back of the New Theatre Royal and saw the shoes of Sophia Baddeley descending, and white stockings above them, and all the glorious remainder of her. She was an actress and courtesan of great fame. A woman they called a 'toast' – the toast of all London.

Until then, I'd been a keeper in Blakestone's Circus menagerie that came to London eight times a year, churning through muddy wastes and dusty summer roads, through towns and green wildernesses such as the place I had been born, field after wood after field after wood. Hills where we slipped backwards as much as we moved forwards. Downward gradients that tore at the brakes on the wheel rims. I tended the twenty-four horses that pulled the tyger cages, and Rebecca tended them with me, child though she was.

And every time I came to London, I longed to stay.

This city is a place like no other, wrapped in fog for eight months a year entirely, where even at noonday carts and carriages and coaches run into each other; but it has given me everything. Blakestone used to send Rebecca and I to Billingsgate and Smithfield twice a week to find food for the beasts, with two guineas folded in a linen pocket handkerchief and kept inside my shirt. We picked our way over the fish-smelling stones of Billingsgate, and when the slow breeze was blowing from the river, caught the black dusty coat of coal from the collier ships moored at the Coal Exchange. There might be seven hundred there at once, come from Newcastle. Colliers and whalers, and the fishwives hacking at whale meat. One year I saw porpoises in the river, many of them, skirting the whalers as if they knew the cargoes.

Fish and coal. Oranges from Spain. Straw falling from market carts, flies settling on the goods in summer, ice coating stacks of potatoes in winter. Red-raw hands on reins, on stalls, on wet fish slabs. Sewer-running streets. Brazier fires. The reek of whoreish perfumes, the close breath of beer. Noise that we never heard in the countryside, of hackney coaches and jostling sedans and coronet-decorated carriages with gilded doors. White-coated painted faces. Pink-flesh masks on men and women. London Bridge bell ringing fifteen minutes before high tide. Sweat-drenched crowds of the theatres: all pressed together in memory.

And one night I walked with Blakestone – he was old then, complaining of the high heat in September – and we went through the streets at two in the morning, in the darkness down through Whitehall Gate where the cows from St James's Park were tethered at night; down the great wide thoroughfare of Cheapside under the dome of St Paul's, past the Tower, and down east Smithfield. We came out by the gardens and orchards of Pennington Tree. And there in the drifting mist from the river, as if a dream had come to life, we saw an elephant brought up from the docks.

The beast had come from Bengal, a gift for the king and not six months old, its handlers on each side and the seamen following like a ghost band of bedraggled and silent admirers. And the animal's head swayed from one side to the other, its trunk exploring the ground and crowding walls. And it touched also those who, like us, quiet-lined the alleys and had come to see. Such a creature. Such a strange apparition.

I looked up at it as it passed, and felt the otherness of it, the unknown of it. I knew at once that I wanted this as my future. Great beasts of the world brought here across the oceans, to walk up London fields and streets, bringing India and Africa and China with them, pulling the whole world behind them. I wanted it all; the remarkable and fantastical. To put my hand upon it. To close my fist upon it. I wanted the circus ring and the theatre audience, and the spellbinding play, and the music, and all the painted faces turned towards me.

My dreams knew no boundaries. And most of all – though I never expected this to be more than fantasy, even in my greatly vaulted ambitions – I wanted the woman that reigned them all that year, greater than all the actresses even though she was so young. I wanted, to add to my phantasmagorical world, Sophia Baddeley.


Sophia's husband was then playing Moses in Sheridan's *School for Scandal*. I don't know that he played much else; not that I remember. He plays it still. Such a one he was for the ladies, and then he eloped with the king's trumpet player's daughter. Sophia Snow. The lovely and debauched siren of the stage.

She was more famous than the prince's current mistresses, however many there were of those. She was Melbourne's, and the Duke of York's and then years later she took the American to her bed who was put in the Tower for high treason. Ah, my Sophia. Foolish, headstrong and dark of purpose.

So, then. An innocent I was, and smelling of beasts. She was a cloud of perfume but under that – yes, under that was an unmistakable soft reek; something from her skin neither unpleasant nor pleasant, but it addicted a man immediately, as laudanum can, as ratafia that is cherry kernels and bitter almonds – yes, something of that, the liqueur that kills a man. Or hashish or hemp that the Mohock men bring to the city. It was such a soft sweet drug when she looked at you. I'm talking of something other than the unwashed smell of those heavy dresses, and the faint aroma of tallow that inhabited even the finest houses; nor the greasy white lead pancake on her hands, to show white fingers in her stage gestures. No, there was something else. Something impossible to resist.

She smiled at me lingeringly that day as she passed on the narrow stair. The servant behind her cuffed me for staring at her, and laughed. She dragged glamour in her wake like a cloak, a train; sweeping up souls as she walked. She was at her height then, and only two years older than me. She had just separated from her husband the previous month, so I was told. But there was no licentiousness in her person. No sign of it. There was not a pock-mark on her skin; and she carried no mask. On that day, as she passed me on the stairs, her hair was more finely dressed than I had ever seen: so elaborate and so high it was hard to believe that it was real hair. Perhaps most of it was not.

The birds embroidered on the shoes were replicated in the hair, a crowd of them with wings spread.

I next saw her again when she played Ophelia. It was a month or two later. I'd not been able to stop thinking about her. Again, I stood at the bottom of the stairs at the theatre, in the guttering light of the oil cauldron by the door. Night after night. Sometimes Rebecca stood with me, pulling at my sleeve. I tried to stop her coming after me from the menagerie, but she would insist. She was just thirteen by then, and a dangerous age to be anywhere near Covent Garden, where there are twenty thousand whores and some of them younger than she, and many a man watching for new flesh. Even a walking disfigurement such as she.

'Why are you waiting for her?' she asked, sulking. 'She's a tart, that's all.'

'And what do you know of tarts?' I asked. 'You shouldn't know them, or talk of them.'

'I see plenty. Swarms of them on Piccadilly, every other yard.'

'That's as may be. Where is the wardrobe woman?'

'Snoring in the dressing room.'

I took two pence out of my pocket and gave them to her. 'Ask her to give you supper.'

Rebecca took the money, but still pouted. She picked the paint from the door, and kicked it softly over and over again with her bare heel. My Lord God, she was brutally thin despite all the pastry she ate. Wrists like sticks, knuckles jutting from her hands; the collarbone showing in an ugly fashion from the neck of the dirty dress. She had stuck a yellow flower in her cap – for what reason I didn't fathom – and she looked clownish, poor gawky girl. 'Where are you going to be?' she demanded. 'Come with me. The wardrobe woman'll feed us both. She likes you.'

'Go away and I'll see you tomorrow.'

Rebecca gave me her lopsided grin. 'Sophia Baddeley won't look at you. She won't give you the time of day.'

'I know it,' I said. 'But go anyway.'

She obeyed me, because she always did. My burned-grey shadow.

I must have had a premonition to give Rebecca that instruction, because it was that same night I was at last rewarded. Just a few minutes later, Sophia Baddeley appeared alone, in a hurry, and in a rage. She was still tying the laces of her dress behind, and two high spots of colour were on her cheeks. She halted on the steps when she saw me. I could hear the play still going on above. 'You, boy,' she said. 'Why do you haunt me? Who are you?'

'If you please, ma'am, I'm the animal boy from Blakestone's Circus.'

'Animal?' she said, perplexed, and then realising. 'Not the one in Tottenham Fields? You smell like an animal, too.'

'Yes, ma'am.'

She looked me up and down. 'Have you ever had a bath?'

'I've washed at the pump this morning.'

'What do you mean, the pump?' she demanded. 'You don't mean the pump in the streets?'

'Yes, ma'am.'

She put her hands on her hips. 'I suspect you to truly be an animal,' she said. She took a step towards me and prodded me with her fingertip. 'What are you, lion or ape? A fox, perhaps? A hound?'

'No, ma'am.'

'A rabbit then.' She laughed. I was astonished to see that her teeth were good, as perfect as her face. 'Do you have a name?'

'Joseph.'

'Such refinement in one so wretched. Just Joseph, no other?'

'Eliot, ma'am.'

She tilted her head. 'Well then, Joseph Eliot, can you call a carriage? Does the rabbit speak more than two words?'

I ran out across the yard and onto Drury Lane, and when they heard who the occupant would be, three or four of them took to fighting to get closest, muddling up the horses so they stamped on the icy ground. It was December, and while the theatre was all boiling heat, out here it was bitterly cold. She came running out, looking back over her shoulder. A door was opened for her. I stood watching, smiling.

'Get in,' she ordered.

It was as if the lion had told me to get in the cage.

'Get in, get in,' she commanded. I did so and crept into the far corner; but it was difficult for I was tall. She looked out of the window and I glimpsed a gentleman coming through the alley towards the cab. Sophia grabbed my coat, pushed me to the floor, hissed, 'Say not a word,' and covered me with her skirts.

Oh my God, my God.

I heard a mild, enquiring voice. 'Sophia my love, I have my own carriage. Sophia my love...'

'Drive on!' Sophia yelled. The cab lurched forward. I heard the man crying pitifully, like a little boy, calling her name, promising her a thousand guineas. A few moments passed, and then she shook me out from under her skirts as she would shake lice from her hem. Her petticoats were silk. Her legs were bare.

'Who was it?' I asked.

'Peniston Lamb. Lord Melbourne,' she replied, full of contempt.


What shall I say of her? What shall I say of the astounding rooms?

A woman called Mary met us as we got out of the cab.

There was a boy in the hall, and a manservant beyond in the shadows.

'Where is His Lordship?' the woman asked.

'I've left him behind.'

'For what reason?'

'He was insulting.'

'What was the price?'

'Only a thousand.'

This conversation was conducted as she took off rings; the woman caught them before they hit the floor. She glanced up at me.

'This is Joseph,' Sophia said. 'He has saved me.' She looked back at me. They both did. An assessment. 'Come upstairs. You look half-starved.'

'There's food in the kitchen for him,' Mary objected. She was a short woman with a cold, knowing eye. She looked something like a man; was broad-shouldered, large-handed.

Sophia fixed her with a stare. 'Come with me,' she told me.

I thought of the thousand guineas as I went up. The nicest of girls in Covent Garden – good girls, whores of clergymen – commanded perhaps two guineas a night. The manservant in the hall downstairs might be paid five guineas a year. I was paid nothing at my own work but board and lodging.

She opened a door. The manservant was running up the stairs at our back – she pointed at me to go inside. She slammed the door in his face.

'His Lordship is at the door,' he called.

'Tell him I am most unwell. I shall receive him tomorrow.'

I heard him going down the stairs, his footsteps crossing the stone entrance hall. I heard voices outside. I was shaking with fear. I had no idea what she wanted with me. I was in the bedroom of Melbourne's mistress. If His Lordship came upstairs she might cry out that I was dishonouring her or worse. He would have me thrown into prison.

'Please, ma'am, I must go,' I whispered.

She raised an eyebrow. 'Are you afraid of him?' She sat slowly on the bed. 'Don't you know what they say of him? He is of no consequence anywhere.'

I stared down at the Turkey carpet Melbourne's money had put on the floor.

She was taking off her shoes. 'You know what he's going to build on Piccadilly, don't you?' she said. 'A three-storey mansion. Do you know what it will cost?'

'No, madam.'

'One hundred thousand pounds.' She kicked the shoes away. 'One hundred thousand pounds! And here am I in such a hovel as this. Do you not think that terrible?' She was looking me up and down. 'Melbourne House,' she murmured. 'And his wife will command it. Lady Melbourne. Elizabeth Lamb. She is a clever one. Don't you know that?'

'Indeed, I do not know, ma'am.' There were roses woven into the pattern of the carpet. They seemed important at that moment. I was three strides from the door, struck with panic, sweat running down my spine.

Sophia was hitching up her skirts. 'Do you know that she fucks Coleraine, and has her eyes on Egremont? Lord Coleraine has spoken of selling her to Egremont for £13,000. Is that not whoredom? Egremont, with his fifteen other mistresses and forty bastard children. A fine upstanding man indeed!'

'Indeed, I did not know,' I whispered. I took a step backwards.

She laid back, propping herself on one elbow. 'Am I pretty?' she asked.

I could not reply.

'Joseph,' she said quietly. 'Look at me. Am I pretty?'

I looked. And there was Venus, framed by the silk of the underclothes and the heavy satins of the bed and the white linen of the pillows, and blushing rosy in the reflection of the fire.

'Even Melbourne's children say he is a drunk, or acts as if he were drunk all the time,' she told me. 'Come here, Joseph. Do you think it is pleasant to be bedded by a fumbling drunk? He is an old man. The women in Covent Garden must tolerate it, for they have no choice. The whole world is drunk there at any hour of the day. But I am not a woman from the streets. He mummers and paws and forgets himself. Do I not deserve better than that?'

Downstairs, doors slammed. To the accompaniment of a clattering of hooves, I heard the carriage pull away outside. 'He would never come in if I say I am indisposed,' Sophia reassured me. 'For whatever else he is, he is a gentleman. A gentleman does not break down doors.' She began to laugh. 'I never saw a man shake so much as you.'

'I must be leaving, madam. If it please you.'

'It does not,' she retorted. 'Am I not as good as Elizabeth, my lady Viscountess? Am I not worth more than a thousand guineas? Would I be worth £13,000?'

'Much more,' I said.

She smiled bewitchingly. 'What would you pay for me, Joseph?' She spread her legs.

'All I had.'

She beckoned me.

'Madam, forgive me, I am not clean,' I said. 'My hands are not clean. My clothes...'

She reached for me. 'I am sick of soft clean hands,' she told me.

I was all night with Sophia Baddeley.

I was told some years later that there was a landowner in Scotland who sold ten thousand acres to pay for twelve night hours with her. And yet I had her for free.

We slept until eleven in the morning. She woke me herself with a tray on which there was a silver pot of hot chocolate. I did not like it; I had never had such a thing.

She laughed prodigiously. 'Why, Joseph,' she said. 'What a face you pull! Are you sure that you are not an ape? I see your teeth when you curl your lip.'

'It's too sweet.'

'Fine, then.'

'No. I must return to Blakestone's. I'm sorry.'

She was lying half on top of me. 'To boast of me?'

'No, never.'

'Is there a show today?'

'Every day.'

'And how long do you all stay in London?'

'Not long. It's December. Christmas in a week. We go to Tilbury.'

'Tilbury? What is there but mud and marshes?'

'The dock. Winter quarters. And a ship is coming from Tunisia. Blakestone is receiving a camelopard. Or says he is. It might just be the skin.'

She sat back in astonishment. 'There is no such thing.'

I was putting on my clothes, despite her trying to keep them from me. We laughed together; we did much of that in the time we had. 'In Mr Hunter's house in Leicester Square there are all kinds of monsters. He means to have a camelopard too,' I told her.

Even then, I worshipped Hunter, the king's surgeon. He used to drive from Earl's Court to London in a waggon pulled by water buffalo. He had many wondrous animals, and he was a genius anatomist both of animals and men. He had stolen the carcase of Charles Byrne, The Irish Giant, boiled him down to bones and displayed him, even though the Giant had paid for his body to be buried at sea to keep it out of Hunter's hands. Hunter kept the bodies of quintuplets in five glass jars, and hundreds and hundreds of other fantastical things. Other men wanted to be like him – there were many freak shows in London, as there are now – but there was only one Hunter.

Sophia sulked on the bed. 'If you do not stay, I shall tell Melbourne that you have attacked me.'

I stared at her, and carried on dressing in a rather quicker fashion.

She leapt up at once. 'Joseph, I did not mean it.'

'It's all the same,' I told her.

She looked astonished. 'You don't care for me.'

'I don't care for threats.' I looked down at her. 'Blakestone waits for me, and I must go.'

'And celebrate Christmas on the dung heaps by the convict hulks.'

'It's not like that.' In truth, it was not. There were some fine hot and lawless inns down in the Essex marshes where a man could lose himself in splendid fashion.

'I don't know, for I've never been out of London,' she told me, circling her mouth with her finger. 'But I shall go and see Mr Hunter's monsters. Does he feed them? Does he sell tickets for the feeding, like the menagerie on the Strand – the 'Change?'

I laughed. 'Sophia, they are all dead. If he gets a camelopard, it'll be stuffed and will stand in his hallway.'

She dropped her hand, and then abruptly threw her arms around my neck. A cunning look came into her eye. 'If you had enough money to buy a living camelopard, you would not leave me. You would be a man in your own right, and not the servant of another.'

'Camelopards are the rarest thing on earth.'

She curled her lip, turned away, and walked to the window. She was thinking. When Sophia plotted, her shoulders hunched. She would put both fists to her face, and only drop them when she had her stratagem. She did that now, and then turned back to me. 'What is the greatest freak in Europe?' she asked.

I shrugged. 'What do you mean, a beast?'

'No. Anything.'

I thought a moment. 'I heard there's a woman in France who has a horn from her forehead, like a unicorn,' I said. 'I've seen drawings of a man in Italy who has a twin protruding from his stomach.'

'A twin?' She gasped in horror.

'His brother. The torso only. I saw in Taunton last year a kitten with five tails, but it died very quick.'

'Are such things worth money?'

'To show them is worth money.'

'And would you?'

'What, show a man with four hands, or a woman as a unicorn? Why not? They show themselves. It's the only way that they can live.'

She walked towards me, smiling. 'Joseph,' she murmured. 'Find such a monster. I will give you money to buy him, and money to display him. A building somewhere.'

'But that would cost a good deal.'

'What we don't tell Melbourne, Melbourne will not know.' She smiled. 'I shall tell him it is for a new hat. The finest hat indeed. He would not know the difference. He has no idea what anything costs. He once papered each tread of the stairs here in fifty-pound notes.' She laughed, and she put her hands upon a part of me that I shall not mention.

I bought an elephant and her newborn calf, and a pair of hyenas, a girl with lobster-claw feet, and a wonderful booth for them at the very top of Oxford Street, just two months later. Sophia said that I was a man of fine sense, as young as I was.

Six months after that, and with Melbourne's money that he cared so little about and had showered upon Sophia, I bought the tygers and the lion on Tottenham Fields from Blakestone.

3

REBECCA

'Becca,' Joseph asks me, 'would you like to go and see the songbirds?'

We've been standing in the 'Change on the Strand with his beloved beast, the soot-spattered rhinoceros, and for an hour he and the 'Change owner, Hallett, have been arguing about the cost of keeping her. I stand next to her cage. Molly's very old and sways slightly with the beer they give her. But I like her more than all the rest. Joseph comes to me and smiles. He puts his hand through the cage. 'Ah, my beauty,' he murmurs. 'You have cost me a king's ransom.'

I look across the room. There's a dromedary here that Joseph hires for the final scene of *Eden*. When Adam's pushed out of paradise, the rhinoceros and the dromedary walk across the stage. Joseph says the dromedary is a very sanguine animal. But I'd say it just thinks that the saunter across the stage at Drury Lane is part of his evening walk along the Strand. Molly is different. Sometimes we have to pull Molly by a rope. I understand her. If anyone tried to pull me by a rope, I'd do the same.

My job is to stand in the wings and try to tempt her with

hay or grass: she eats a hundred pounds of this in a single day, and it's a worry to bring the grass into London. Hemp arranges it; but most of the storage is in our backyard at Long Acre. We once had a field along Mary Bone Road, and a kind of stable there, but boys tormented the beast and she broke the fence. We found her wandering down Henrietta Street towards Cavendish Square. A woman climbed a tree to avoid her. It was a more interesting sight than an old and befuddled animal looking for a place to lie down. All I could do was stand by a fence and laugh, and Molly sauntered over to me and put her head down. The woman up in the tree screamed, but all Molly wanted was for me to scratch her ears. That, and the jug of beer that I was carrying.

She is a sweet-natured animal. I stroke her shoulder and wish they hadn't called her Behemoth on stage. She is much more a Molly: round and dour, clumpy-footed, square-rumped.

Joe is standing, one hand on his hip. I can tell he's plotting something by the way he frowns. 'There are four thousand birds in a warehouse in Ratcliffe Highway,' he says. 'Think of them let free at the end of the tableau.'

'And how would you catch them again?'

'We wouldn't,' he says. 'Some could be caught by the audience, and the birds that die overnight we could sell the next morning. Greenfinch pie.'

'Four thousand? In one night?'

'It could be a special performance when the theatre reopens. Special prices. To see the usual, plus the birds.'

'Sheridan would like it? Four thousand birds shitting on his newly furbished theatre?'

Joe laughs to himself. 'That's a point.' He looks disappointed for a moment, but then his face brightens. 'We'll go and see them anyway. It will be a walk, and on the way I might think of something else to do with them. Prentiss is shutting down and wants rid of them.'

He's happy now, a new project in his head, absurd as it is. He usually finds a way to make the absurd work, I'll give him that.

I turn back to our behemoth. Her breath's very ragged. I think she's been affected by the smoke. Her breathing sounds like water running down a drain. But she likes tobacco. In the theatre, when she smells pipe smoke, she occasionally lifts her head and moves it from side to side, and an expression of quiet ecstasy comes over her as she lays back her ears. I look now in her blank, unquestioning eye and wonder what worlds are within.

She came from India twenty years ago. She was captured as a baby, and kept as a pet, a conversation piece. Like all small animals, a baby rhinoceros is playful and much liked. When she got larger, she was traded to an Afghani merchant and then on to the Mediterranean, walking some of the way, carried in a cart in others. They told us she had a goat that walked with her, and that the goat was taken on board the Portuguese ship that carried her to Lisbon. Molly was chained to the deck and kept in a cage, and the goat wandered about and between her legs, together with chickens. If the goat was there, Molly was quiet. Only in Lisbon did she get bad-tempered, and that was when some fool slaughtered the goat and cooked it on the dockside. And that was when they apparently discovered the rhinoceros could be calmed with spirits dissolved in water. Kind that we are, us humans.

She came up through Spain and France, and was seen by the French king, and sold to a circus. But she wouldn't perform tricks like the elephants, and she took to grinding her head against walls and turning her back on her keepers. That's when Joseph heard of her. By this time – what would be four or five years ago now – she'd have been at least twenty years old, and with much fanfare and triumph we brought her to London, walking her up from Dover and selling tickets on the way.

It was like the old days that Joe and I spent sleeping under Blakestone's waggons when we were young. It rained a great deal, but I was happy. I was happy to be on the road again with him. I stayed with the beast, for sometimes in these ignorant rural places in Kent they wouldn't admit me to inns because of my face. And sometimes Joseph went in anyway and left me, and sometimes – once or twice and when perhaps a little drunk and the weather was better – he came and laid down under the cart with me.

Not in the way that men and women lie. No, never that. Never that.

But it was a good time. In the countryside, we tried walking at night, for we were less held up that way. We would stop at daylight near some village, and Joseph would have sent some lad on ahead to the gentry. Ladies and gentlemen, he charged a guinea to see her – a guinea! And they paid. The working people he charged a penny, and sometimes nothing at all just to see the children laughing.

We were invited to all the great houses along the way, walking Molly up long shady driveways and across beautiful gardens and up to the doors of some fine mansions. We saw Penshurst Palace, took Molly into the walled garden, and Mr Shelley – he that's a poet now – then was just a boy and the place was decaying. But it was his playground and oh, how he did love our beast. I see him still; he sat on my knee and never minded my face, and he begged, poor little rich boy, to come away with us. I remember I looked over at Joseph, and I thought, *I should like to stay here instead, with you, Joseph, and it be a fine romance and passion here, as it was for Henry and Boleyn.*

We moved on, and I left my nonsense in those gardens, and the poor little rich boy left us at the gate, a face like sin on him.

One night, just before we got onto the road to Lambeth, up Newington Butts and across St George's Fields, we laid and talked for a long time.

Joseph had brought food out of the public house. Hot food, for once. He watched me as I ate.

'Rebecca,' he said. 'Why are you so good?'

I laughed. 'Good? You're addled, Joseph. Bad wine. Some such.' I couldn't say much more, because with one hand he waved absent-mindedly, and the other he had fastened gently around my bare ankle. I don't think he even knew he done it. But the touch scored through me, and the agony of wanting more, that I knew would never come, was shameful. Not the wanting more, but the ache of wanting it at all.

He rubbed his hand over his face. I think he was bone-tired. It had been a long way from the ship; eighty miles. Twelve days. He fumbled about, pushing straw this way and that to make himself comfortable. He took his hand from me. He shook his head from side to side as I have seen the elephants do. A sort of shaking-in-sorrow motion. 'Becca,' he said at last. 'Why is it that you aren't angry?'

'I'm angry often enough.'

'Not with me.'

I started eating again, looking down at the food.

'Becca,' he prompted. Getting no reply, he shifted a little towards me. 'You stay with me.'

'Do you want me to go someplace else?'

'Of course not. I promised to keep you, and I will.'

'Keep me?' I didn't like the sound of it. Keeping me. Like a beast.

'Look after you, then. Yes, look after you.' He was smiling slightly. He is a tall man, broad-shouldered. When we left the workhouse – ran away together – he was still scraggy and juvenile; but somewhere along the way he had sprung straight into adulthood, filling out. I like his fair hair, and sometimes he's let me cut it. It has a lovely thick feel to it. I've put my hand through the bars of the cages and stroked the lion when it was asleep, snapping my fingers away as soon as it woke. Joseph's hair is thick and the lion's colour; but it does curl astonishing-like in the rain, very wayward, springing out from his head. I always want to stroke it down and smooth it. Of course I never do. He acts humiliated even when I lean on his arm.

'Yes, you promised that.' I finished eating and put away the plate, and I looked out across the empty spread of land at the very edge of London. *Things I shall never do*, I thought.

'What I mean is, if you wished to be elsewhere. If you met a man…'

He frowned, wiped a hand across his face, and pulled off his hat. He knew it was mad to say that a man would want me. I gazed at him, and such a fear ran through me that he would turn me out. That he had at last grown tired of looking at me. Looking at his own guilt every day. To tell the truth, dear God, to tell the truth, I think he always looked at me as he looked at the animals, a thing to care for, a speaking thing, a freak of a sort – a thick-hide animal that could form words. As others saw me. An animal in a shoddy dress. An animal wearing boy's boots, who had never owned a pair of lady's shoes such as Sophia had. I dug my nails into the palms of my hands and willed myself to stay still.

'Maybe it's you that wants a wife,' I murmured, very softly.

He grinned. 'Me? A wife? Think of that.' And all of a sudden he sat up straight, nearly banging his head on the bottom of the cage, and he grabbed my hand. 'You'll marry me then, Becca.'

'I will?' Hot blood rushed to my face.

He was smiling broadly. 'We're a grand team, though.'

'That don't make marriage.'

'No?' He jiggled my hand playfully in his. 'I think it does. It's the one thing that matters. What say you?'

Ah, but a thousand things rushed into my head. I saw myself in some nice gown in a church and saying the vows, and carrying a posy of pretty flowers. I saw myself climb into his bed. I saw the light go out on the nightstand. And then I saw that afterward – for ever afterward, for all our lives – he might be shamed; he might have to point me out to some fine gentleman or other, or some fine lady, and he would have to say 'This is my wife'. And they'd look from him to me and I'd see it on their faces. *Poor man. Is that the best he could do?*

It wasn't the best he could do, not by far. And it came over me like horror: it was asked out of pity. Because he knew no one else would. Or maybe it was out of pity and convenience, too. Always at his side. Might as well marry her to keep her from straying. Because she knows the business, and that's a blessing. And then I thought, maybe it's that he's drunk. He smelled of drink, of course. All men do. Small beer or watered-down wine. Tis more safe than water. And my heart sank into the ground because I come to convince myself it was only the drink and pity talking together.

I took my hand out of his. 'I won't marry you. Never.'

Maybe there was disappointment in his face. It was hard to see in the shadows. I turned on my side away from him.

He never asked me more.

The next day was a trouble, because we got to Watling Street where it crosses the Medway at Rochester and there was no ferryboat that could take the weight of Molly. There was all sorts of shenanigans trying to get a boat. And when Joseph saw that there was money to be made out of the delay, he set up a fence with bales, and he charged the crowd to come in –

sixpence this time, for they all looked well-fed; and we pranced about a bit, he and I, doing an African dance – or so we supposed. And Molly stood there, oblivious, just eating her way through the field she stood on. And afterwards we laughed so much at each other, dirty faces and a feather in our hair.

He put his arms around me and lifted me up when he found we had taken nearly two guineas in just one afternoon.

He said that I made him laugh.

And he said nobody else could do that.


I never knew my mother. Joseph knew his. He told me he remembers being stood in a laundry basket to keep him safe while his mother was at the laundry in the parish workhouse. He said he remembers a piece of paisley silk, and that it was sewn inside his jacket. But by the time that we left, the paisley and the jacket were gone, grown too small for him. He said that whenever he has his hand on a piece of silk, he still thinks of tar soap.

The first thing I remember is also tar. Sitting on a bench next to a woman who had a coil of hemp at her feet, and my toes grazing the pile, and her hands, sticky with the tar, batting me away. I did that job all my early years. As soon as you could manage to pick the coil, they set you to it. They said we were keeping the Navy afloat, because it went into ships, sealing cracks between the planking. I don't know if that was true. Keeping ships afloat, I mean. It seems a far-fetched story to me.

I've heard from others since that in some workhouses the children are allowed out; but that wasn't so with us. It was only a small place at the edge of a village in Nottinghamshire. Three-storey, with children on the top floor, women on the next. The men were in another block that laid side-on to ours, and there was a yard, bordered on two sides by the inmates and on one by the manager's house. On the fourth was a brick wall with a gate in it. Beyond, a stone path winding through a field. And the roofs of the village below, down the hill.

The children on the top floor were divided on two sides of a corridor. The whole floor was locked in at night. The doors closed at eight in the evening. I was a good girl then, saying my prayers. I actually believed someone listened to them. The woman warder would drone on – I think she was simple, if you want to know – about Jesus and his little angels who watched over us, and about how God saw all that we did. She never mentioned the devil or hell. The vicar did that on a Sunday morning, but I can't say I paid much attention to him either. I was always away in my own little world. 'Dreamer,' they'd say, in the kitchens, in the corridors, or out in the vegetable garden. 'Dreamer.' Sometimes it got me a whacking blow on the side of the head. Designed to wake you up. More often it knocked me off my feet.

There was one properly good thing about being on the top floor.

Every year, a show would come to the village. We weren't allowed to go out to see it, but we could see it go by from our rooms. The first time, I was probably no more than three or four. Great carts came rumbling along the track – you could hear them long before they arrived. Biggest carts in the world, tearing little branches off the trees and cow parsley out of the hedges, they were so tall and wide. On the front of the waggon was a board painted with a red and yellow sign, and a team of ten horses that dragged it. There was a horse chestnut tree outside, and there were hundreds of white candles swaying among the leaves, the blossom. Oh, I wanted with a fierce hunger to climb that tree. To sit in the leaves and the candles and look down at the cages going by.

The next year was the same: we saw the carts go by, and we

heard the noise in the village below the hill. We heard music at night and we heard the roar of a great beast. It was the third year they came that I wanted to see them so much, because the men – who went out into the fields – said there was an elephant. I longed to see it. I imagined it to be all kinds of shapes and all kinds of sizes. All I knew was that it came from Africa, and just that made it something to wonder at, to want to touch. At first, I thought it might be like a big dog, and later that it would be as big maybe as one of the cows that came by for milking. When they told me it was taller than a cottage, with tusks that swept the ground – oh, then, I was properly consumed. I must see the elephant. I thought that even if I couldn't run down to the village, I might run to the tree and get up into it somehow, and then I might see more of what was happening in the village. It was a tangled plan that made sense to my small mind.

Sometimes, the man who locked the upper floors at night would forget. He was an old man who would sing to himself. And he would mutter away. 'There's all you chicks in your beds.' He would nod, pulling on his beard, checking the windows were shut, snapping the catches. He had a kind, faraway look. When he shuffled about, his slippers swished along the floor because he never lifted his feet.

We would lie in bed and listen to him coming up, step by step. Go into the boys' room, slap his hand on all the big windows, shuffle along, open the door, close the door. Fumble in his pocket for the key and sometimes forget it. Open our door, and the same shuffling absent-minded routine, a slap on each window, and a wistful smile or two, singing his strange little songs that had no beginning and no end. Open door, close door. Sometimes we could hear him doing a little dance to himself on the landing, living a day that had long gone, talking to himself of harvest fair or Christmas. Or summer. *Sumer is icumen in*, all that, and making little cuckoo noises to himself.

Well, this night. This night.

I got out of bed and crept to the door and tried it. It was locked tight. Having got up the courage to leave my bed at all – it was forbidden – I wanted to get outside so badly. All I wanted to do was to get on the chair on the landing by the big window, climb on it, and see if I could see the horse chestnut tree and the menagerie fair. They had said there was a big striped tent that was bigger than the workhouse yard. I wanted to be in it. It was like being so hungry you could faint.

As I stood at the door, I heard the boys' door open. I heard voices, whispers. Shuffled footsteps. They were standing on the landing, talking softly among themselves. My heart leapt. 'What are you doin'?' I said. I banged gently on the door with my hand.

A voice came very close. 'Who is it?'

'Becca.'

'Which one is that?'

Sounding as if it was by his side, another voice. 'Give me them.'

A scuffle. I got myself down to the keyhole. 'What you doing? What?'

I saw there was a pair of hands close by, and they were carrying handfuls of wood chips. Behind, the shadowy bodies of other boys. The hands disappeared, and were replaced by a face I knew. Joseph Eliot. 'We're lighting a fire.'

'A fire!' Wonderful excitement. 'What for?'

'For making smoke. If we light it, they'll come running. The door downstairs is always locked. Master sees to it. I just tried it. So we've got to get a fire started.'

'Why?' I asked. 'Where are you going?'

He laughed. 'To get out. Be a right set-to, and we can get out. Get down to the village to see the beasts.'

Joy ran through me. To see the beasts! To go to the village and to be in the striped tent! I saw straight away what he had planned. Light a fire, make it smoke; the master would soon unlock the downstairs door. In the confusion, we could run away. Such stupid little short-sighted plans. Children's plans. 'I'll come with you,' I said.

He hesitated. Then, 'No.'

'Oh please!'

He disappeared. The shadows changed. I felt hot tears collect behind my eyes. The boys would get away; Joseph would get away and see the beasts. And I would be left here. 'Joe,' I whispered fiercely through the lock. Desperate with the injustice of it. 'Take me with you. Joe! Joe...'

A face I didn't know replaced his at the keyhole. I could make out a fleshy mouth, but I didn't know the boy, couldn't place him. I saw the lips working. 'Go back to bed. No girls. Go back,' he hissed. 'And shut yer mouth.'

I kneeled down on the floorboards and clutched the door handle, but it wouldn't budge. Oh, I wanted to see the beasts as much as they. It wasn't fair. I wanted to climb the trees as much as any boy. I hated my thick pinafores and skirts during the day, their clammy coarseness. The boys had more interesting jobs to do, too. Chopping wood. Shovelling coal. Digging in the vegetable garden belonging to the master's wife. If allowed out, we girls had to sit quiet and sew. Lately, the women had been trying to teach me to knit, and the wool was so sticky, unravelled and unpicked a hundred times before it came to us. We were supposed to knit blankets but I knew I would never be able to do it. Those thick wooden needles, that dirty-feeling wool. I hung there on the door handle in the dark, and wanted to be a boy so much.

They were shuffling backwards and forwards. They had got the wood chips from the log pile, but God only knows where they got the flint.

It took some time; I drowsed by the door.

I smelled the smoke before I saw the flames.

Today, we reach Prentiss's warehouse by early evening.

We've walked through a busy London coming alive for the night.

We've come to see the songbirds.

Prentiss himself sits outside his warehouse: a fat man who's drawn a good Jacobean chair out into the road and sucks on a pipe and watches the world go by. Joseph told me that Prentiss is sick; that he has a liverish disease. He's quite yellow. He seems content, however. He has had his threescore-and-ten, by the look of him. Or perhaps that's the illness.

Joseph shakes his hand. I step back, waiting.

With huffing and puffing effort, Prentiss gets up and fumbles a while with the keys about his belt. 'You be not afraid of so many?' he asks.

Joseph says nothing, but he laughs. Maybe Prentiss has forgotten the rhinoceros, the Barbary apes that screech, the great wallowing Herefordshire hog we had that charged down anything in its path. It made good money, that hog. I hear Hemp now, walking up and down St Martin's Lane crying, 'A most surpisin' and astonishin' great wallowing hog, the greatest natural curiosity alive! Measurin' nine feet ten inches in length and eight feet five inches in girth, six feet arun' 'is neck! Sixpence each person at The Bell...'

'Be careful, Becca,' Joseph says to me now.

The door from the street is an ordinary one, a plank door such as we have in Long Acre. Inside there is a small corridor, and another door, and then when we are inside that, all of a sudden I catch the smell. I thought I was past being gagged by any smell, but it seems not. Seeing me, Joseph takes a linen handkerchief out of his pocket. It's one that I've washed and pressed, and he smiles when he gives it to me. My eyes are already smarting, and I push it to my face.

Prentiss opens the next great door just a sliver, and we creep inside.

It's a huge barn of a place, at least four or five storeys high, and on each side it has racks and racks of bird boxes like the inside of a honeycomb, and they are all white over. On the floor is a thick layer of straw but the straw has not been fresh for many a week, and has a curious look to it, like snow-crusted fields. Here and there, for just an inch or two, a board floor shows through.

There's no song, but as the door shuts there is a whirlwind in the place; the air thickens with wings, and flurries of green and grey, blue and yellow. Through the storm of birds, I see two large brushes against the far wall, and beside them, looking like a tide that has washed up on the shore, a great stack of bodies, the same green and grey and blue and yellow. I gaze around through the dipping and rising of birds, past the flutter of thousands of wings, and I think this place is like some strange ocean, white over on the waves, and caught in a strange blue light by the shore.

It ought to be terrible, but despite the guano floor and the tides of dead, there's joy in the birds, the blizzard of colour, the evening sun coming in through the high glass windows and pooling around us. We're all struck dumb with the sight. Prentiss leans against a wall and nods to himself; an animal dealer who deals no more, but has loved his possessions, even though he's past caring for them. He closes his eyes and it's such a strange sight: the old man, yellow-skinned, sleepwalking almost among his fluttering captives.

Joe puts up one hand. And in a miracle, after a minute or so, a bird alights on his outstretched palm. It's shaking, poor little thing. He gently closes his fingers, and shows me. From inside the lattice of his thumb and forefinger, a frantic spirit suddenly, a thrash of head and wings.

'For you,' he tells me. 'Take it.'

I put my hand on his, and under my touch he opens his hand. I look up at him.

Why are some beloved, and others not? I think that some must be born so. That makes one person give their heart readily, without a thought. Without a will of their own. And so some are natural keepers, and some are naturally kept. And it's never known soon enough who has the keys, and who is locked in. Before you know you're a captive, the bolt is thrown, the promise made. I threw my heart into such an enclosure long ago, and I hope that nothing will alter it.

For what could break us now?

'I shall buy you a cage,' he says kindly.

*I have one*, I think. But I'm pleased to be in it.

4

BOY TYGER

Night-time in the Exchange, and the painted walls come alive.

Big trees bend to the ground, and sand ripples. High up is a light from the street, flickers of fires, clouds, or the moon trundling over the sky between the smoke. Sounds of the crowds, the drunks, and the streetwalkers on the Strand.

Beasts don't like smoke and they don't like fires. They like nothing. They lie in sloven-like hate. Not hard to guess what they hate and why they hate it. Smell that? Suffocation. Tarred chains and ice. The floors of the cages here at Exeter Exchange are cold.

Anything's cold to a lion, or a leopard. Or the tyger. Or Jumby, the elephant by the big door. But he don't mind. He does his tricks, like taking a gentleman's hat off his head and putting it back on just where it was. He does them sometimes to himself in the dark, like tonight. Like he was practising. He don't mind lifting his feet like he was dancing.

He's just a good sort is Jumby. You know, a good sort, like some people are a good sort? He don't care. It's not that he's forgot. They don't forget. It's a true saying, that is. He don't forget but he don't care so much now because he's old, very old.

Look at his eye, all clouded over. He feels you with his trunk, warm and friendly.

A long, long room with painted walls. And on one side there's windows and small cages, and on the other there's big cages. Middling dark in here now, at four in the morning, and hard to see what's behind the bars. There is a wall to stop the folk – all the fine ladies and gentlemen in the daytime – going too close.

I'm not afraid at night.

Not much afraid. Cross my fingers. They'll come, but I won't move. I'll stare back at them, I will. Trying to stop breathing in case they hear me.

Sometimes the two women come first, drift through the wall, got short skirts on under the knee, very dirty. Come in through the Jumby wall where he dreams, walk right through him. Once he shuddered. They pass the big door, always looking like they're talking and laughing to each other without any noise and one got red hair and one is black, very pretty, very tall and they walk towards the windows and disappear. Then sometimes a man comes straight after. He got a red cloak right to the ground and a gold cross and his head is shaved. He has a book. And I'll see him start to run. As soon as he does – running straight at me – he seems to go up, like there's a hill. But there's no hill and he goes into a shadow but so close I can hear the sound of his shoes and a bloody terror I can feel – falling off him like leaves fall from trees, shedding bits of himself. He did wrong once – stole something. They took off his head for it, spiked it on the bridge. I see what he sees, his own head with eyes open.

I wish they wouldn't come.

I wish they wouldn't walk through the cages and the beasts.

I lie at the back on the floor. Try to make myself little. Put my head down and I can hear the water under the ground, and feel like there was something else here once, somebody by a stone wall making glass. See it shining in the flames. Under them, pavement. Under that just a field. Way over, cattle and a track lane. Tall grass in summer. I see it ripple. Maybe I dream it. I turn my head so my ear ain't pressed to the ground. Curl in a ball.

Got a bit of hay to lie on that they took out of a cage, smelling of shit. But then so do I. Shaw says so. He takes me out in the yard and washes me under the pump, slapping me, saying I'm costing him money. Puts me back in clothes and stops to have a feel and grins like a great ape right in my face, clay pipe in his teeth. Now and again he looks at me, thinking. 'What are you?' he says, and pinches a bit of skin on my back. 'Cover it all up. You're like a disease. Got some fuckin' disease.'

I hide when ladies and gentlemen come and pay their shilling at the door. I stay back in the feed store. Shaw says I'm not fit to be seen. Neither is he, but it makes no odds. He plasters his hair down and shoves his face under the pump and coughs and spits while he dresses. The woman brings a clean shirt every day and he puts it on over his dirt. Worse than the animals. At least they clean themselves. Apes pick at their fur. Cats clean with their tongues. But not him. Put a tongue to his flesh and you'd poison yourself you would.

He don't do none of it when Mr Hallett comes. He's the owner, Shaw's the keeper. Then there's ten others, ten keeper men. Then there's me, I do errands. Feed getter. Shit sweeper. Don't know how long I've been here. Once there was a woman and there was another place out of the city, out past a lot of fields, by some water, maybe the big river. And I dream of hands that was gentle. Not soft but gentle. But then, like the women and the running man, she goes away like the smoke in the top window, or the moon or the clouds.

The keepers have sport with me. There's a door in the cages, a little door, and they open it and they're meant to bring the cats or whatever in with a chain and sticks, but sometimes Shaw puts me in there in the corner and they open the little door and leave me there and the cat or the ape or the bull will come in so they can clean out the other bit of the cage. But first they have their laugh watching me trying to climb out of there. Lucky I can climb, and faster than a cat, up to where there's a hatch in the top. I learned it quick when I was younger and got stuck there by accident, and now they do it sometimes just to watch me clamber as fast as I can. 'Go on up, yer bloody monkey, bloody freak!' But only one cat ever leapt up after me. That was the tyger. She shook her head back and forth but she never tried it twice.

I think the cats hate the keepers much more than they hate me. They hate them and remember. Slow, sloven-eyed, sloven-backed house cats you'd think they were. But you get too close, they fix you. They smile. *Let us out. Then you'll see us proper like up close, and feel us too.* The leopard, draped like a worn-out dancer in the corner. The lion close to the door. *Come and see us close. Come close, boy. Closer.*

It's getting light outside.

The tyger eyes follow me.

I get up and crawl. Not make a sound or else I'd be waking Shaw, snoring back along the room in his truckle bed. Thinks he's a soldier with his campsite there: kettle, bottle, chair, bed and the curtain between. He kicks out at night when he's dead drunk, and swears in his sleep. And stinks, and groans. It's an hour before he'll shift himself.

The edge of the tyger's lip twitches, very small, very small. Yellow eyes, beautiful, ringed in black, the same colour as her coat: yellow flecked with black, like round wet drops that fell on soil and spread in lines. Small round drops of black rain on yellow ground. She shifts a little bit.

When a tyger looks at you, she don't see you. And she don't care about it neither. She sees a shape. She don't care what that shape is, only that it smells of meat. They say she will take you quick and clean, if *you're* not quick. And that's what's in a tyger's eye.

'Here, tyger,' I say.

She stretches but she don't get up. Even though I'm down here under the wall now, in the gulley between the wall and the cage, she sees that she can't quite reach me. She looks at me and all of a sudden I see her shine. It come pouring out of her, yellow on yellow, black on black, black on yellow, and she thinks of running through sun and tall grasses, light and shade she is, and hard to tell her from the tall grass and the sand under her feet. Very fast she comes, and when she leaps, she stretches. Then she's alive. Then she's got a loud heart, and blood pounding in her. Tyger, yes. I lean forward and feel the trickle of breath over me. Hunger. Rage. I feel her dry throat, hear the air rasp as it leaves her. Hate and thirst and hunger. Patience cold as death.

I'm stood pressed up against the bars, and she's stood on the other side. 'Come on then,' I tell her. 'Let's go running.'

She's stock-still, breathing that dry hot air she remembers, her lip pulled back over the gums.

'But we got nowhere to go,' I tell her. 'Not you, and not me.'

# 5

JOSEPH

Late July. And a week ago, The Yellow House on Soho Square was put up for sale.

I've always loved that square. There's an oak tree that grows in the road that leads up to it, and it has a bench around it. For the last ten years or so, when I've been in need of quiet thought, I have sat there and watched the cattle being brought down to drink through the meadows. On summer evenings I like to walk out of Oxford Street and up Mary Bone Place towards Green Lane. There were orchards just here when I first came. They are taken down now, and there is much building in this area; great houses, terraces, and shops, and mansions, all of a riot and jumble, are going along Berners Street and The Green Lane. Green Lane! It won't be green much longer. However, there is nothing new on the Square. I hope it'll always be a small heaven in the city.

The Yellow House is very pretty. It has railings at the front, all with leaves and vines and pineapple fruits, and three broad white steps made of Portland stone. It has two fine wide windows on either side of the door, and a Flemish roof of dusky red tile. Far off in the distance you can hear the noise of the city, but it's very faint. In the square itself are some gardens where boys sell cherries and strawberries. Last year there was an artist, very young, who sometimes set his easel on the grass, and you could pay a shilling and have a portrait done while the sun filtered through the branches of the lime trees and cast racing shadows on the ground.

I had a friend who owned this house. Sir Thomas Miller.

His son Henry inherited it, and is a friend of mine.

Sir Thomas was, in life, a great physician. But he was a humble man. The world was to him, as it is to me, a place of wonder and discovery. I never had an education until I met him. Soon after meeting Sophia and beginning my own business, I developed a bronchial spasm that he diagnosed as exhaustion. He was charming; his wife, Catherine, too was all sweetness and calm. Because I've always wanted a true education, I would go to The Yellow House of an evening and he would explain life to me. And I would learn of science and how to think and how to speak like a gentleman.

He treated Sophia once, too. I called on her one afternoon to find Sir Thomas in the outer room. He was, of course, younger then, and bore the jaunty air of a worldly man, and was known for his forthright manner and kindliness. I was surprised to see him; thought him at first to be one of Sophia's many admirers. But it was not so. He was leaning on the casement window in a weary, thoughtful fashion, and he turned when I came in the room.

'Sir Thomas.' I held out my hand. He took it. I looked back towards the bedroom. 'Is Mrs Baddeley ill?'

'She is delivered of a stillborn son. Of five months or so.'

I hadn't known. She had hidden it so well. No man would have known, I think.

'I'm sorry for her,' I said.

He said nothing more. He visited her, that I know. He told

me she had called him because she knew his name from me. But she and I never once discussed the matter: I did not think it was my business at all. She recovered. Within three weeks she was back at the masked balls and parties, glad as ever. Even a little wild. She and I parted in a friendly fashion around that time; I was busy and she did not press the matter. She has never once mentioned the child.

Neither did Sir Thomas ever recall the stillborn birth whenever I saw him. I do not think he connected me with the event in the least. He was a man of the world, used to its trials and tribulations, and the very model of affability.

He would have parties; intellectual evenings to which he began to invite me. At one such – as an entertainment – he brought electric eels that had come from Surinam. He had paid an extraordinary sum for them – sixty guineas. There were twenty-two of us at the gathering, and he asked the ladies to sit by and the gentlemen to form a circle and hold hands. He produced the eels and the shock passed directly through the eleven of us. It was the most amazing thing, and delighted me so much that a creature could affect us, that it had such power. God is indeed great in his infinite speculation.

'What is it for, the impulse?' I asked Sir Thomas.

'To facilitate movement.'

'And our muscles – our limbs, our hands – are they too moved by electricity?'

'No doubt. Of a kind.'

What kind? I wondered. I looked around at the hands of the ladies nearby, and at their faces, and beyond them to the trees moving beyond the window in the breeze. 'And the trees, and the growth of flowers and of grasses?'

'Propelled by light and the wind itself,' a man next to me surmised.

Was there not something else? I asked myself. The impulse

that drives the upward-shooting mechanisms of grass, for instance. Something in the root, or the plant itself.

That night, it made me go out to Tottenham Fields before I went home, and I stared at the sleeping forms of the great cats that we had in our cages. The movement of muscles beneath the skin, the flexing of the feet. What was the impulse that drove any animal to breathe, to grow? There it was again, some vast secret. The impenetrable secret that haunts my thoughts.

I had little enough education in the workhouse; but I've learned in life, listened to many. Learned to read and write, and how to talk as the gentry do, as Sophia instructed me, though she said she could still hear a Nottinghamshire burr in my voice. I've even gone to lectures in the city. Drunk deep of the world that thrills me.

London is indeed a great city – the greatest on Earth – for bringing new mysteries to our doors. Ships come from all over the globe loaded with new conundrums, and it's a blessing both for me and the business. There's always something new to buy and to show, something strange to incorporate in the tableaux and dramas. I have walked along the Garden with the capuchins on my shoulders and a great quilled porcupine on a lead, giving out handbills with Hemp. What a fuss, what a distraction that porcupine caused! It's a pleasure to do these things. No doubt I'm still the boy who, years ago, longed so much to see the menageries. In the Garden, as I walked, the merry women leapt out of the way, and the street boys tried to pluck a porcupine quill with much squealing and shouting. It stopped in its tracks and raised its hackles. I sold every ticket for that night, and for many nights afterwards.

Over the dinner table, we talked about Cook. I wished I had travelled with James Cook, to see the Marquesas and Tahiti and Norfolk Island and the Sandwich Islands. Omai of Ra'iātea, a native, returned with Cook from Tahiti. All the bagnios are wild with Tahitian stories; the bawd Charlotte Hayes concocted a show, a 'Tahitian Feast of Venus'. I was told of it by a young fool who had paid a hundred guineas to attend it. He was supported in his cultural endeavour by twenty other gentlemen of the highest breeding, which is to say twenty young idiots whose brains – what they have for brains, which is little – reside in their stomachs and arses, to see what Hayes had devised.

'There were a dozen couples,' he told me. 'I recognised most of the women behind their masks, and – if you like it! – the Earl of Avon's nephew was one of the men. Inordinately fond of brandy, which impeded his performance.'

The pot calls the kettle black.

'They danced a little, with grass skirts and whatnot,' the buck continued. 'On a satin sheath of blue and gold. To represent the sea and the sand, don't you know. And there were palm trees and ferns and fronds. And what mayhap you call 'em – orchids, what?'

'And then?' I asked.

'And then, why, and then!' He started his interminable hawking that passes for laughter. 'Why, the sea and sand got tangled up you might say, and the orchids were crushed and the ferns fell over, and *rites were enacted by all!*'

I hear from Charlotte Hayes herself that she made three and a half thousand guineas profit from the idiot young flowers of the aristocracy, and from food and lodging and the profit on the wines. She has bought a house in Dover with it. She is no fool.

I ask Henry when I see him this evening what else Cook has learned on his latest travels.

'Oh, the chronometer. The Southern Ocean.'

I don't know what he means about chronometers. I suppose it must be important for ships in some way. Henry is an intelligent boy. I think it won't be long before he owns the shipping company.

'What of the Southern Ocean?'

'Ah, this will interest you. There are many seals and whales. Vast populations.'

'To capture a whale would be an interesting feat.'

'It can't be done. Not to be brought back alive.'

'No doubt. But I should like a whale skeleton to display.'

'Would it make money?'

'Dead animals make more money than live ones. We made a good amount two years ago when our hyena died. People can touch them then, you see. Dear little children may climb upon them and pull their ears. Of course, the display is a short one before the corpses start to stink.'

We sit looking at the square. Dust ripples along the ground; the great trees in the centre of the square hang down, weighted with their own abundance of leaves. It is growing dusk.

'You might apply for the next voyage,' he muses.

'I? On what basis?'

'Your knowledge of animals.'

'But I have no book learning, Henry. Besides, Cook has already gone.'

'Others then. The next ship is going to the Gold Coast. There are many unusual beasts roaming in that country.'

We watch a boy go past, bowling a hoop and not very well. It keeps falling over in the road. We can hear his mother calling across the square.

'Did you always live in London, Joseph?'

'No. I come from near Nottingham.'

'And you have a family there?'

'No, none at all.'

'And none here.'

'No.'

'Just Mrs Baddeley.'

The mention of Sophia makes me turn to him. 'You know her?'

'All London knows of the latest scandal.' Surprisingly, he begins to blush. 'And I know that you were once... friends.'

He does not know that we are friends still. Melbourne – cad that he is – has lately left Sophia in a quandary. London does indeed talk of nothing else. She finds herself in debt, and Melbourne won't answer her pleas.

I did go to see her the other day and she was in floods of tears. 'Oh, he has deserted me,' she sobbed. 'And left me in such desperate straits.' I looked around at the lodgings. It was true that they were not a patch on the previous ones, but they were very decent. And there were several gentlemen's calling cards on the hall table.

'You will right yourself soon enough,' I told her.

She smiled up at me. Some coarseness shows now in her countenance. It can't be helped. She's had fifteen years at the peak of her profession. I wonder if she looks down from that peak now, and sees the dizzying heights down which she will – of necessity – fall once her looks are completely gone.

I patted her delicate hand. I left a five-pound note on the same table in the hallway.

Henry turns now in his seat to smile at me. 'You are an enigma.'

'Why so?'

He waves his hand, a gesture encompassing myself from head to foot. 'Why, here you are, a fine sort of fellow. Tall. Always so broadly smiling. His own business, and a head for that business. A brain, though you protest at your ignorance. A perceptive person.'

'Thank you, Henry.'

'Who mixes with the lowest sort. A man who might have

any respectable woman of a middling kind. But who keeps company in the sewers of the theatres and the fairs.'

'I meet many fine women. I don't have amours, however.'

'But that's my point, Joseph. Why do you not marry?' He slaps his hand down upon his thigh. 'Marry, and buy this house,' he says, his face lighting up with the idea. 'My father would have loved you to live here. Have you not always liked it?'

'It's too far out from Covent Garden.'

'You see,' he says. 'That is another thing I don't understand. You might have any good house, and yet you live – where is it? – Long Acre.'

'It suits my purpose. I've no need of a fine house.'

Sir Thomas died a month ago. His dear wife has gone to live with her sister. Henry is to live on the Thames, where he has bought a good double-fronted terrace that looks over the water. We both look back now at The Yellow House.

'My father's collections are all here,' Henry murmurs. 'Would you not like to have them? I don't want them to go to the Holophusikon in Leicester Square.'

Oh, I should so like the preserved insects and the eels in particular, now bottled in brine. And there is a vast glass case of hummingbirds. It's not a collection like Hunter's. Not sixty thousand specimens. But it is a fascinating observatory of life, kept in the library.

'If you married, you should have a nice wife to oversee it all,' Henry murmured. 'You did not answer the question. Why don't you marry?' He pauses. 'In fact, why don't you marry that helpmate of yours, Rebecca? She is a good woman and a fine right hand of yours.'

All that he says is true. But Rebecca once refused me, and with some insistence. That stung me to the core. I have my pride, like all men.

'It is the disfigurement, perhaps?'

Moments pass. He looks into my face and holds out his hand. 'There's a good fellow,' he murmurs. 'Take my apology. I see that it is not the disfigurement. I am sorry.'

'I am responsible for Rebecca.'

'Yes, yes, of course.' Another pause while he searches my face. In anyone less personable, it would be an affront, this close inspection, these probing enquiries. But Henry is a naïve and friendly sort of fellow. And besides, I forgive Henry the impertinence of his question, because I know that he will soon marry Miss Parrington, a daughter of his father's partner in his medical practice. I look in his face and see a genuine enquiry, and – God bless the boy – a concern. I think of giving many trite answers. 'Ah, but she feels for you, Joseph,' Henry murmurs. 'You must consider that.'

I look away, back to the boy trailing his way home through the twilight. I don't want to think of this. Rebecca might be fond of me, but it's not the love of a man and wife. And so I tell him a lie. 'I do not marry because I don't feel the emotion, Henry. I have seen you with Miss Parrington. I don't feel that. It is a foreign land to me.'

'But children. A family.'

'I shall never have that.' This at least is true. I have seen what happens to children abandoned after poor liaisons and failed marriages. I have been one. I let Henry go ahead of me into the house, and look at his well-clothed back, his lightness of carrying himself, his jaunty air. I can't remember if I ever had that. Not the lightness of spirit that goes deep inside.

I think of Rebecca silently putting food in front of me each evening. The quietness of our domesticity. When I look in her face, I see my own, that seam of horror that must not be disturbed. It is an understanding that we have. An understanding impossible to explain to others.

I have an impulse suddenly to catch at Henry's arm, turn

him back to me, and say, 'You see, we were forged in something else. It is hard to overcome. I failed her once. I made her looks what they are now. I dare not risk failing her again.' But I do not.

Then, suddenly, Henry turns in the hallway of his own accord and smiles at me. He tells me of a ship coming from the Gold Coast this week. 'Come down and see the captain,' he says, and grips my arm. 'You must do that, Joseph. Perhaps he will take you with him on his next sailing. A sea voyage, an adventure! Just the thing for a man jaded by the city.'

In the morning, I accompany Henry to see the ship.

She's a fine East Indiaman, a working vessel much scarred about the bows, but sitting in the sunrise on the Thames mid-river like a blushing maiden, a rosy shade, very unusual. And the figurehead is of a child clutching a posy, gilded but the gilding now weather-beaten.

We are rowed out to her; it is a beautiful morning and the water like glass.

'She's seen storms,' Henry murmurs. 'She is much bruised.'

Our ferryboat pulls up alongside. Ripples tremble along the river, and are reflected on the hull of the ship. She seems very high to me, but all round us and as far as the eye can see there are other ships. Most are sleeping in this five o'clock light. On the shore, the people passing along the streets seem very far away.

I'm thinking all the while about buying The Yellow House. I shall speak to Rebecca. I don't want to make her feel embarrassed by fine living. She is, it seems to me, comfortable where she is. She is a most practical woman, and not given to the things that ladies preoccupy themselves with. She's accomplished and sturdy, and not shallow. I wouldn't make this decision, at any rate, without speaking to her and gauging her ideas. All this goes through my mind as I gaze at the river and feel the small boat rocking gently underneath me.

'*The Peony Child* has seen many trips for us,' Henry confides as he stands to catch hold of the rope ladder. 'We take chains and manacles out to Ghana, and manufactured cotton, and guns and all kinds of metalwork from Birmingham. Daggers, and handles and spokes and nails. Swords occasionally.'

'Swords?'

'For Ghanaian chiefs. They relish a fine sword, especially in a good scabbard.'

'In return for – what?'

'Do you mean what comes back?' Henry looks down a little guiltily. 'Some slaves from the slave dungeons built along the coast. Some animals. I daresay Captain Fisher has a few apes for you on board.'

I lay my hands on the rope, and suddenly I am overcome with the most extraordinary feeling of grief. The sadness saturates me as if I had been drenched in a storm. I put down my head; the ferryman asks – it is as from a far-off place – if I'm well. 'Yes,' I tell him. I make my fingers grip the rope until the fibres bite into my skin, and the feeling passes. But it was a real sensation, a true emotion; as vivid, as sudden, as clouds racing across the sun.

As quickly as it comes, it's gone.

I climb the ladder, and the captain is waiting to meet us.

6

REBECCA

A woman takes her life in her hands walking to Southwark by
the new-built Blackfriars Bridge, and yet this is what Joseph
wants. A boy has run all the way to Long Acre with the
message.

I've got a lot to do, but it's a sunny day and what Joe wants
Joe gets, so I dry my hands and I take Hemp with me. I wrap
myself well against pickpockets. Just at the end of Long Acre we
find a farming man coming back from the Garden, taking his
empty cart towards the orchards south of the river. There are so
many fields and fruit trees and gardens there on the roads to
Camberwell and Clapham. I sit beside him and watch the old
horse slip and slide along the road in the heat of the day.

When we've crossed the bridge, the old man tells us how it
used to be in a way that never gets to the point and sets Hemp to
fidgeting at my side. I slap Hemp's leg; he stares at me and picks
at his fingernails. Hemp is a tall man, and his limbs unravel like
wet string, drooping down until his forehead almost touches his
lap. This is the way he sulks. I steal a glance at him as the
waggon rumbles along. He's big, but you should hear him
muffling through his prayers before he goes to sleep. Nothing

but a boy in a man's body, and as ugly as sin. I've seen him sleep at the side of the stage when our God's thunder bellows, so unconcerned is he.

I first saw him among the crowds that watched the queen's zebra go by on the way to her gardens at Kew. He was standing by Newgate prison, and so cheerful was he that I turned to look at him.

'What are you smiling at?' I asked, even though I knew. He was smiling at my face. As soon as he saw that I would smack the smile off him, he changed. He started wringing his hands. 'I don't mean nothing,' he told me.

We'd been looking for a man to help us for weeks. Mostly they came and went: vagabonds, thieves. Old men who were hungry. But Hemp looked different: like the big child that he was. 'What do you do?' I said. 'Have you any work?'

He nodded up at the prison. 'Here,' he said, 'I work here.'

'What as?'

'For the women, to plead their belly.'

'To plead...?' It dawned on me, then, what he meant. 'You mean to stop them being hanged?'

'Yes,' he said.

'You help them when they are with child in some way?'

'No, missus. I help them *get* a child.'

Surprising how industrious a man can be who is nothing more than a helpless idiot. Every prison has one or two child-getters but it was the first time that I'd met one.

While we talked, he told me that he was tired.

'I don't wonder,' I said. And I thought, *He'll not last long, even with a constitution like a bear*. He was lucky he hadn't caught the pox as it was. He probably would have lasted not more than another year. He was a lucky man to have escaped unscathed, which I tell him if he ever complains at something that I ask him to do. And he'll smile his stupid smile and say there were some respectable women in prison who lived now because he saved them.


It's midday. The river smells sour, and smoke trails out across it. You can still hear the city; but here on the south side you can trace apple trees in the air. It's so sweet. The old man talks of how it was fifty years ago, when there were lighted paths across the marshes that have now been made into streets. 'Haunted marshes they was,' he tells us, and laughs. 'Dead souls all looking up at you through the water.'

Hemp gawps at him, round-eyed. I remember those lights, too: they were there even some left five or six years ago when Joseph and I sat talking that night, when we brought Molly up from Dover.

Just lately I wonder if I could bring him to talk to me like that again. Joe has not wed, and we are as close as ever. I dream, as the cart goes along, of the pitifully shy and anxious thing I was then – not so long ago really – and I think, if he would ask me. *If he would ask me.* I think of myself saying yes to him, and what that would mean. We might be quiet, in time. Move to the country, raise children. It could be possible. I sit and turn this picture over and over in my head, looking at it from this way and that. We get no younger. I feel my life slipping gently through my fingers, and I look at him each day, and I turn his bed each week, and I think... oh, just that. I think.

We pass the ugly octagon that is Rowland's Surrey Chapel, once in the fields close to the river, and now with houses all round it. I remember that we had to take Molly across the river by boat, before the bridge, and that as we stood waiting we could see the land running with water as the Thames tide came in and out. There were cornmills here too, reflected in the Thames, and windmills. I realise as we come down Great

Surrey Street towards Melancholy Walk that I don't see windmills any more in the city. There used to be some behind Oxford Street, but they're gone now.

'The melancholiest women come here,' the old man says, flicking his horsewhip lazily to one side of the road. He's pointing at the house where the women are kept. Them that the Walk is named after. 'You can come here for the singing – they sing very fine behind screens – but you mayn't see 'em. You can pay a sixpence but you'm only ever glimpse they hats. Straw hats they have and sacks to dress in instead of they hitched-up skirts you'm see on the Strand.' He laughs to himself in dirty fashion.

The word passed to us in Joseph's message is to come to Melancholy Walk, and it's only then, as I sit up and look out for him – look out for a cage, I suppose, or some great lumbering tethered beast as we once had in that bear that died so sudden, fell down and couldn't be got up no matter what – and something of that nature tied to the fencing at the side of the road... well, it is that when I see Joe. And at the same time, I see where he's standing.

Outside the Magdalen House for Penitent Women. What the old man is calling the Melancholy Women. The repentant whores that the priest – the scandal that he is – houses here. Oh, he's kind towards them, I don't doubt that. They dress very sombre and they don't speak of their past, and they are let out at the end of their terms to decent houses in far shires who don't know what they are, and I suppose that they prosper there. Survive at least, instead of dying in the syphilis wards. But it's always fired me up that visitors are charged to look through the window lattices just to catch sight of those bonnets and covered-up bodies. I suppose it pays well.

As if summoned by me, I see the priest himself. William Dodd, what they call the macaroni priest because he dresses so fine and stoops so low with all his fine hats and suits and lace and whatnot. We've seen him at Drury Lane many a time, supposed to be saving souls and gathering up women as he goes. He carries a wonderful Malacca cane with a silver top in the shape of a heron with its wings outstretched. The first time he saw me, he stepped back in surprise, then came close and ran one hand over my face and the other down my back. 'Ah, you poor child,' he murmured in my ear. 'Come to my rooms and let Christ cure you.' When I laughed he looked so shocked, and then he laughed too, seeing how he'd been understood and he not ashamed at all. What a whore once called 'that meddling peddling bastard'. He will be caught one day and strung up in the street, I don't doubt.

But here he is in the sunshine outside the Magdalen House, twirling that heron-headed cane, smiling that smile that shows his bad teeth. I get down from the cart, Hemp behind me. 'Ah, it is the redoubtable Rebecca,' he says. 'And her ape.'

'Don't insult him,' I say. 'He's worth a ton of you.'

Dodd just smiles all the more. He comes close as he always does, looking hard at my face. 'Such a pity,' he murmurs.

I turn to Joseph. He looks like he's sweating hard. And Henry Miller is with him. Joe rushes up to grasp me by the shoulders. 'Thank the Lord.'

'What is it?' I ask. And something strikes me hard. The look on his face, a look I've never seen before. From inside the Magdalen I hear something: a woman wailing. *She must be repenting whole-hearted*, I think.

I glance again at Henry. His face is the colour of cold ash.

The woman inside starts screaming. It's an unearthly sound. Such a high grinding cry, piercing my head like a nail. I clap my hands to my ears. 'Have mercy, who's that?' I ask them. 'What're they doing to her? And what are *you* doing here? Where's the animal? What is it?'

'It's an ape,' Joe tells me. 'We have brought an ape here.'

'Why didn't the captain bring it out to us?' I ask him, confused. 'Why do it yourself?' Anger starts to simmer in the pit of my stomach. I've been brought all the way out here for no reason.

'He refused.'

'What, to sell an ape? He only had to pay a waggoner, chain it up, drive to Tottenham.'

'He would not.'

I lean forward and look in his face, partly turned away from me. 'What sort of ape?' I ask him. 'Not them from Africa.' I mean the silverbacks. They can kill a man, easy. We don't take them because while you can get a big cat drugged or drunk, it's harder with an ape. They have more sense. And they fight like men. They have hands that can snap a neck, break an arm. The big silverback ones, they don't care for sticks or chairs, and I been told they can break locks. So no thank you. Not them.

'No, not from Africa,' Joe murmurs. 'Sumatra. They call it an orang-hutan there.'

That's many a month at sea. That's many a mile of ocean.

Joe looks at me. 'She's a female.'

'So what?'

Henry is standing near us, and he looks as guilty as a boy caught stealing apples. I get up again and walk over to him, and he at once colours up.

'Henry,' I say to him. 'What are we all doing here?'

'I'm sorry, Rebecca.'

I turn back to Joe. 'Have you left your senses?' He glares at me, but I don't feel like apologising to him. For one thing, I've sat next to an old fool who stinks of horseshit for the last two hours. 'Hemp was at Tottenham making good the stage for tonight, and your message dragged him here,' I hear myself objecting. 'There's a feed delivery this afternoon. Why don't you attend to your business?'

Inside the Magdalen House, a woman screams again.

Henry blanches. 'It's a special case,' he murmurs. 'The ape... she is dressed.'

'Dressed? In what?'

'In... clothes. Ladies' clothes. A dress. A shawl.'

I've heard of such things. We dress our capuchins, after all. And I say this to Henry.

'Oh,' he says. 'But not like that. This creature is the size of a human woman.'

Joseph has stood up and walks over to me, dragging his feet. 'You must tell us what to do, Rebecca.'

'I? But what for?'

'The captain...' He stops, takes a deep breath. 'He bought her in Martinique, where he bought two women who came with him on the ship.'

'For what reason?'

'For... company.' He sighs. 'They thought it was sport to dress the creature and treat her as one of them.'

For a second, I can't speak.

'It is a poor stricken creature and she won't let the women near her. But you have a touch, Becca. You're good at calming.'

Henry takes hold of my hand. 'It had to be taken away from him,' he explains. 'He sold it.'

I look at Joe. 'To you, I suppose.'

'No,' he tells me. 'Not me.'

Dodd has sidled over to us. He stands leaning on his cane with a sneering expression on his face. What he has to be superior about, I don't know, and I tell him so.

He looks at Joe. 'You have a need to tame this one,' he says.

'I know what you are,' I tell him. And I mean it. I've heard the stories. Not just about this place, but about him spending what he hasn't got and lying to them that put him on a preacher's path and give him pulpits to preach in when he had no living of his own. They say he lied to men like Chesterfield, and even the king. Oh, it's many a place that a worm can wriggle into. I hear he takes an unholy interest in women like those behind us. I hear he knows the bawds and aye, he visits them. Yet he stands up in churches and tells folk to repent.

'Becca,' Joe murmurs. He gets up, takes me by the elbow, and we walk a few paces. Dodd stands in the sunshine fussing with the lace on his collar and smirking to himself.

'Becca,' says Joe. 'The captain paid me to come here or take the creature to Hallett. Dodd bought her but within five minutes she backed into a corner and bit him. Now he doesn't want her.'

Henry has walked away from us all. He stands looking up the track towards London.

'Henry looks right ashamed,' I say.

'He only meant to visit the ship to see the exotic birds. He has got caught up in this mess.'

I lower my voice to a whisper. 'How much did the captain pay you?'

'Ten guineas.'

'Ten guineas!'

'Ssssh...'

I sigh at his trickery. 'How much is Dodd paying you?'

'Five.'

'Because...' I think about it, not taking my gaze from his face. 'Five to keep quiet about what he tried to make the creature do. What no bloody doubt the captain wanted her to do.' He raises one eyebrow.

'What godforsaken dirty beasts men are,' I whisper, wholly disgusted. 'Worse than pigs.'

'We have to take her to Hallett,' he says. I see that he don't contradict me about the filth of men. But he does take my arm, links it and brings his mouth close to my face. 'Not all men,' he murmurs. 'Not me.'

'Oh, not you? Profiting by the beast's misery.'

'That's very harsh, Becca.'

'And how much are you going to sell her to Hallett for?' I ask him.

He pinches back a soft knowing laugh, and taps the side of his nose.

Sometimes I think I don't know this man at all. Nor want to know him.

'He'll make her take tea, though, and be laughed at,' I say. Hallett, who once had two little apes take tea sitting at a table. The crowds loved them. Made Hallett a lot of money – shows four times a day and sixpence to see. They seemed to be, like our capuchins, cheerful little beings. Hallett may well like this great ape-woman in her clothes. But for all that, I wished she would not go there to be looked at.

'She'll be a star,' Joe tells me. 'And far better than what Dodd might else have done with her. He didn't want us here. I had to argue for an hour. He was going to sell her to Charlotte Rawlings.'

My heart sinks at the mention of the name. We've sold Rawlings parakeets and found her cats – ordinary cats – but she has a fondness for them, the only fondness she's ever shown for man or beast and that's the truth. She got rich selling virgins in her place off Cheapside.

'Oh God, the shame of it,' I tell him. 'And you should be ashamed, too, to be any part of it. What's wrong with you?'

'We have to make a living too, Becca,' he says.

We go in to see the animal.

She looks at me, and I see strange eyes, piercing and calm.

The women, four of them, are huddled in a corner of the room. 'She'll grab hold of you,' one of them warned. 'And not let go.' She held up a bruised hand and arm. 'Look.'

'Anybody would grab someone screaming,' I said. 'You're lucky she didn't do anything else.'

'It's not natural,' the whore retorted. 'Dressed like that.'

They're right. It don't seem so bad when it's just a little creature. But this. She's stood crouched over – I later see that she can't straighten up like a man – but even then she's four feet or more, and comes up to my shoulder. She's broad round the hip and her feet are wide-splayed. Her hands hang low. The dress makes her grotesque. It has no sleeves and is cut low at the front.

There's something so alive in the face. Knowing, understanding. She looks solidly at me and I feel so sorry for her mournful journey, and I wonder where she had been living before the traders took her and sold her on at some port or other, some string of huts on a shoreline or in an alehouse.

She holds out her hand.

'Oh,' the women say. Like a great sigh.

Behind me, Dodd is tapping his cane on the floor. Impatient. 'We have a service at three,' he tells us.

'You mean you've got paying punters,' I retort.

'She's taken a shine to you,' he replies. 'One poor raddled creature to another.'

The ape drops her eyes and won't look at me more. Maybe there's something in what Dodd says. Some of the apes are perfect clever, you know. They act like human beings sometimes. Tender, like. With children. I gave a doll to one and he carried it everywhere. I look down at the creature's hand now, gripped so tightly to mine.

'Hurry up,' Dodd mutters. 'You, or Rawlings.'

I take a step towards the door, and bless the creature she follows, quiet as you like. Before we get out to the daylight, I take off my shawl and wrap it around her, and tie it in front to cover her up.

I feel Henry's hand on my shoulder. 'You're a good woman, Becca,' he says.

I watch Joe as we get into the cart. He's a clever bastard and no mistake, taking money from the captain and Dodd and Hallett to boot, all on one animal. He's done things like that in the past. No wonder I had to come here quick before anyone else got wind of it.

The ape sits next to me with the shawl over her head and shoulders and her face turned down, as still and helpless as a baby, and I know what the crowd in the Strand might think when they see us together, *two ugly sisters God have mercy!* – and I don't care for me, let them say what they like, I've heard it before – but I care for *her* and I think aye, it is ugly. An ugly business all round.

7

BOY TYGER

They don't come through the front door. They come in the back.

It's late but there's no closing today. We stay open for Jumby's walk. They take him out into the street. Not to take money, but to walk him right to the edge of the river. He likes the river. He washes himself there. Once, there used to be a polar bear that swam in the Thames, belonging to the Tower, and they would let him out on a great chain and he would swim, but he died after a year or two. Now the crowds come to see Jumby. They get him down to the shoreline between the great houses there, and he likes to play. They let me go with him sometimes, but not today. Shaw says he don't like me today.

These people come in as the light is low, and they bring with them an ape that Shaw thinks is a woman and then he laughs for a long time, first time we've seen a smile all day. He picks up the corner of her shawl and peers at her. She's holding the woman's hand.

I know this woman.

Mr Hallett is upstairs. They send a message and he comes down and looks at the ape, and he gives the other man money. I don't know how much, but there is a lot of talk and Mr Hallett puts his arm around this man's shoulders. I know the man, too.

Hallet's smaller than the other one. He dresses very showy and he makes me worry. Turns my stomach over. He never looks at me but there's a feeling off him, something that bothers him, some reason why he *won't* look. Like Shaw, he's all shadow. Like the torches you see from the playhouses, burning far off in the river on the far side. Coming and going is his mood, like the torchlight in water.

The other man who brought the ape... sadness. Heart sewn up inside. Very tall and fair-haired but plain in his clothes, and wears a greatcoat today even though it's summer. Cold in his veins, afraid of warming. I don't know how I know these things or see these things or feel them. I don't ask for them. Curious about this taller man. It's as if there are many children at his back. Why that is I can't reckon.

I'm behind a feed stall, where Shaw put me and told me not to come out. 'You feckin' eyesore,' he said, and give me a clump to the head on my seeing side. It was a joke. I got something in one eye this week, all gummed up and it weeps on its own accord. I scratched it sore. So that's Shaw's joke. 'Sit down and don't come out.'

But the woman, holding the ape's hand, looks at me. She's looking for somewhere that the ape could be, a space where they could bed her down. They bring out a chair and the ape sits and the men begin laughing. Oh. Oh and oh. The creature has got nothing in her. Oh. Just empty. She's got no hope, that's what it is. I know because I got none either. I want to go over and tell her, but I daren't. She don't look my way so sunk down is she, so sunk and low that I want to cry. That's how low.

The woman steps aside. No one is watching her. She comes across to me and I shrink back into the wall.

'I never seen a child so dirty,' she tells me, hands on hips. But kind.

She reaches down and touches my shoulder. 'How old are you?'

I stare at her. Wreaths of smoke.

She crouches down so that we're face to face. 'Don't be frightened of me,' she says, quiet like. She looks me all over. 'Did you see our Molly, the rhinoceros? She's here in the stables.'

I'm not allowed in there. All I'm allowed in is the pisshouse, and then to clean it, put down ashes. The soil man comes at night.

She puts out her hand. 'Want to see it?'

I do, but here comes Shaw.

'Best not touch that,' he tells her. 'Got a disease.'

She stands up and looks at him so straight that he drops his gaze. 'Have I got a disease?' she asks.

'No,' he mutters.

'Well, neither has he.'

'Best not, it's a bad child, it's a bad one...' he says, and pulls on the arm that holds me.

Oh, smoke. Fire. 'Take your hands off me,' she says, and he drops it.

Nobody holds my hand. Not ever. I forgot all about it, how one hand can take gentle hold of another. And she's got a grip even stronger than Shaw. He makes a bad face at me behind her shoulder, and I know what's coming tonight when everyone else has gone.

She takes me out into the yard at the back, with Mr Hallett and the man in the greatcoat. The yard is big. It has tall wooden gates that lead out into the street. I don't know where the road goes from there. I've not been out since I got here and I don't know how many years that is. I remember three Michaelmas Fairs. I trail behind her, watching my feet follow hers. The back of her dress drags a bit and it must always drag a bit because it's dirt nearly as far as her knees. I never seen a woman with a dress as dirty as that.

We come to the door. A half door. She looks back at me.

'You can't see, can you?' she says, and she comes and she picks me up. She holds me in her arms and I am tall and I see over the door and there is such a beast, bigger than a horse, not as big as Jumby but a hide that looks thicker than him, like he's wearing something thick and grey.

The woman reaches over with one hand and she opens the door latch. Mr Hallett says no, but she does it anyway, laughing, and we go inside and she sets me down. There's such a stench, but it goes quick and then it smells of earth. Thick wet earth. Breath rumbles inside it.

'Nobody knows her real name,' the woman says to me. 'But we brought her here. We walked her here when we brought her here a few years back and she has been on the stage at Drury Lane.' She put her hand on the beast's head and touched the great spike on the end of the nose then she puts that same hand into the mouth and rubs the gums. I shake even though I can see this mouth won't hurt her. The man in the greatcoat is leaning against its back, patting the big wrinkled rolls of grey.

'Feel her coat,' he tells me.

No, I can't do that. She knows them but not me and I can't see into that little eye, half closed.

'The theatre burned down, did you know?' the woman asks me. 'And we got her out and Mr Hallett lets us keep her here for a little bit.' She smiles. 'We won't take her into the cages,' she tells me. 'I don't think she ever saw a tyger. She might get them all feared in there.'

I start to grin. Tygers don't fear any beast. Maybe the tyger never saw a behemoth, but she'd see that soft space under her mouth. She'd see that alright.

'Oh,' the woman says. 'Am I funny?'

I smile at her and I see what she used to look like. Pretty with curly hair, reddish brown. She looks back at the man and I see more: threads that bind them, as clear as ropes. Bind them together.

She takes me out again into the fresh air and she walks straight over to Shaw, who's standing in the middle of the yard sulking, pulling at his jacket with a face like thunder.

'Does this boy speak?' she asks.

'Him?' he says. 'Not much.'

She looks back at me. Her eyes travel head to foot and back again. 'Why don't you put shoes on his feet?' she says.

'Boys grow.'

'That they do.' She pinches at my clothes. 'And what is he dressed in? A sack?'

Shaw says nothing.

'Do you wash him?'

'Sometimes, when I do the horses,' he says. 'But he's a devil, that boy. He won't stand still long enough. And what's the need? Boys only get dirty again.'

Just for a second he looks at me in the way that he does when he gets me by the waist. The woman sees it, too, and her mouth sets in a line, and she lets me go.

The man in the greatcoat walks over. 'Come, Becca.'

And then it comes very strong from them both.

Smoke and fire, smoke and fire, smoke and fire.

8

REBECCA

I don't know what time it is when I wake.

Night. Dead of night.

Sometimes months might go past before I have the dream, and I don't know why I've had it tonight. Except that it's something to do with the boy.

There's still a little heat left in the embers, a faint glow in the ashes, and I bring the kitchen fire back to life from the stack of wood. I go to the door and the foot of the stairs, and don't hear anything from Joseph's room. The house with its yard seems to settle down into the ground at night, as if it's sinking a bit, pulling up the earth around it. It's old, maybe two hundred years; the back was once a barn on an open field, so they told Joseph. You can still see beams in the walls and roof: faded, wormy. At the door to the yard there's lath sticking out from between the brick.

I imagine this house once sitting alone on the edge of the field that used to belong to the king – him that chopped off his wives' heads, the fat bugger – before he stole the lot from the church. Think on that, just fields, think on them in summer and spring down to Covent Garden, all green and smelling of cow-wheat or orchid, and Joe says on the papers it was once called Elme Close and later on there was turnings – Feather Alley and Knockle Alley with ramshackle stuff built. Nothing to see of all that now. There's an inn going to be built on the corner, and in between we have coachbuilders. It's a rare education to see what they make and the iron wheels and the seats inside – sometimes velvet or other fancy stuff, silk maybe – and they come and paint a livery on the doors. Sophia used to have a carriage like that, silk seats inside and white silk walls, too, and silk curtains on the window and Melbourne's coat of arms on the door. What every high-class whore works for: a title on the door and her inside like Lady Muck.

I sit in the dark and think of what Joseph has said, that he wants to move away and into Soho Square and that The Yellow House is up for sale now Henry's father is dead. I've never been inside – never wanted to be. He's always gone to dinners with the old man and said that Sir Thomas was kindly and taught him about things scientific, and how to speak like a gentleman, and he told me the story about the eels from Surinam, but I never wanted to see them on account I might be the one that got a jolt that made me faint or worse. 'You should come, Becca,' he'd say. But not me. For one thing I've no fine clothes and want none; and for another I don't want to shame him. My face disgusts people.

When Joe tells me his stories, there's always a light comes into his face of wanting something else, something better than the slurry of the Fields or the backstages of theatres. I wouldn't call it greed. I'd call it what he has always had, wanting to be out of one place and into another. To be climbing upwards, and to know things and to find the strangest, the furthest, the thing that makes him ask why and what for and how can he have it. That's what drives him to do his deals, sometimes dirty ones, with Hallett or a ship's captain. Sometimes good things. It makes him so passionate, so interested in the beasts, and I've seen him sitting with them if they're not faring well, even talking to them in the dead of night by the cages when he thinks I don't see him. He wants a bit of their world, you see. Just something from them, a little bit of the exotic. He holds it to him like it's something precious.

He's no wish of being like the lords and ladies. He calls them sheep. 'And backward sheep at that,' he says. 'You never saw a beast half as stupid and backward as a young man with a fortune, worse still a title.' And he always laughs. No. He wants to be something other. Something clever like the surgeon Hunter, and if he can't be that then something like Sir Thomas with his money and discoveries.

It was the wanting that brought the fire.


It could not have been more than nine in the evening. It was still light outside – a beautiful still summer evening. The workhouse was on the very edge of a small town. I never even knew its name, although I knew that horse chestnut tree seen through the third-floor windows, and I knew that somewhere nearby was the travelling circus that came every summer. That was what was driving the boys to light the fire. That was what I wanted to do more than anything else – see those carts and the great striped tent. But as for the names of the places beyond the tree and the wall and gate, I knew nothing.

I must have been dozing a while on the floor by the door when I smelled the smoke. I put my eyes again to the lock, but I couldn't see the boys or the fire. But I could hear the crackling of the wood chips. Then, as if they were standing at the top of the stairs, the boys began to shout.

'Fire, fire!'

They waited a while and shouted again. Then you could

hear thumping on the doors downstairs. It was the women on the second floor. They were locked in, too. The smell of smoke got worse. The boys shouted louder.

'Fire, fire!'

I don't know what put the sudden thought in my head – I was barely nine years old, after all – but I suddenly knew there was no one downstairs with any keys. I knew that they had gone out – the old man, the kitchen women, the two big boys that worked in the yard – I knew they had gone out to see the fair in the field. They had gone out and left us locked in.

It was then that I heard the big chair on the landing being pulled across the floor. I battered on the door with the flat of my hands. 'Let me out!'

Nobody answered. Other girls had got out of their beds. Some of them were big ones – eleven or so – ones that would soon be sent off to work in service in houses or factories or mills. I'd wanted to be older like them because I wanted to see something other than the workhouse, the tree and the wall and the gate and the lane that ran down the hill. I wanted to be big. They came close now. There were five of them, and they pushed the little ones back. 'What's happening?'

'The boys lit a fire,' I told them.

'Sweet Jesus!' the biggest exclaimed. 'Pull on the door.'

They all tried it. It wouldn't budge.

'Open the shutters!'

None of us had ever touched the latches on the shutters. We were supposed to wait until one of the women came to do them in the morning, and the old man did them at night. They were big: cast iron, and there were three on each window. Only the tallest girl was big enough to reach the top latch, and when she finally managed it, we saw out into the darkening evening through the narrow bars. There were lights on in the field:

torches. You could hear a lot of people down there. We all started to shout at once.

'Help, help us!'

There was no chance of anyone down the hill hearing, of course. There was music playing and every now and again you could hear people clapping, and there would be a burst of laughter or the sound of the crowd shouting at whatever it was that they were watching. I thought of the elephant and the big cats and such a bolt hit my heart – I can feel it now – a bolt of realisation that I would never see them at all, and I would never walk down the hill, and that I was going to die in this locked room.

Then there was the sound of glass shattering.

Only the window on the landing had glass in it.

I ran back to the door.

I put my hand to it. It was warm.

There were a lot of voices now: women screaming downstairs, boys shouting outside our door. And the muffled crackling sound. Smoke began to drift under the door.

'Let us out!' the older girls shouted. The little ones began to cry.

I put my mouth to the keyhole. 'Joe... Joe...' But I breathed in the smoke and fumes, the sticky, scouring taste of burning limewash from the walls. I turned and a bigger girl was trying to squeeze through the bars of the window. We might all have been able to do it, we were that thin. Others scrabbled at her clothes, saying it was too high. She hesitated on the sill, looking down, and looked back at us saying, 'There's flames coming out of the landing.'

The girl nearest her squatted on the floor and began to pray in a high-pitched voice. 'Gentle Jesus meek and mild, look on me a little child...' I ran over to her. Gentle Jesus wasn't looking down on us. He never did. Nobody did. I'd kept this horrible burn-in-hell blasphemy to myself for a long time, ever since we had the Bible read to us on Sundays. I didn't believe it. I didn't believe Jesus was watching from his cloud in heaven and cared about a run-down workhouse where people were carried out all the time in winter in deal coffins and where no angel of the Lord had ever been known to strike the doctor who drank in the superintendent's office with the parish priest and who said it was all right for us to eat the porridge with the black bits in it that I never knew what they were, but I guessed dirt off the pans. It was all just a story. And I suddenly knew, looking at this girl praying on the floor, that God was busy somewhere else. I looked at her bare feet and my bare feet and the calico shift we both wore, and I wanted to slap her. We were going to burn.

She stopped praying and looked up at me as if she'd read my mind, then looked past me suddenly with a gasp.

For as long as I'd been there, I'd watched that door at night, and in the early mornings. My bed was right opposite it. All my life I'd counted its cracks and knots and made maps up in my mind to pretend the door was a picture of islands and seas. It was mid-brown with a brass lock. But not now. It had gone pinkish and flakes were falling from it. And then God finally remembered us. The panel by the lock fell in, and a boy was standing on the other side, boot smouldering where he'd kicked in the door. The girls plunged towards him, all of a mass, all gouging and treading on each other to get out. The big ones got there first. All these girls raised on the Sunday Bible didn't give a rat's arse for anyone else. The little ones were pushed aside, and one was very small, maybe three or four, and she sat down with a bump, mouth open in a little stunned O shape. I picked her up and never felt anything shake like that little girl was shaking, trembling like in a fever. 'Come on,' I told her. 'Hold on to me.'

At the door, hardly able to see, I felt her being pulled out of my arms.

'Becca,' said a voice. I couldn't fathom who it was. But it was a boy with a blanket and he put it over my head. It was sopping wet. 'Jump,' he said. He propelled me to the window where the smoke was worse, drawn out by the evening air in a churning torrent.

'I can't,' I told him.

He took my hand. 'Jump out. Out, not down. Watch me, right? Watch me. And then I'll catch you.'

Joseph Eliot got up on the sill. And he jumped. For a second, he hung there against the sky that was still half-light, and then he stretched his arms out. *Here's the angel*, I thought. An angel all of my own. I heard him yell. Then a whoosh, a whoosh that came up behind me. I pulled back the blanket to see what it was and a wall of flame hit me, a wall of blank white brightness. Never in my life had I thought about what fire could do. I'd only ever seen it in the superintendent's fireplace, or out in the yard when they burned the rubbish. I never thought it was a whole world of bright like this and just for a second, I wondered where the little girl had gone.

'Becca!'

No more time.

I climbed up on the sill then jumped.


'Becca, what are you doing?'

I look up. Joe is standing in the doorway wrapped in the Flemish coat, a thick tapestry coat right to the floor.

'I couldn't sleep.'

He walks to the fire, warms his hands, and then takes the other chair. 'Is it Shaw?'

'Shaw?' I repeat, thinking at once of the dirty bastard at the Exchange.

'You don't like him.'

'No I don't,' I tell him. 'Who would?'

He smiles to himself. 'Did I do right yesterday?'

'What, with the ape?'

'Yes, that.'

'It's your concern.'

'Not really,' he says and looks into the fire. 'It's ours. Tell me what you think.'

'I suppose it made you a good deal of money.'

'That it did,' he says, nodding. 'Money we need.'

'Aye, I know.' And as has been our way for years now, Joe lays it on the table: five guineas. It goes into my own purse that hangs from a string around my waist inside my skirt. That's our way, and there's an old reason for it. We sit and look at each other for a moment, both thinking of the dwindling account at Child & Company. Drury Lane means we don't have a theatre show any more, and Molly looks fit to drop, so I hope to God that we get more crowds at the fairs at the Fields. Meanwhile, the animals and birds there eat us out of house and home, and Hemp and the other bruisers we have to guard them complain constantly, and the gentlemen at Child's begin to frown, so Joe says.

'We shall get through,' Joseph whispers, almost to himself.

'Let's hope Hallett don't find out. Nor Dodd.'

'Purely business,' he says.

There is a long silence in which I watch him, seeing how the years are beginning to tell. There are grey hairs in the blond. He holds himself differently now, much as an older man would, a little slope-shouldered, a little weary. It's no surprise. He must be thirty and more. The kind of life we have, it's a wonder neither of us have dropped in our tracks, hauling about horses and cages and tarpaulins and tents and the wood stages that we set up in the Fields. I must have heard 'Becca, take this' a thousand times. More. After Sophia set us up in business, we did it all until we could hire someone to help us.

'But...' Joseph stretches out his legs and rubs his knees. He has gout in them. 'That ape.'

'Aye, she was different.'

'Will Shaw mistreat her, d'you think?'

If there's one thing that Joe prides himself on, it's keeping the animals fed, watered and warm. We spend a fortune on dry meadow grass and he had doors made for the lion cage to close at night. I've seen him brushing down the backs of hogs, and cleaning out pens, and shovelling food he's got off tavern bins in Covent Garden. He's particular. The men know it. Though if a man asked him if he cared, he would say he cared about money alone, but I've seen him blindside Scrub, our driver. Knocked him down when Scrub took a whip to one of the horses that couldn't pull no more.

'He'll try.'

We both know what he means. Shaw is a pig, and that's an insult to pigs.

'Will you go in sometimes?' he asks. 'Find out.'

I smile at him. 'If you want.'

The water on the grid is hot. Though I go to reach it, he takes the pan from me. We have tea locked in the cupboard, only because of Hemp who'd steal it if he could. He can't pass it up, he's that addicted to it. Joseph gives me the filled cup: black, steaming. I think of the continents that it's crossed. I think of the poor ape and the oceans she came by. When I heard about Joe going to the ship, I had a half thought that he might come back and say he was going away, pulled out of London by the stories of heat and discoveries. I see him look at the blackamoor on the side of the Custom House, him that does dances and plays the whistle, and I see Joseph plainly wondering where it was that he came from, Africa or more like the plantations. There are a lot of freed blacks on the London streets. Freed and escaped, or ones that grew too big to be pageboys and got thrown out of fancy houses, or got some sickness that made them no use. Maybe Joe wants to go to the Gold Coast. Maybe Jamaica. I daren't imagine.

'Remember the boy?' I ask him.

He glances up. 'What boy?'

'In the 'Change. The one I brought to see Molly.'

'That dirty child? What of it?'

'Shaw told me he had a disease.'

'No doubt. He had a death's head look.'

'I think the only disease he's got is hunger. That, and...'

'Well, what?'

I don't know. I can't say. But there's something. 'He said something strange to me, that boy.'

He has finished the tea. He's taken the bread, slathered it in butter, and has his mouth full, so he answers by raising his eyebrows in a question.

It was all because of him that I'd returned this night on that hot ash floor, back turning to the sheet of flame that burned me, that caught hold of my shift and ran up the sleeve and streamed over my head and scorched me in a moment and made my skin melt, and came after me when I jumped and landed in Joe's arms in the candle-heavy branches of the chestnut tree. It was Joe who smothered it out with his own body, and Joe who bullied me down to the ground, and Joe who carried me out into the road and through the hedges and over the cornfields to a stream an acre away. It was Joe who cried when he saw me. We cried together and watched the smoke rise across the fields, and heard the crowds shouting and the horrible silence afterwards.

Nobody ever came looking for us. 'We're just ash,' Joe

would say whenever I worried that they would come searching, even when we got to London. 'We're nothing no more, Becca. We're nothing but ash and dust.'

He was right. We would sit under the windows in Oxford Street and pick up scraps of food, beg for them like dogs beg at butchers' doors. I think how invisible we were, how pitifully low. I think of the cold in winter and how we first came to the theatres because there was always carriages outside at closing time and braziers that kept the drivers warm. We used to run errands: bring an actress to a carriage, go fetch anything wanted. We got inside and made ourselves useful and became a kind of pet, though still nobody looked at me with pleasure. Joe kept the wandering hands away from me. He would stand there, all five foot five and eleven years old, bringing up his little white fists. We came as a pair and said we were brother and sister and the sad story of the fire got us food sometimes. Even shoes. None that fit, but they was still shoes.

My thoughts run back through our past and straight to the boy at the 'Change.

The boy took hold of my hand yesterday and he said, 'You jumped from the fire. You jumped into the tree.'

I tell Joe this, and his face blanches. The hand holding the bread slumps to his lap.

'He knew, Joe,' I whisper. 'That boy knew.'

9

BOY TYGER

Asleep in the feed store in the dark.

Summer. In grass and the grass is tall. Taller than me. Soon going to be cut. Path by trees. Two hands hold my waist, steadying me. Maybe I'm walking, or trying to walk, and the hands go tight and a voice close to me says, *Easy little one.* My mother. Dark skin, pale voice. It's coming down to evening, everywhere is soft in the heat. Not a heat like I see in the eyes of animals, not heat scorching the soil so that the ground underneath you is dry like sand, but a soft heat of a long day. The grass under my feet is crushed and there's the edge of a piece of cotton, the hem of a skirt. Her skirt.

'Where is he?'

We're not supposed to be here.

We're not supposed to be outside.

For a minute, a man's voice is tangled up with *easy, easy.*

Then I'm lifted out of the dream – a glimpse again of summer and then – like a crash – the darkness of the inside of the feed store, and Shaw's face coming up, greasy and red. He has me by the hair.

'Here he is,' he says. 'What did I tell yer? Little rapscallion,

81

sleeping on the feed.' There's someone behind him, a smaller man. I can't see his face in the dark. The smell of drink and something else rolls off them – something rotten, like bad meat, something knuckle-raw – I feel the fight in them and a splinter, like a nail hammered down through them, a splinter of greed and mud washed from the streets.

'Aint he like a girl, though,' the other man says.

'I told yer.'

'Little pretty girl.'

'He ain't pretty. What's got your eyes?' Shaw says, laughing. 'Got a pox, gummed up yer eyes, is it?' He pulls me towards him. 'But what you can't see in the dark, you can't see, is that right?'

They holler yes to each other. I try to duck out of his grasp, but he pulls tighter. I think my hair is coming out by the roots.

When Hallett comes into the 'Change, there's always a smell of fear round Shaw, but there's no smell now. Hallett makes him nervous. Afraid of losing his job. But there's no fear here in the middle of the night where there's no Hallett to see him. There's just the other stink – the one he has when he's washing me out in the yard. Angry and slithering, wet with spittle, a mouth stinking of whatever he ate last – herring or roe or oyster or pork – ale and gin on a night-time, and thin beer for the day. He breathes close to me now.

'Show us what you're made of,' he says.

I get out of his hold, and he stands there with a hank of my hair in his hand, and he looks at me, and he looks at the hair, and he laughs all the more. I make for the door, running, slithering on the beer that they've spilled, and I reach up and unlock the latch to the cage room, and they come after me.

Light bars fall on the ground. Moonlight from the windows. It's a still, warm night out there, and I think almost dawn, for there's a pinkish line at the top of the first window.

'Come here, pretty girl.'

The other man stumbles after him.

I back away, four steps, five steps, and my back slams against the bars of the first cage and the monkeys inside it start to screech. They open their mouths and cry like banshees, like ghosts, like wind caught under the outside door whenever there's a storm, and the sound feels like a nail driving into your head, and they run around inside the cage, one after the other, screaming and screaming. And they've woke the new ape in the next cage, sitting far back clutching on the shawl that the woman gave her. Just for a second I hear her – a little faint thread of a thought as if she's going far away, or is thinking of something far away and all her heart has gone with it over miles and miles of water, over miles and miles of land to a green place – but I run too fast to listen to her.

Shaw's nearly up to me and he looks like a devil. The only thing he hasn't got is horns and a tail, but he looks like a demon that Mr Hallett showed me in a Bible when he got me here and told me to be good else one of demons would come and get me one day. And I think that maybe today is the day because the picture in the book looks like Shaw, red-faced and grinning and waving his ham-like hands in front of him, trying to grab me. There's no way to get away from him, or the man at his back, and the sour stink rolls off him and I know it won't end.

And then I remember what the keepers used to make me do. I grab hold of the nearest bars and I climb them. There's another rail that runs across near the top, and another one after that, and I get hold of them and pull myself up and I'm sitting right on top of the cage and I look down.

The tyger is standing below me.

Her mouth is open.

I think she's waiting for me to fall and I don't want to fall, or feel what it is to have that mouth close around me or have her make sport with me if I run around the cage until she leaps on me, and I hold tight to the bars, green paint and rust under my fingers, sweat in my eyes, fear rolling off me that I know the beast can smell.

But I don't fall. And the tyger doesn't leap at me.

Shaw is trying to reach me and while he's looking at me and yelling and cursing while the other man shakes the bars, laughing.

'That's no tyger,' he says. 'That's no more'un tyger than a fookin' tabby cat.'

And he puts his hand through the bars.

I don't remember.

I won't remember.

Close my eyes.

Can't see.

Can't hear.

You'll see them on the street all the time, always women. Some of them sell flowers and then try to take your hand to tell your fortune. If only a small portion of my being believed in such things, I still wouldn't take those hands willingly, for once they have hold of you it's the very devil to get away.

We have one at the Fields regularly, and two at Michaelmas and Christmas. People like it, though the appeal has always evaded me. The crowds give over their pennies or sixpences, money hoarded and wrapped in little pieces of cloth and unwound with deliberate care, their eyes fixed on the woman at the table behind the curtain. They give her the money and wait with their foolish mouths agape waiting to hear that they'll end up rich, or some man will come along and marry them and take them out of London to some house somewhere where they'll be lady of the manor. I've seen them come out of the tent with their faces flushed with excitement at the rosy future that's been given to them. A gift that's washed away in daylight when they're back to scrubbing steps or making braid in their crowded rooms or washing other women's clothes.

I've even had one such gypsy tell me that I'll die far away

from London, out in that same countryside that they paint as if it's paradise, and I told them that the nearest I'll get to an earthly paradise is painting palm trees on theatre scenery and tethering a monkey to a tree.

'Oh,' she said, 'you'll mark my words one day.' I gave her a penny for her absurdity.

So when Becca told me about the boy, and said that he saw us jump from the flames and some other arrant nonsense, I stopped eating and stared at her. You never know with women. Even sane women like Becca. They seem level-headed but inside they want to believe the world will come right for them. Perhaps it will. Perhaps it does. But it's not through believing the world is all dancing and daisies. The world comes right for women like the madams who pocket the money and buy themselves a nice little estate by the sea. The world credits the brain, not the heart.

'You should talk to the boy if you see him again,' she replied. 'And see what he says to you.'

I had no intention of going back to the 'Change any time soon, and would not have done until I heard the news this morning.

Hemp knocked on the door at about eight o'clock.

'There's been trouble on the Strand,' he said.

'What kind of trouble?'

'You'd best come see.'


The body still lay in the street.

It had been put on the back of a cart, but Hallett had no idea what to do with it afterwards. Nobody had come to claim the man, and it wasn't likely that anyone would. By his clothes he looked as if he had had lived on the streets, as many thousands do. He was filthy and despite all his terrible injuries, the reek of alcohol was still around him.

A crowd of boys had gathered around, as boys always will, and every now and then one of them would lift up the sheet that covered the body and the whole lot of them would step back, hissing and squealing. They do the same at Hunter's dissection rooms at the back of his house on Leicester Square. They wait for the waggons from the hospital and then they dare each other to go and see what's being carried in. One day, so people tell me, an amputated leg fell to the ground and a dog ran forward and took it. Hunter was most displeased, but then there is human nature. The boy wants to see the bodies and the leg. But most of all, the boy wants to see the dog run away with that leg. I ought to know, I am a showman by trade. If there's one thing that draws the crowds more than naked women and strange beasts, it's blood.

As if to prove my point, the cart and the boys had begun to attract everyone else on the street, and soon there was a whole concourse of other carts, and tradesmen, and even carriages whose drivers had been instructed to find out what was happening. The horse of the waggon that held the corpse began to fret, and the driver began to curse, and soon the whole street was shouting enough to deafen any decent person passing by.

'What's Hallett going to do with him?' Becca murmurs beside me. 'He can't leave him out here in the street.'

'Waiting for the parish constable, no doubt.'

Becca snorts to herself. The parish constable is probably drunker than this man was last night.

'Would Hunter want him?'

'That may be. If only to see what a tyger can do to a human body.'

Inside the 'Change, there's a curious atmosphere. It's quiet. Silent, even. No visitors have been allowed in today, and Hallett is standing with two keepers and Shaw and they are staring into the tyger's cage. We go to stand alongside them, and I understand their problem.

Hallett looks pale. It's for certain that he never imagined he would be faced with such a task, and the keepers have that same irresolute expression.

Hallett takes my hand. 'This is a bad business, Eliot.'

'An accident, surely.'

'Have you ever had such a thing?'

'Never.'

'No accidents?'

'None.'

Hallett takes a step or two towards the cage, and then steps back again. 'I can't understand how the man got in here,' Hallett murmurs. 'Shaw says the yard door was open, but he never heard a thing.'

I hear Becca take a long, deep breath. I glance at Shaw, who looks as if he has put his head under the water pump. Even the collar of his coat is wet, and his eyes blink at me with an unaccustomed innocence, red-rimmed. If Hallett can't smell the drink on him, I can.

'Did you know the man?' I ask him.

He does a little shuffled dance, hopping from one foot to the other. 'No, sir.'

'You say that he came in during the night, and you never saw him?'

Shaw lowers his voice to a whisper. 'It was the boy, sir.'

'What boy?'

'The wild boy, sir. Scavenging boy not to be trusted.' He glances at Hallett, looking apologetic now. 'I think the man must'a come in with the boy.'

Becca finds her voice. 'Are you saying the boy brought a

man in here, at night, under your nose, and took him in to this room and showed him the tyger?'

'I can't say, ma'am.'

'But you just did say that very same thing!'

I take Hallett's elbow and we walk away from the group. 'You had better show me the ape.'

This, more than the tyger and the dead man, was what had brought Hemp hurrying to the door this morning. On the floor of the cage at the far end of the room lies the body of the ape that we only brought to Hallett yesterday. She lies on her side, curled up, much like a human woman, knees drawn towards her chest and her back to the wall. Her eyes, mercifully, are closed. You might be forgiven for thinking that she was asleep.

Hallett is chewing on a fingernail and looks at me narrowly. 'Did you know she was ill?' he asks.

'No, of course not.'

'Had some fever from the ship?'

'Since I don't know the ship, I can't say.'

I'm not at all sure that he believes me.

'You bought her from Dodds?'

'Yes.'

He gives a little shrug and stares at the floor. He's unsuited to this business; his old trade was inanimate objects: silks, fabrics from the Orient. He probably wanted a more exciting life. But not as exciting as this, perhaps.

'The king's surgeon, Hunter, will take her,' I tell him. 'The body outside, too. You may give my name – he has dissected an animal or two of mine. He has a passion for it.'

Hallett is continuing to gnaw on his thumbnail. 'You might offer me the money back that I paid for her yesterday.'

I put my arm around his shoulders. 'Why, you'll be a rich man before the day is out,' I tell him. 'Open your doors and let the crowds see the man-killing tyger. Leave the bloodstains on the floor and... whatever it is that the beast is eating there in the corner of his cage.'

I had an inkling that he had a weak stomach, and so it is now proven. He turns away from me abruptly, runs a little way out into the yard, and vomits in the dust. Out of courtesy I turn away from him and look about myself in the rooms here at the back of the building. There is a small place with a truckle bed and a poor set of cupboards, with a dirty rug on the floor. I take it that this is Shaw's room, for it stinks the same way he does. On the other side are a set of stables where a horse gazes out with an almost philosophical expression. And there on the far side is Molly's stabling. Taking care not to notice Hallett drying himself as best he can, I go to visit our faithful old behemoth.

She is standing asleep, looking as if she was carved out of rock. Our great chain is still about her neck, and a bucket by her feet is testimony that she has been given the same beer diet that always kept her so content. I lean on the half door and think of Becca and I walking her across Kent, and something in my heart constricts for the youth we had and the optimism and carelessness, and I see Becca lying under lit windows in London begging for food long before that, and a ravaged and burned child long before even that, who I held in my arms by a stream in the darkness. I think on the fact that Becca never cried much but always clung to me.

There's a noise behind Molly, there in the shadows.

'Who is it?' I ask.

I look behind me, hearing footsteps. Becca herself is striding across the yard with a look of fury on her face. 'That Shaw is a bastard,' she tells me.

I smile at her. 'You're probably right.'

'Oh, I'm right,' she tells me. 'Blaming the child!'

'It's feasible.'

'Feasible?' She rolls the word round her tongue in disgust.

'Saying he knew the man and went to the yard gate and let him in. Look at the bloody gate!'

I look. It's eight feet tall and bolted top and bottom.

'Have you seen the child?' she asks. 'Has anyone?'

It strikes me then. I beckon her to my side. 'Look past Molly.'

We see nothing at first, but we hear it again. A scuffling like a dog scratching to get out. I open the half door and we both peer down into the gloom of the pen.

Becca walks past me. She skirts around Molly and kneels on the floor. I hear her say, 'You know me, remember?' But there's no reply. Her voice goes on. 'You like Molly, don't you? Has she been good?' And much else of no consequence. Then, 'Come with me.' I hear a movement, and then a cry. Becca stands up and waves her hand at me. 'Mr Eliot,' she says.

I know then that there's trouble. She calls me that when she's wanting something, or it's a business matter. I've been called Mr Eliot when a customer won't pay or when someone has teased an animal through the bars of a cage. Or when a performer won't perform, or wants more money, or is ill. It means that I'm to deal with whatever matter she has before her.

I open the door and see that the boy is halfway to his knees but has stopped, and Becca, beside him again, looks up at me. There's no condemnation or pity in her glance. But there is an expectation that I'm to do something about this child.

And then she picks him up. I hold out my arms, and she transfers him to me. He is as light as kindling.

In the daylight of the yard, I look down on the face that looks up at me. I see an infected eye that streams pus. I see gouges in his scalp. I see a long bright welt on his neck, much like a rope burn. His breathing is ragged, and he puts a frail hand to his stomach. The legs are so covered in dirt that it's hard to know what injuries are on them. His feet are bleeding.

Such a rage comes up in me that I almost drop him. Becca has run out with a piece of cotton that I fear – and afterwards know – is torn from her petticoat. She wraps it around him as best she can.

They say that when you are considerably angry you see red, and even though I have been in many situations where despite everything my gaze is clear, now I see a curtain cross my vision for a fleeting and enraged moment. I walk across the yard and into the back rooms, and I see Shaw there by his makeshift bed, and when he hears me he stows a bottle under the grey blanket then turns to me. He has his mouth open to say something, but what it is I shall never know, for I don't stop long enough to listen. I go out into the long room with its cages to where Hallett and the two other keepers are standing at the door of the cell, staring at the body of the ape, and they have the grace to look sorrowful. Hallett glances up at me.

His eyes range over the child.

'What is the meaning of this?' I ask him.

Behind me I hear Becca yelling at Shaw, but she comes out to me quickly.

'Do you see this child?'

'Aye,' Hallett murmurs.

'You are a father, are you not?'

'Yes...'

I know that he has four sons and they are all as young as this boy. Too young to work. Young enough to be schooled. And I know that his children are at home in Spitalfields, where Hallett still makes a living from the silk weavers, and I know that his wife is Huguenot and of a family that gave Hallett his money in the first place, and that she is God-fearing and keeps their children out of the vice of the city.

'I'm taking this child,' I tell Hallett. 'Shame upon you.'

It's noon by the time we get home.

Not much attention is paid to us. The day is hot, the street busy. We sidestep the pure-gatherers shovelling manure off the streets, and the flower sellers giving a better perfume, and the crowds drifting towards the 'Change with a rumour of something to see. Now and again, I glance down at the boy and his eyes are wide. I wonder how long it is since he was last out in the bright daylight and among the noises of the city. Once as I look down I see tears in his eyes, but he makes no movement at all and is light as a feather to carry.

Becca opens the street door with her key and hurries ahead of us. She stokes the fire in the range and drags a chair forward. The lad slumps in his makeshift covering. He looks at the fire and tilts his head, just like a dog sniffing the air. We have more time to examine the wounds on his head now, and Becca hisses to herself as she cleans the mess.

'We had best call the apothecary,' she says.

'You go,' I tell her. 'Bring him back with you.'

I open the window. The range smokes more than it ever used to. I think it is in this moment that I finally decide on The Yellow House in its clean, quiet little square. I have no idea how to pay for it – our income could not stretch to it and I must borrow – but Becca deserves more than this house and yard. I want more for her. I want her to hold up her head and have something more than the stink of animals about her. Lately it irritates me at how she makes her plainness and poor clothes a kind of religion. It does not suit me. Perhaps I am getting old and want no more of this life. Drury Lane wakes me sometimes in the night, the fear and upwards struggle of it all, when once it propelled me. It rankles somewhere deep down like a bad meal in the gut for too long.

The smoke goes out the window and the heat rolls in. This is the warmest summer that I can remember. And all these thoughts – the summer, the stubbornness of Becca, the tyger in the 'Change, Shaw's puffed, choleric face, Hallett's thinness of character, and the longing for the better house and the worry of money – churn like a carousel until, suddenly, they stopped. Hunter, the king's surgeon, slapped into my mind. Hunter and a portrait that he has on the wall of his study.

I grab a bowl and fill it with lukewarm water, the residue in the range kettle. I take it to the boy.

'There's no need to be afraid,' I tell him.

Why had I not seen it until that very moment? Or had I seen it and looked past it, registered it but not given it any weight? I take one of his feet in my hands and wipe the water over it. It is indeed thick with dirt, crusted over. It is a slim, narrow foot with a high arch. The boy takes a deep, long breath but other than that made no sound.

'I shan't hurt you,' I say.

And as the filth is taken away, I see what I saw in the portrait in Hunter's study. The foot and the leg are a patchwork of light and dark. There's no difference to the feel of the skin, but the contrast is unbelievable. I never thought to witness such a thing in life, and I've even doubted the reality of Hunter's portrait. But this is real. I begin on the other foot and leg, and they are the same. Not the same pattern but the same variegation.

I hear Becca come in through the street door. She enters the kitchen saying, 'He's not there. He'll come in an hour or so, and I told them...' But she stops short.

She stares at the boy and then at me, and, perhaps seeing her shock, the boy begins to whimper.

'Oh my God,' Becca whispers. 'What is it? Oh my God.'

11

JOSEPH

It used to be that a decent person could walk along Long Acre without being troubled, but all that is changing. Becca, the boy and I set out at seven thirty, an hour at which one might think the streets would be clear of working women – bawds and brothels alike are shut at this time of day, unless it's to let out some fool who has paid for a whole night – but this morning I see four women, two by two abreast, making their way towards Leicester Square as they cross St Martin's Lane.

They see us, and stop, and watch us pass by, and finally one of them runs up behind me and pulls at my arm. I'm not carrying the boy. Becca insisted that she should today, and she holds him close, well-wrapped even though the sunlight is streaming down. I know the way of these girls – one taking the arm, the other robbing you.

'Sir,' one says. 'Will you buy us two poor girls a drink?'

'Good God,' I tell her. 'Can't a man be left in peace before breakfast?'

Nothing is open, not even the Blue Periwig at Southampton Street. I know that for a fact. I stop and look at them, not dressed well, and not more than eighteen or twenty. They're glancing at Becca; the two others behind them now draw close. They take her for a servant. Already one is eyeing my shoes. I feel another reach into my pocket for a handkerchief.

They remind me of others working in pairs and fours along Covent Garden and Southampton Street and into Haymarket. Others I used when I was young myself. They weren't of Sophia's calibre, but she was often busy fleecing Melbourne for whatever she could get and then be inclined to give to me, if she was in good humour. Pretty girls from the countryside who took jobs in little shops that supposedly sold clothing. It was the usual thing to go to the Royal Exchange and into one of the milliner's shops along there and be taken to the back. It was in one such shop that I learned it was not so much her that was for sale, but my own money that was being robbed – clothes peeled off me and returned without the purse I'd carried.

I offer no apology for myself. I was young and anxious and living from hour to hour, and if something came into my possession from buying a bird and showing it at my lord and lady's house after dinner – we did such a roaring trade in that once, with our first cassowary, what Hemp called 'that lumpin' bird' that could do an injury, it was so strong – then it was likely that money went to the milliners a day or two later if Becca couldn't get her hands on it. I came to think of money as stupidly as Sophia did, puffed up with pride at running a nice little business showing animals and training them to do tricks, and hiring little booths along this very road – Grain Street going into Leicester – where we had one or two human miseries: the girl with the deformed feet and a man with eight fingers on one hand, and a blind old boy who had been at sea all his life and told fantastical stories of cannibals, and sang a few songs.

It was Becca who stopped my spending. She hit me square across the face one day, split my lip. I'd come back from Haymarket without the money we'd earned the night before.

For ever after, money went to her and she paid me an allowance. It's not something I like the world to know. Becca's not allowed in the private banking houses like Child's, but she comes with me to the door and watches me go in and demands to see the receipts. And then she'll tell me I must buy a better coat and look like a gentleman and we'll walk to Pall Mall and she'll watch me go in to the tailor with the same suspicious scrutiny. The arguments we have had, the struggles over what she sees as my public face and hers. I am sick sometimes when she stands in doorways, but she is obdurate. I bought her six fine lawn collars last year. She put them in a drawer in the kitchen and there they have stayed.

And so both she and I know these girls. Becca is on them in an instant. With the boy held close to her chest she tells them, 'Don't touch him.'

They laugh. 'Oh, missus?'

'Yes,' she says. 'See this boy? Have a care.'

'We ain't harming him.'

'It's him that'll harm you,' she retorts. 'We're going to Dr Hunter's.'

They spring back at once, horror on their faces.

Becca smiles at me as we walk on.

Dr Hunter's house is number 28 in the fine square. It was once very stylish to live here, as the Prince of Wales did, but since Leicester House was turned into the Holophusikon it is slowly moving downhill into gambling houses and brothels, which is perhaps where the girls were headed. I like it better, I think. I like going into the Holophusikon and looking at the curiosities, so much more refined than mine. It's painted all over with botanic drawings, and there are thousands – some say twenty thousand – delights to look on. A bird of paradise, a pink gull, shells from Cooke's voyages and striped rock and insects and bottled beasts such as Hunter also has. It is a place of wonders, this square, although Hunter's house has two faces: the one that has a lofty entrance through which Mrs Hunter's guests may enter, and the back door on Castle Street where the corpses come in.

This morning is still quiet, though barrows are trundling through the streets, each man pulling one towards the market, head down. Hunter's man, Clift, shows us in, an apron tied about his waist that he wipes his hands on. We go towards the back of the house and into Hunter's consulting room. Becca places a hand on my arm and inclines her head towards the boy. He is shaking, eyes wide with fear.

We put him down. He stands rigid, shoulders hunched.

'It's all right,' Becca says to him. Though it makes no difference.

Hunter comes in. He may be the king's surgeon but he looks like a rogue. That's what I thought when I first saw him, at least. He has an untended beard and uncombed hair, and there is dust in the material of his sleeves. But he's smiling broadly.

'Now then, Mr Eliot, what brings you here? Have you another dead animal for me?'

Somewhere in the back we hear a buzz of noise. Students are entering the dissecting room and gallery directly in front of us along the hall. There will be a corpse in there, probably come from the gallows yesterday. The boy lifts his head and puts it on one side, listening. Just as a dog would prick up its ears and listen.

'No, sir. This boy,' I tell him, 'reminds me of your portrait of the patchwork girl.'

'Mine?'

'That you own, sir. In the room upstairs.' He had a lofty gallery built with a skylight, and he has filled it with specimens that he shows to visitors. I've been shown the bodies of rarer animals than my behemoth. And he has human monstrosities too. I recall – sometimes too late at night to be good for me – preserved dissections of male phallus. Hunter is a master researcher into syphilis. I try not to think about those at all.

Hunter has leaned down so that he is face to face with the boy.

'It's of a girl,' I say. 'Your portrait.'

'Not theoretically a portrait,' he says. 'An engraving from the *Histoire Naturelle*.' And he waves his hand behind him to the bookshelves. He stands up. 'Mary Sabina is the girl. I see no resemblance in this boy.'

Gently, Becca takes the coat from the child. He has closed his eyes tight so that he can't return Hunter's look. She kneels and rolls down each stockinged leg below the breeches. Both are loose; we took them from Hemp's drawer. They hang on the boy like curtains, but it was all we had.

Hunter looks from Becca to myself, and back again. 'Put him on the desk. My knees don't allow me to kneel.'

As soon as Hunter touches him, the boy begins to cry. He makes no sound, but the tears roll down his face and he starts trembling again, flinching each time Hunter's fingers touch him.

'Does it hurt him?' Hunter wonders to himself.

'I don't think so,' Becca says. 'I think he's frightened.'

Hunter smiles and puts his hand on the boy's shoulder. 'Are you afraid of me?'

The boy opens his eyes a fraction and nods.

'Why, I'm as jolly as you like,' Hunter says, continuing to smile. 'Is that not so, Mr Eliot?'

'Yes, indeed.'

The boy suddenly looks at me. I feel caught in a lie. There's something terrible – a wordless grief – in his expression. And then he screws his eyes shut again. Becca glances at me, and puts a hand on his shoulder.

'Most interesting,' Hunter murmurs. 'Piebaldism, if you

like.' He pulls on his beard. 'After magpies, you see? But Sabina is patches, as you rightly say. The curious star shape on her forehead. The large areas of white. Born to slaves in Cartagena, and taken from them as a prize. Jesuit plantation.' He looks away from the boy and back at us. 'But these are stripes. Most curious.'

'Like a tyger,' I say.

'Yes, quite. A tyger. I have never seen the like, nor read of it. Stripes and not patches, you see?'

'Is it a disease?'

'Oh no,' he replies. 'Inherited, it's supposed. Who are his parents?'

'We don't know.'

'You see the dark stripes; he is most likely from slave stock. That, if you like, is the natural colour. It is remarkable that no dark colour shows on the face.' He considers the child for some time. 'His hair is rather close. Perhaps a white father. I wonder if he came here as a prize, for gain?'

'Gain?'

'Mary Sabina was stolen by a privateer. She was exhibited.' Hunter looks closely at the boy again. 'Or perhaps the boy was born here, even to a freed slave.' He is thinking aloud. 'Where did you find him?'

'At Exeter Exchange.'

'And these?' Hunter points to the wounds on the boy's head and the marks on his neck.

'That's why we took him away.'

'Hmmm. They sold him to you?'

'No, sir,' Becca says. 'We took him. On account of his treatment there.'

She is re-dressing the boy, and lifts him down and puts him in a chair, where she stands guard over him like a mother hen.

Hunter half sits on the edge of his desk. 'A difficult exercise, to take a child,' he tells me. 'An offence in law.'

'You see the injuries,' I say.

'Nevertheless.'

'They are not his parents.'

'Have a care,' Hunter says. 'Kidnapping a child is a capital offence. One you might swing for.'

'I shall take my chances,' I reply. 'You're a witness, sir, to the injuries.'

'Well, well,' he says. 'I suppose it won't come to that. And... yes. I see the injuries.'

There is a knock on the door, and Clift shows his face. 'Everything is ready,' he announces.

Hunter stands up with some puffing, as if he's run a distance. 'I'll be there directly.' He shakes my hand. 'Come back in an hour. Clift will have a poultice for his injured feet. And the wounds on the head.'

'Thank you, sir, for your time.'

'And let me know how he gets along.' Hunter's gone in an instant.

Along the corridor, we can hear applause as he enters the gallery.


I send Becca and the child home.

I hesitate on the doorstep and watch them go, then turn back to the stairs. I don't think Hunter will deprive me of another look.

The tall doors are already open. The room is full of the sunlight that streams through the glass roof, and it is deathly quiet. And there in the very centre of the room is what I have come to see.

When I was first with Sophia, there were many who told me

that a camelopard was the stuff of legend. That such a thing did not really exist. That descriptions of it were only inflated rumours. For a while I'd discussed with Becca how we might make such a creature. I thought we could buy some kind of beast with a long neck – I'd heard of camels in Egypt – and paint it. Becca had actually considered it for a moment until she burst out laughing. She was only thirteen at the time, and Sophia sometimes allowed her to come into her house and sit in the kitchens where she was fed prodigiously by the cook who had no children of her own. It was clear she quietly despised both Sophia and myself, such was the disapproving frown that she would give me. But she pitied Becca and she was a great fund of gossip. Other men were slid into Melbourne's house right under his aristocratic nose, and the cook knew them all: the Duke of Portray; and the astronomer, Maskelyne, who was addicted to the tripe at Slaughter's coffee house, which one night nearly killed him. He was laid flat on the floor and treated by none other than Hunter. And, of course, those simpering fools Lord Wokingham and his sister. Because it was not all vice at Sophia's. She held afternoon teas, very civil, which lecherous husbands would attend with their stiff wives in tow, frowning just like the cook at Sophia but unwilling to let the opportunity go of meeting powerful men.

If I have to say anything at all about these wives it is generally that they are as capable of idiocy as their husbands. Mrs Casell – she who has The Boar's Inn in Piccadilly and a tribe of girls – has a small house on the road to Holborn. It is said – although I've never seen it – that the house is very select, with a little garden in the front, and that ladies may visit there and be shown to upstairs rooms where Mrs Casell has invested in strapping country boys for their amusement. And, of course, there are more visible practices – the great Messalina Ball, for example, tickets one hundred guineas, held not so long ago. One titled gentleman, masked as they all were, is said to have enjoyed his wife unawares, and that when they both realised the unfortunate liaison, they were reconciled and have lived very happily since. Sophia would probably quote this as the restorative effect of her profession.

I'm thinking of all this, of those early years with Sophia and the frowning cook and the stick-thin Becca who almost ate them all out of house and home, as I look at the glory of the camelopard now in Hunter's upper floor. I was part of the reason Hunter came by this wonder. A traveller called Paterson came back from South Africa, bringing with him a trophy – the skin and skeleton of a male camelopard that he had shot on his journeys.

By then, such beasts were called a giraffe by men of science. Lady Strathmore had paid for this expedition of Paterson's, but it was I who stood on the dock on the morning that his ship moored at Tilbury, trouncing those who were waiting at London. Lady Strathmore was a strange stick who had an adoration of plants and called herself a botanist. She had taken a shine to the young gardener near her home in Glamis and given him more power than he merited, and one look at this Paterson in the dawn of the morning told me all I needed to know of him.

He was unwashed and surly, sleepless from a rainy Channel crossing, and looked down at me when I hailed him from the dock. The ship was loaded with specimens for Her Ladyship and the hide of the camelopard was the prize. I told him that Lady Strathmore had sent me and showed him the note given to me by Strathmore's agent, the drunk and lazy man that I had met in Cheapside the night before. Because I was burning with curiosity at the news of the camelopard carcase on Paterson's boat, I had sought the agent out. He was well known and not hard to find, red-faced and singing, with a tart on his lap. I had offered to do the unpleasant task of going to Tilbury in the morning, and he had jumped at the chance and given me the note with the Strathmore seal and a guinea for my trouble.

Paterson took the note, grunted at the sight of the wax seal, and told me he would give me the carcase.

'But if it don't get to Lady Strathmore, I'll come after you,' he said. His Scottish accent – an accent so reviled in London – was so strong that it was hard to make out what he was saying, but the grip on my shoulder and the look on his face made the message clear. 'If ye don't give it over,' he continued, gripping me ever tighter, 'and I find you've taken it yourself, I'll hunt you down just as I hunted down the beast.' He kicked the packing case that held it. 'And you'll end up like that.' You could never have met a man more lacking in charm. He's in the army now and has gained a vicious reputation, which I do not doubt.

I gave him my word that Lady Strathmore would have the animal that morning. I took it in a carriage to the Strathmore agent who was waiting in Cheapside, and he paid me another guinea having forgotten that he'd paid me the night before. I can tell you freely that I had thought of how I could get that beast's skin and bones away for myself, but I did not doubt Paterson's word. There in the coaching inn, the agent and I took off the nailed-down lid of the case, and were rewarded by an unholy stench. But what a sight! The patterned hide alone was something to behold.

'Thank God I won't be taking that to Scotland,' the agent told me.

'Are you not?'

'No,' he said, holding his nose and backing away. 'Lady Strathmore wants me to give it to Mr Hunter.'

And that is how I came to be standing for the very first time on the steps of Hunter's last house in Jermyn Street, a packing case loaded on the cart behind me, holding out my hand for the price of the carriage.

Hunter was so overjoyed he paid me two guineas.

I can't help smiling to myself now at the memory of that lucrative day.

Four guineas – what a labouring man might earn in a year – for doing nothing much. The kind of trick I employed at the Exchange, of course.

I stand now in the morning sunshine looking up at the animal, eighteen feet high, and I think how I'd like to see it moving. See the plains in Africa where Paterson found it. There must be more. There must be many more. I stand gazing at the miraculous pattern and try to imagine those places where I will never go. It takes another Melbourne fortune to pay for such a trip. Ships and guides, porters and supplies. I would need to be able to fire a gun, and have no idea how to learn. And then I think that perhaps after all that travel, I could never kill such an animal. When our beasts die it's not for want of keeping them alive. I dread the day when we have to cart Molly to Hunter's and see her perhaps stuffed and placed in this very gallery. Poor Molly mournfully chewing on the hay that we pay such a price for, and drinking the ale that we were always assured she enjoyed.

But no matter. These feelings are no subject for a man of business. I wish now that I had asked much more from Hunter to bring him the carcase. I hear he plans to open the gallery to the public next year. He will make a fortune, of course.

I turn away and make my way down the stairs to the street, and just as I look out onto Leicester Square I think that while I can never exhibit the camelopard, I do have something else.

Something curious.

The astonishment of the age.

Striped like a tyger.

A fortune maker.

*'Taken as a prize, and exhibited.'*

12

BOY TYGER

The words are jumbled.

She's singing.

Someone other sang this once.

*When the bough breaks*

*The cradle will fall...*

Warm and dark. We are inside a place. A house maybe.

A man came to see me, washed my eyes. A dry mixture. Then honey.

'Hush, it is only honey.'

*Down will come baby*

*Cradle and all.*

Over and over again. Sitting on a kind of bed.

'When the old women had something in their eyes, they used to blow into them with dried hen's dung,' she says, and laughs to herself. Arms around me. Rocking backwards and forwards. 'It will all be all right,' she whispers.

Morning.

A room with a fire.

Too hot.

She comes with a bowl of water and she takes off my sacking shirt.

'We must get you other clothes,' she says, as if to herself.

I don't know what I dreamed of last night. Perhaps it was her. It's hard to sleep without the women who drift through the animals' room and pass through the walls, or the running man, or even Shaw's grunts. I wonder if I talk in my sleep like he does.

But there was something. Maybe the man yesterday. The doctor drenched in stains. Blood. A knife. Something hardening in his heart that pumps so sluggishly slow. Afraid of his kindness, afraid of him. Hands on skin, on broken things. Bottles, bones. But far away in someplace else he has his hands on a living hide. A horse. In the daylight, in the country.

She cleans me. The water smells of something very good. She is crushing up a herb and putting it in the water.

'Oh, want to see?'

I look at her. She smiles. She holds out her hands.

'Rosemary. Smell.'

It's strong, nice.

'We'll have you smelling like a rose,' she says. She washes my back. 'Oh, look at these. Stripes and scars.' Again, to herself.

I look past her to the table, where there is a jug. It has things – flowers, but like none I've ever seen before – that are bright and they look like the patterns on some women's clothes. Ladies that come to the 'Change. I've seen them sometimes. I've looked beyond the door. The ladies flutter like birds when they move, with gauze around their faces, and bare shoulders in summer. They're pretty. They're pale as skies. Their skirts have colours. I've no name for colours. Lovely rustling and rippling sounds. Young ones bleed pleasure. Light hearts, light as their gauze. Not always. But most.

Still the tyger hisses at them. Jealous that they can come and go.

And to her, it's still meat however it's dressed.

The woman puts a cloth shirt over my head. It's strange to be covered. Loose cloth pantaloons. She smiles. 'I'll find something to fit you when I can go out,' she murmurs. She pauses at my feet, strokes them. They are patterned, but not as clearly as my legs. I try to pull away and she pats my hands. 'There's nothing wrong with you,' she says. 'Don't take no notice of what people say, understand? You see, you're not dirty. I've washed away the dirt.'

Still, I try to pull the cotton down over my feet.

Warm and wet, tears fall on me.

Some other cried. Mother, pushing me behind her as large hands tried to touch me. In a room, a cold room. She hissed at him. Lioness with a cub. I felt her curdling fear, fear in the gut turning insides to water. I see his face come close and hear his words on his soiled, dark-stained breath, eyes fastened on me. 'I can kill him in an instant,' he says to her. 'Do as I say, and remember that.'

# 13

JOSEPH

I have a plan this morning, whatever Rebecca says.

It's another beautiful morning, and dust rises already from the streets. I'm walking towards the Pantheon and Sophia's house.

Times have changed indeed since we were together all those years ago. Her rented rooms here are a poor version of what once she had.

I remember going with Sophia – at her heels, anyway – to the opening of the Pantheon. A grand place, a marvellous place run by a rascal who had made a minor fortune robbing his way through India and who has since married into the gentry. It was supposed to be an exclusive place when it was being built. Nobody lower than a lord would ever be able to get in there, they said. It would be a place of utmost refinement, a very genteel way to spend an evening.

But as soon as it opened, it got out of hand. An aristocrat might recommend a friend by way of a calling card, and that was supposed to keep the rabble out. But those cards went all over the city. How Sophia managed to get hold of one, I can only guess – under her pillow, probably – but she presented this at the door, and was barred by some buffoon. The next day she came back and had forty admirers with her. They had raised a crowd at Teresa Cornely's – a masquerade house, a shop for immorality – and when the Pantheon opened its doors, the young nobles drew their swords and Sophia was admitted.

She queened into that green-painted room like a ship in full sail, looking about her with a smile. It was just entertainment for her. On other nights, she would stand at the gaming tables and, instead of the boredom of a game, she would simply stand and suck her forefinger. Just that. London likes to be shocked. It likes most of all to be shocked by a beauty, and one who scorns it.

I think of Sophia now, holed up in her three rooms, weeping over the writs from her bankers and letting coarse actors paw at her. Life is brief.

The one thing that marks this street out as a prostitute's paradise is the way that the ladies sit in their windows and allow themselves to be seen. Dressed in what might be taken for finery as long as a customer does not look too closely. It's near to the staging coaches: taverns on the corner with their wide, high arches to admit the carriages. Now, at seven o'clock in the morning, the Red Bull is already busy.

I stop and look into the inner yard. Horses are being tacked and the drivers are overseeing the loading of luggage. Voices rise in the air, groups gathering in the bright morning sunlight to take the coach or say their farewells. I see a wedding party come out, the new husband puffed up with the pride of taking his bride out to his home in the provinces. He's smiling as he helps his wife into the carriage, and I'm pleased to see such a pretty picture of bliss. A love match, it seems. There's pitifully few of those.

Sophia's house is halfway up the street.

There's no one in the window, and it takes an age for anyone to come to the door. An older woman, dressed plain but neat, tells me to wait on the doorstep, but before she's gone two paces I hear Sophia's voice from the first room on the left. 'Come in, Mr Eliot,' she calls.

Well, what time has done to us. There are no more embroidered shoes such as those I saw descending the theatre stair. In fact, there are no more stairs. It seems that Sophia lives on the ground floor, and somewhere at the back of the house footsteps are going up and down to another tenant.

I incline my head towards the sound. 'So early in the day.'

'Yes,' she says. 'Only young. Left by a clergyman. Promised much.'

'Poor girl.'

'It's just the drovers now.'

She's sitting on a large couch. In the corner of the room is a washstand and a fancy armoire. On the floor is a carpet that, for a moment, takes my breath away. The very same that once was in her fine bedroom when she belonged to Melbourne. But the bed beyond it is half the size of the mighty four-poster where we used to lie. The curtains on it are plain. The fire is yet unlit. Sophia is wrapped in some sort of bedcover, I think, and her hair falls down her back, no longer the pale colour it used to be but some kind of reddish brown. It looks, to my eye, revoltingly fake. God knows what she uses to make it so.

I remember how long it used to take to dress her hair. She had a hairdresser of some fame who came to do it. He would pile it high, combed over padding and resplendent with all kinds of decoration. I sometimes watched these creations, and was beaten out of the room once for laughing at a concoction like a garden, with little painted wooden trees and a meandering stream made with shards of glass. It was the very devil at night. We rebuilt the garden on the floor, scattered its greenery, and pulled apart its glittering stream. She was so sweet under the London layers, but always so vengefully childish.

She's watching me. 'The same Turkey rug,' she murmurs. 'But all else has changed.'

I take a seat opposite her. 'How are you, Sophy?'

She spreads her hands. 'As you see.'

'No coronet on your carriage?'

She laughs. 'No carriage, Joe.'

'Melbourne is very old, I should think.'

She pouts. 'His son is all the rage,' she says. 'He has a brain, unlike his father.'

'Did the old man leave you anything?'

'Nothing. He shut me out of the house and left me on the streets. Luckily, a name or two came to the rescue.' She gives a great sigh. 'And what of you? The Fields are doing well, I hear. How many beasts now?'

'A few.'

'And dancers, and acrobats?'

'Always.'

'Three nights a week?'

'Five.'

'Ah, you'll be quite society soon.'

'I don't think so. Society won't muddy their feet.'

We pause, looking at each other across the years.

'I'm sorry for the fire at Drury Lane,' she murmurs. 'I hear they blame you.'

'It can't be proved.'

She laughs. 'Ah, Joe, you always did find a way to wriggle out of your woes. And mine.'

There is a discreet knock at the door, and the woman comes in carrying a tray. 'Chocolate,' she says.

Sophia's love and my distaste. But I take the offered cup this morning.

'I'm going to the Fields now,' I say. 'Would you like to take the air and come with me?'

'Before noon?' she retorts. 'No.'

'Would you like to see Molly again?'

'Not if you've put her in the Fields.'

'I have not. She is comfortably stabled at the 'Change.'

'I haven't been there in an age.'

'You might ask a beau to take you there. Say that I've said you're to be allowed to see her.'

'You won't take me?'

'Not at the moment. This week at least. Hallett and I aren't on the best of terms.'

'Dear me,' she says. 'You have too many troubles.'

The irony of her saying that, with all her worries, makes me smile.

'Do you still have that girl with you?'

'Rebecca. Yes.'

'As a wife?'

'No, no.' I finish the drink.

'A housekeeper?'

'A partner in the business.'

'Given money?' She puts hand to her mouth. 'You don't pay her. Shame on you, Joe. Not wife, not housekeeper, not paid.'

'She is content.'

'Oh no,' she tells me. 'Neither woman nor man would be content with that. Be careful. Even a lapdog bites.'

'She's no lapdog. And she *does* bite.'

Sophia laughs. I'm glad to see it.

'Sophy, I hear that you know Mr Clement.'

She raises an eyebrow. 'Yes, I know him.'

'With the Galleon Theatre.'

'Yes. What of it?'

'I'd like to talk to him. Will you effect an introduction?'

'"Effect an introduction". How well you speak.'

'You taught me.'

'Ah, but you've added refinement, I think,' she says.

'I knew a scientist in Soho Square. He was kind to me. He taught me a great deal, and he had many friends.'

'And you know his son, and you're thinking of moving there. Buying his house.'

Despite all Sophia's contacts, this still surprises me.

'I listen to conversations,' she says, by way of explanation.

'And is that all you hear?'

She smiles, and stirs the gritty remnants of the chocolate in the cup. 'I hear that you'll be bankrupt very soon, once Sheridan has finished with you. And that you'll never have enough money to buy that house.'

'Not if you help me, Sophy.'

She puts down the cup and frowns. 'You ask a lot, don't you, Joseph?'

'I know that you have a kind nature.'

'I'm too kind. I've been too kind with you.'

'I remember,' I say. And I look pointedly at the carpet.

She wags a finger at me, and then bursts into laughter.

'Could you please introduce me to Clement and sing my praises?'

'Why can't you do it yourself?'

'Because *I* hear that he can't refuse you. You're not the only one who listens to gossip.'

She considers, drawing the heavy sheet around her. 'He's not as generous as he might be. If he were more generous, I wouldn't be here at all,' she complains.

'You can work wonders.'

She gives a great sigh, glances at the carpet, and smiles a little to herself.

'Oh, Joseph,' she murmurs. 'Very well. For old times' sake.'

# 14

REBECCA

We gave the boy a bed in the eaves of the house.

I thought he might try to run away, but he's quiet and obedient. I suppose Shaw taught him that – to be afraid. And not to speak.

I want Joe to buy him something better than the truckle bed that's so like Shaw's. I think the sight of it must remind him, but the boy did as he was told and lay down and I fetched good blankets, and I know that the little mattress is all right. No fleas, no lice. It's fresh.

'Come downstairs,' I tell him now. He follows me.

In the kitchen, he sits down and watches me as I put food in front of him. He seems puzzled by the noise that my wood pattens make on the flagstones. I put a glass bottle, bulbous at the base, in front of him. 'Pig's trotters and ears in Rhenish wine,' I say. 'To eat. Or I can heat them on the stove.'

He looks away, puts his hands over his eyes.

I take the glass away. 'They're bloody expensive,' I tell him. 'Not such a clever idea then, Mr Clever Eliot.'

I sit down and sigh. Gradually, the boy uncovers his eyes.

'What am I going to call you?' I ask him. 'Do you have a name?'

When he looks at me, it's with eyes like you see sometimes on faithful dogs. Big, wide open, waiting. Such an innocent-looking face for all he's suffered. But still he says nothing.

'Shall I guess?'

Nothing. Only the look.

'Jack. Or John? George, like the king?'

Nothing.

'Don't you know?'

He glances away, and stares at the loaf of bread on the end of the table. 'Bread. You must know bread,' I say. 'Shall I cut you a piece?'

Nothing. I cut it and put it in front of him. 'You've got to eat. You're skin and bone.' He touches it, but doesn't try it. And it dawns on me that all he's ever seen is rough grain bread, not white like this. Gentleman's bread. I go to the cupboard and bring him a covered dish. Inside is a honeycomb. I bought it in the market five days ago. Preciously expensive, but so good. Bought it from a woman who'd come in from Kent. When I lift the lid, you can almost smell the farm that it came from: all flowers. They say that whatever the bees feed on, you'll taste it. I put some on the bread and push the plate back to him.

'Try.'

He does. Those puppy-dog eyes widen at the taste, and then he begins to wolf it down.

'Not all of it,' I tell him. 'You'll make yourself sick. What else? Cheese?'

The eyes lower. He sits back in his chair.

It's getting warmer. It's going to be a hot day. Joseph asked me to stay in the house and not show the boy, but I wonder if it would harm if I take him away from the busiest part of the city. Away from theatres and the Strand. I sit for a while in silence, thinking of what it is that Joseph went out for so early. He had that look on his face that tells me he's plotting something, and it rankles with me that he wouldn't tell me. Ever since seeing Hunter he's been quiet, even when someone came to the door last night. The street door, banging and calling his name for a long time.

'Don't answer it,' he told me. 'It's likely creditors.'

I thought so, too. Or maybe Hallett come for the boy. Perhaps Shaw told him what his skin was like underneath the grime. Maybe to get back into the man's good books.

I look back at the boy. 'Where's your mother?' I ask.

Finally, a shred of an answer. A little shrug.

'Do you remember her?'

He rocks a little backwards and forwards in the chair.

'Is she alive?'

The line of his mouth straightens, then folds in on itself. The kind of expression that a small baby might have before it cries.

I don't like to ask if she's dead, though his face tells me so.

'What about a father?'

He crosses his arms, hugging himself.

'Does he live in London?'

Nothing. He probably doesn't know.

'Somebody must have took you to the 'Change. Was it Shaw?'

I don't know what else to say. There are thousands of children on the streets. Somebody told me that a gentleman was so unhappy at the dying and dead children he saw near one of the prisons that he's going to build a hospital. There's already one of a kind up the Hampstead and Highgate Roads, the Foundling Hospital. Where women bring their babies and leave them at night, and the Foundling takes them in.

But I don't think that's what happened to this boy. I think

maybe Shaw found him, maybe begging, and he's taken a fancy to him and Hallet took the child on because they needed a do-it-all. Maybe Shaw was convincing.

Just the thought of Shaw makes me feel sick.

'I don't remember my mother and father either,' I tell him. 'I grew up in a workhouse. Mr Eliot and I both did. We got out when there was a fire...' I touch my face. 'This fire.'

Suddenly, he nods.

'You said it to me. In the 'Change. You said "you jumped into the tree". And that's what happened. Mr Eliot jumped out first and then I jumped and he caught me. But you know all this, don't you? But *how* do you know?'

He raises a hand to his own face and feels it as if he were touching mine.

'Talk to me,' I tell him quietly. 'You can talk to me.'

The blank look comes back.

'Can't you tell me? Are you afraid? Why?'

He holds my eyes and for the first time I see a small smile. I don't know why it makes me so happy to see it. I mean really happy, happy right through, like it's Christmas and I've got a present.

Like sitting with someone who knows much more than you, although why I should think that, I can't make out. I've never been with anyone who's so... *still*... I mean as if that's how he has to be. As if he's listening to something that I can't hear. As if he knows what I'm thinking.

That thought makes me shiver. I rouse myself, stand up.

'Let's go out,' I tell him.

15

BOY TYGER

Hot under the feet, like the city sweats.

We walk, and she tells me all the names: Long Acre, Drury Lane, High Holborn. All the hills and valleys. Water runs under us, under the stone paths. When we stop, I smell green space. I stand still even when Rebecca pulls at me.

'Down here,' she says.

Along Long Acre. Noise. At the corner a coach is coming out of a yard. Six horses. Going a long way. 'Edinburgh coach,' Rebecca says. 'Late today.'

We come to a quiet place. A square set about with houses, and there are gardens. We stop in front of one. 'This is The Yellow House,' Rebecca tells me. 'This is where we're going to live, very soon.' She pauses, then says under her breath, 'Well, *you* are.' And softer still, 'There's no money, but he tells them there will be. The Fields don't make enough for this place even after five nights. We'll have to sell the animals, and they bring more people.' She stares at the house for a long time, and puts a hand on my shoulder. 'Will you like to live here?'

I hold her hand. She looks down at me in surprise, and smiles. 'Want to be a gentleman?'

'Stay with you,' I tell her.

She lets out a little cry of surprise, and drops to her knees and puts her arms around me. When she looks back at me, she tells me that wherever Mr Eliot goes, I must go with him.

'No.'

'Yes.' She stands up. 'You'll have a better chance growing up here,' she says. 'People will look at you differently. I can't stay with him in a public square like this, where folk can see your comings and goings. I can't be in a house with a man I'm not married to in a place like this.'

She waves her hand towards the house. 'The carpenters are in there now, making it right. Joseph persuaded Henry to wait for the money.' She looks long and hard at it. 'I'm not being a housekeeper neither,' she says. 'Cook-housekeeper. I don't know how to cook. Not properly. Not fancy. People talk in places like this. You've got to fit in. Have evenings and dinners and suchlike. What would he do with me, lock me in the attic? I don't know nothing about science. I don't want to know. He doesn't really want me in a life like this. I'll go on as I am. Hemp and me will find somewhere.'

There's a tree in the middle of the square, and a bench underneath it. We walk towards it. 'Above our station, that's where he wants us to be. Something eats at him. Wanderlust, maybe.'

'Wandering.'

'Yes.' She looks at her hands, spreads them on her lap, and then hides them in her skirts. 'Wants to be better. I hold him back. Maybe always have done.'

I want to say no. I don't know why his heart is running so slow, wrapped up inside him.

'I know my place,' she's saying. 'I like it. Why doesn't he? What would I do in a house all day?'

Arguing with herself.

'Why was there a fire?' I ask.

She turns round on the seat, puts her elbows on her knees, and stares at me. 'In Drury Lane theatre?'

'No. Long ago.'

She bites her lip. 'Small boys and girls and the wanting to see tygers.'

'Tygers?'

'And lions that roared, and red waggons, and dreams.'

'This made a fire?'

'The boys lit the fire thinking someone would come, and they'd be let out and could go and see the circus. It was only two fields down the road.'

'But nobody came.'

'Nobody came.'

I feel a pain over my heart. I put my hand to it. Years and years and years. Waiting.

'To be married,' I say.

'Oh,' she breathes. 'Oh.' And she stands up and takes hold of my hand again. 'I don't want nothing from him. Nothing.' But she is lying.

We walk. So tired.

We pass by a yard where women stand next to wood buckets. There is a line strung up, and some taint I know nothing of. Out of the bucket comes a sheet like there is in their house, sheets that go onto beds. Piece of big cotton, very long. Wet and heavy with dripping water.

'They're washing the floors,' Rebecca says. 'And washing the linen.' I put my hand to my mouth. 'Ash, lye,' she says. 'And they're burning roll brimstone and Indian pepper. You can smell it? They've got bugs in the house, then.' She snorts, thinking this house is not good. 'Wall-lice,' she tells me, and looks at me questioningly. 'You must know about lice and fleas?'

It makes me think of something. Washing linen. Big house

with a special place at the back where they brought all the bedsheets and the clothes. There were big pots full of steaming water. Brass pots, or iron. Some metal that shone. The air full of steam and soap.

Around another corner. I can't get white sheets out of my head and then suddenly, colour. Can't remember the names of colours.

'Tenter's field,' Becca explains. 'Dyeing fabric. Making it another colour. Putting it here to dry.'

Try to soak up her words so I can learn the way of it. We watch the colours flap in the wind. On and on in rows. Watch the moving waves, and the coloured shade on the ground. There's a wind, and in the sky there's smoke chasing cloud, and on the ground there's dust curling under. Women go between the rows, carrying poles and baskets. Here at one place, they turn a long piece. It ripples as it turns.

'What do you think of us?' Rebecca says, but to herself. 'I wonder what you think of us.'

Another long street, and she stops. 'Are you tired?'

Feel bad. Feel everything swim and stretch, swim and stretch. See across the street a red-brick place so high and on the roof is a lion. A lion staring across the city. Catch my breath hard. 'But it's just stone,' Rebecca says. 'Just stone. Don't be afraid of it. It can't move. This is Northumberland House.'

She squats down and looks in my face. 'You've not said a word since we passed the place washing their linen.'

I press my face into her shoulder and put my arms around her waist.

# 16

JOSEPH

Night is coming on, a beautiful night full of stars and the sun long set but still casting a strange pink glow in the streets. Such a haunted, lovely night and Clement and I are walking to the Fields.

He's a tall, thin man, hollow-cheeked and yellowish looking, as if stained by the pipe smoke of his theatre and the candle smoke of the footlights. He must be all of fifty years old. It wasn't my choice to walk; I was prepared to hire a carriage to stay in his good estimation, but no. Clement walks. He walks *prodigiously*. It's all of seven miles to Lordship Lane in Tottenham. He claims it keeps him in good health. I stride out at first and afterwards tire; but Clement walks on, cane in scrawny hand, hat far back on his head, boots splattered with dust.

We've been talking about my idea. His theatre isn't large, but it's well fixed for my purposes since it has a wide yard at the back and a ramp for scenery and – in our case – an open waggon to bring in the cages. It's close to the Strand and word will spread fast. I'll go through the streets as I used to, giving out handbills. Calling out the show like the old days. I'll sell tickets

123

on the streets, and Clement and I have just agreed this, which is pleasing since I'm only known at the moment for supposedly swindling Sheridan.

'I saw the show at Drury Lane before the fire,' he tells me. 'So I don't doubt you'll bring in money.'

'Tickets double price.'

At last, he stops.

We're out in the country now. Overhanging storeys and narrow alleys give way to open views. They're cutting hay across the lane, and the sweet smell adds to the pleasure of the evening. There are few houses but, curiously, many Greens in this part of the world. Greens that perhaps were for long-forgotten grazing but are now are idle spots around a patch of grass or under trees: Beans Green, West Green, Wood Green and Chapmans and Scotland, relics of some former time. Becca and Hemp and I come here by waggon – and they've gone ahead tonight – but I had to wait until Clement had seen the first acts at the Galleon at four o'clock.

We're looking towards West Green, almost there, and here a few buildings are at the side of the road. Sometimes wealthy traders from the city build here – Wanley, for instance. A goldsmith. His house has wide, well-tended gardens in the midst of all this meadow and wheat, and standing here I can glimpse his roof.

'Double price?' Clement asks.

'For the special attraction.'

'You haven't yet told me what this special attraction is,' he reminds me, leaning on his cane. 'You'll bring the beasts...?'

'Aye. The lion. The behemoth, and the serpent. I'll have scenery painted at my own expense.'

'And the attraction?' Clement persists.

'We'll see it shortly.'

He huffs and gives me a pained smile.


Darkness is coming by the time we get to the Fields.

We leased this land years ago. It was, and continues to be, very cheap. Nobody was much interested in it then: it was supposed to flood from the River Lea, but we've never found so. It was supposed to stink too, being called The Marshes, but the air is good, with no trace of bad smell. Maybe it was marshy once, but the river's further away than it used to be centuries ago.

At first, we kept our stabling and storage on it in a falling-down farm building, but since then we have fenced it and keep our cages there. Five years ago in the autumn, I had a shelter with locking doors built over the cages. We had a watchman, and then two. It wasn't the animals that were in danger of being stolen, but the foodstuffs. A thief can't very well handle a lion, but a couple of likely lads can make off with mash or hay. No, the shelter was to keep the beasts warmer. I've known snow up to my knees here and it can be the very devil to get a waggon along the lanes. I've cracked ice on the water butts, and stuffed straw waist-high in the cages to keep them warm. The lion has grown old with us, and we have water buffalo bought from Hunter who are as docile as you please.

Bartholomew Fair comes to London in the last week of August, and we precede it by a week. A taster, if you like. Booth-holders are already here, or on this road at least. They like our stabling and they like the inn on the way to Tottenham Hale. It is all, if I say so myself, more pleasant than Bartholomew's. Local country folk come to us from all the way up the Lea Valley: Edmonton, Enfield, Barnet. Enfield has its own market and a fancy market cross and Fortescue Hall – you'd think they might be too high and mighty to come to see us, but they still do. The same for Edmonton, with its own fair and its houses with King William gates and red-brick walls. They still want to see us.

Our booth-holders come from far away; they tour all year. We have Tahitian girls (which I suspect are Welsh) and fire-eaters, performing horses out of Oxford, and dogs from East Anglia. We have the usual tightrope walkers and singers. And, of course, our oddities and monsters. This year I've found a calf with two heads. I travelled all the way to Warwickshire to buy it and had the devil of a hard bargain struck for it from a gawp-faced farmer and his sons. The beast isn't weakly at all, though I rather expected it. It grows, although the second head seems not to grow. I've known two or three faint at the sight of it – one a man who simply went down like a fallen tree. It's ceased to surprise me what people like and what people have a horror of. Although they do mightily love to be horrified.

The sun is slowly going down. The fields are full: families and apprentice boys, and here and there some tradesmen. The jeweller from Bond Street who works for the king and has a passion for beasts is showing off his gargantuan wife; she could be a beast-show herself. He has her on his arm and she smiles like a queen at her subjects.

The cook-stalls are busy. Hemp brings me a potato pudding in a little earthenware pot. It smells of nutmeg and orange and brandy before I even put it in my mouth. Clement and I stand eating like proper heathens, each using a wooden spoon. The evening light comes down, and we are surrounded by moths. They batter their wings against the tent walls for the circus, drawn to the torchlight inside.

I can't see Becca at first. There's so much noise and music. She likes this so much better than the theatres; perhaps she was even glad that the fire stopped us from parading Molly every night and throwing ale down her throat. Perhaps she'd always like to be here or somewhere like here because it reminds her of how we began, and of journeys before we had carts or waggons for transport, and of shows we put fleetingly on foot as we walked with some animal or other.

I wonder what it is that Becca really wants. She swears that she won't come to The Yellow House, and I think she imagines that buying it is some cockeyed way of mine to humiliate her. I look in her poor face and I can see there's a wild girl in there who never complained about the muck and the work. A free spirit who sees The Yellow House as a cage. And yet she's been with me all these thankless years and if that isn't a cage, I don't know what is.

One thing I do know is that she's been good for the boy. She tends him and washes and feeds him. She wants to take him to have clothes measured. She fusses over him. The boy looks at her with trust and some invisible bond has wound them together, some kind of understanding. He doesn't look at me that way. His eyes slip from me and he won't shake my hand. Becca says he is frightened of Hunter, and that's one thing I certainly will never understand. When I was a boy, it would have pleased me no end to see Hunter's house, even to climb those steps to the door. But this boy cried after our visit, Becca says. Cried and shook. They went for a walk and when they got home, he curled up like a baby on his bed and shut his eyes and made a moaning sound. She stood over him for some time apparently, just as puzzled as I would have been.

But he does my bidding. He'll come and sit by me, though stiff-backed and with his head slightly bent away from me. I've shown him my books – the few that I have, an atlas and a picture book of animals and the Bible. I don't think he can read, but he reached out and touched the creature portraits: the bright blue hummingbird, the green pea-fowl from Java, the Indian red-headed crane. The leopard, the lion, the elephant. He held his hand on the page at the elephant.

'He's thinking of Jumby, from the 'Change,' Becca murmured.

'There's a lot of elephants in the world, they say,' I told him. 'Wild ones.'

He looked up at me, and he smiled suddenly.

'He's never seen an animal free,' Becca said.

I sat back in my chair and thought of the shame of it, to never have seen any creature running wild. But then neither have I. I've seen them offloaded from ships; I've seen them at the Tower in chains. The king and queen have zebra. The only animal I saw out of a menagerie – if animal it is, or fish, I don't know – was the whale that swam up the Thames beyond London Bridge once and got stranded at low tide, and Hunter went up to dissect it. I watched him from afar, just a boy hanging on the rail of the docks while Hunter slithered his way across the carcase. The 'stinking whale' London called it. Hunter told the *Gentleman's Gazette* that he tasted the whale milk and it was rich, like cow's milk but with cream added. I wished then, and I wish now, that I had seen it swim.

What it must be to take a ship to the places where birds are no bigger than your thumb and are bright blue and feed from flowers. What it must be to stand where few men have ever stood. I'd give a king's ransom to go out on the convict ships that are starting for New Holland and find that most mythical and half-believed thing, the kangaroo. I've seen Mr Stubbs's portrait of one, and it looks like a rat sitting on its hind legs, but it cannot be like that – like a rat, I mean. It's something else entirely. My friend Henry claims it has the head of a fox and the hands of a man, but that can't be right either. Surely one day the convict ships will bring one back, and then, if my plans with Clement succeed as I know they will, *then* I could buy myself a kangaroo.

I looked down again at the boy.

I told him about the beast in New Holland and how I would bring one back one day, and he stared down at the floor.

Becca set her mouth in a line and put her arm around his shoulders. 'Perhaps one day there'll be no cages,' she said. She stood up and wouldn't meet my gaze, and she took the boy upstairs.

I don't understand her. We make our living from caged beasts.

*Very well*, I thought.

I got up and damped the fire and kicked the chair back to the table.

'We shall make our living some other way,' I muttered. 'And see if you like that.'


I see her now.

She's standing with Hemp by one of the stables. They're laughing at something and they have pots of ale. I watch her as she drains the ale, puts the pot down, and untangles her hair, letting it out of the scarf that usually holds it back. She holds the scarf between her teeth and undoes the fastening, raking her fingers through the mass that looks reddish in the firelight. Not Sophia's false red but a lovely chestnut that falls halfway down her back. I can't remember when she last undid her hair. I'm surprised how long it is. She puts her head down, draws up her hair and fastens it again, smoothing it back, all the while still holding the scarf between her teeth.

I know exactly why it touches me so. As a little girl the hair above her forehead and on the left-hand side of her face wouldn't grow for a long time. She used to cry, as girls will when they're starting to be women, about it and her looks. And then as if by magic her hair came back, and it was a darker colour, and she took a pride in it and used to show me. I remember Sophia's cook combing it and telling her how pretty she was, and that little face beamed as if a light had gone on behind it.

But it's so long ago now. I watch Hemp lay an arm over her shoulder and she shrugs him away, laughing. They gaze out over the fair. Some fellows nearby start a haphazard kind of drunken jig, and they come over to Hemp and Becca and try to get her to dance. To my surprise she goes with them, links arms, does a few trotting steps, and then adroitly squeezes herself between the onlookers to get away. She is a kind girl, a strong girl. And just for a second my heart runs out to her before I catch it.

She turns and looks at me.

'Becca!' I call.

She runs over, glancing at Clement. 'You're late,' she says.

'It's my fault,' Clement tells her.

'Mr Clement likes to walk,' I say.

Becca gives me a puzzled smile, her gaze shifting between me and Clement. She knows who he is.

'Where's the boy?' I ask.

She inclines her head towards the stable. 'Sleeping.'

'In this racket?' I take Clement's arm. 'Come and see.'

'See what? A boy? Is that all?' I can hear the disappointment in his voice.

I open the stable door. There's no lantern, but I can make out the child lying on the straw. He is curled up tightly.

'Watch.'

I pull back the blanket. Becca is suddenly at my side. 'Don't wake him.'

Clement squats beside me. 'Tell me if you've ever seen the like,' I say.

In trying to peel back his clothes, I wake him. The child jerks up, half stands and then scrabbles back into the corner.

'It's all right,' Becca soothes him, though she looks at me as if she'd like to swipe me. 'It's only us. It's Mr Joseph and his friend. Shh... shh...'

The pattern on his skin looks otherworldly. Hazy in the shadows. Flickering in the flame.

'What's the matter with him?' Clement asks, staring.

I can't help smiling. I help Clement to his feet. 'Half human, half tyger,' I tell him. 'The tyger-striped boy.'


It doesn't take much after that to convince Clement.

Over hot gin, I paint him the picture.

The new *Eden*. Not at Drury Lane but at the Galleon. A show that will dig me out of debt. The crowds leaning on the doors and filling the streets. They say that Elizabeth Farren is fair, and Dorothy Jordan and Sarah Siddons. They say Mary Hamilton is fair, and Emma. They draw the crowds. But London has not seen this sweet-faced child, completely white in his face, who will wander across the stage and then emerge showing his body, perhaps crawling on all fours as if he's transformed into a beast. I can use the firecrackers that I used when we made a volcano. That was a triumph. After the singers in their little operetta, we made a panorama of Italy with Vesuvius in the background that spat fire. The people in the front screamed, then clapped. We did it night after night until the attraction paled.

And then, such an idea comes to me. A wonderful idea. An idea that makes me laugh out loud. Clement looks at me, and Becca too, holding the boy and stroking his shoulder.

'The tyger,' I said. 'The tyger!'

'Joseph,' Becca said in a low voice. 'Don't do this.'

I barely heard her. I took Clement's arm and turned him to look at me full face. 'The tyger in the 'Change. The man-eater.'

'What of it?'

'Have it on stage. Have it change the child into a half child, half tyger. It roars... something. We shall make it roar. The child disappears and reappears – changed. He can be a frightened child to begin with – he has strayed into a jungle, he is lost – we shall have trees, palms like those that burned in Drury Lane. We can show it as a panorama at first, I can buy more capuchins–'

'Joseph,' Becca says at my back.

We have moved to the doorway. 'You see the tightrope walker there, the girl?' I ask Clement.

He looks through the crowds to the crepe-hung stage. 'I see her.'

'Dressed as a monkey, walking between the treetops. And you see the lion? We put the lion on stage left, the tiger stage right – we can bring the cages on rails, and pulleys – the child gasps when he sees them – we can disguise the cages with vines. And there is an old bear south of the river once used for baiting, I know the man who shows her – just for showing her he takes five guineas a day – he will bring her. I'm sure she's docile, she's so old. And our behemoth of course–'

'The creature that caused the fire? No,' said Clement.

'She shan't be left in the theatre overnight.'

'How will you get the tyger? It belongs to Hallett.'

'I shall arrange it, never fear. Give him a portion of the takings, perhaps. A small portion. It will be an Eden of animals, a garden of flowers, grass laid on the floor, a waterfall–'

'It can't be done.'

'I've done much the same before. With a little effort, with a little will, all things are possible. Trust me. Imagine it: as the tyger roars, the child vanishes in smoke and reappears without clothes, transformed into the beast creature. He steps forward to the edge of the stage – take out the seats so that you have a pit again and you can fit in hundreds more – the child shows himself – we'll flood the streets with drawn pictures of him, but to see him in the flesh will be bizarre, outrageous, thrilling – and he lets out a scream, a roar of his own–'

'No.' It's Becca, standing in front of me with her hands on her hips.

'What?' says Clement.

'I won't have it,' she tells him. Then turns to me. 'Since when do you make a decision without me?'

'I know my business,' I say. I don't like her tone of voice.

'It's *our* business.'

'It will make us all a fortune.' I smile at her. 'Don't oppose me.'

I watch her take a deep breath. Her mouth works a little, as if she's trying to choose her words but can't get them out. 'You will not make money out of that boy,' she tells me.

'Becca,' I say. 'We'll talk about this later.'

She rocks backwards and forwards slightly on her heels, like a prize fighter readying himself for a blow. 'He's not yours to make a show of,' she says.

'He belongs to both of us.'

'He belongs, if you push the point, to Hallett,' she retorts.

'No longer.'

'You think he'll allow it, once it becomes a success?' she asks. 'He'll want him back. And you think he'll give you the tyger? Never.'

'He'll give me the boy and the tyger if he's paid enough.'

'Oh,' she says. 'There's a lot of people getting money from this escapade.'

'There'll be plenty left for us and Mr Clement here.'

'And what about him?' She points towards the boy, now cowering with his arms crossed and his shoulders hunched behind us. 'Do you think he'll want to be part of it? Have you asked him?'

Now, a man doesn't like to be crossed. He doesn't like his partner to question him in front of another businessman. I can talk Becca round – she'll see the sense of it; she'll be relieved at making money again – but I won't have her talk against me. Stubbornness brought us this far. Doing things that others said couldn't be done. And we will do this.

'He'll do as he's told,' I tell her. 'And be glad of it. Glad to be with us and not Shaw. Glad to be fed and watered.'

'Oh, fed and watered. Like a beast himself!'

'And clothed and educated.'

'Educated in a bad business,' she replies. She puts her hands to her face. I swear she's crying, though it's hard to see in the shadows. Perhaps the ale has addled her brain.

Hemp has walked up to us, and looks between us. 'There's a fight at the gate,' he says. 'Over tickets.'

'God's wounds!' I yell at him. 'Knock a few heads together. What do we pay you for?'

He slumps off, grumbling. I hear him calling a few of the others to join him, and they disappear in the mass like a troop of chimpanzees, knuckles scraping the ground.

It's getting late. The fires in the braziers are getting low. No doubt the gate is complaining at paying at all when it's so long into the evening. A weariness suddenly comes over me. So much to think of. The Fields here, the stabling, the animals. The setting up of another theatre show. The moving of our home from Long Acre to The Yellow House.

Clement is talking but I hardly hear him.

I look around for Becca and the boy, but they're gone.


It's early morning by the time I get home.

The whole street is dark – the whole of London is dark aside from the lamps on the night-soil waggons. The scavengers are out, cleaning the streets.

It used to be, once, that this horse dung that they're clearing so fast now was left in heaps along Piccadilly and as far as Sloane Square in winter. Its heat was thought to be able to prevent frost from breaking the pipes underneath the paving stones. It didn't work; the water still flooded the streets and turned them into ice rinks. But I remember the piles of dung, and Sophia turning up her nose at them. I was sitting next to her in an open barouche at the time, a flighty form of transport for the evening. She could be seen in it, and that was all that mattered to her. It was Melbourne's, as everything was Melbourne's. She was Melbourne's from the top of her head to the soles of her feet. But she still went to Carlisle House with me at her side, and I was all dressed up in fine breeches that Melbourne's money had bought.

Times change. The streets change, and green land is built over, and what were once villages are part of the city, and most of all women like Sophia change and fade and are lost. As we all change ourselves. As I have changed from the barefoot boy. The only thing in my life that has not changed is Becca.

Despite the lateness of the hour, a light is shining in the house.

Becca is standing in the kitchen. The kettle is on the range. She has laid bread and cold mackerel on the table. She looks up at me as I come in the door. 'Sit down,' she murmurs. 'And eat.'

I sit but I've got no appetite for food. I'm bone-tired. 'You must see my point about the boy,' I tell her.

She's still standing. 'Oh, I must, is that so?' Very quiet, very slow.

'Let's not quarrel.' I try to get hold of her hand, but she moves it. 'We never quarrel.'

'It's not the boy's duty to do as you say. You're not his father.'

'I can't get us out of this debt without him, Becca.'

'Oh, you could. If you had half a mind to.'

'How?'

She bites her lip, then straightens her back as if she's delivering a speech that she's rehearsed. 'Don't buy The Yellow House. Sell this one, and sell everything else, and move out of London and...' She pauses. 'Be done with it all.'

'What?'

'You heard me.'

'What, the animals? The Fields?'

'Yes.'

'We took *fourteen* pounds tonight, Becca. Fourteen pounds.'

'I know.'

'You'd throw money like that away?'

'No,' she says. 'We'd sell it on. Animals, cages, Fields' lease.' She sits down at last, opposite me, and clasps her hands in front of her. 'Buy somewhere in the country and take the boy.'

'But...' But I can't finish the sentence, it's so much of a shock to me.

'Buy a farmhouse. Buy a lodge in the Highlands. Buy a fishing boat. Buy anything but more of this.'

I shake my head. 'No, no.'

'You can be a gentleman out of the city, Joe. Think on it for a bit. You can buy scientific instruments and have talks with great men and visit Hunter. You'd have the time. You can even go on voyages.'

I look at the table, at the knots and whorls in the wood, and I think of seas and shorelines. Roads in far-off countries. All the dreams I had as a boy in that godforsaken workhouse. Drawing maps in the chalky dirt, or what I thought might be maps. I'd never seen a globe then, never even knew that the world was round. Never seen a sailing ship until I came to London with Becca. The beasts gave me wonder. Gave me pride. Gave me what I couldn't see for myself.

'But it's all we've ever known, Becca.'

'Aye, it is.'

I put my head in my hands, trying to make sense of her. 'What we made together.'

She looks at me, unmoved. I know this expression. If I'm stubborn, then she's worse once she gets an idea in her mind. 'I can't show the boy. Not like an animal. Not to be made out to *be* an animal.'

'He's worth a fortune.'

'He's a child.'

'So what? He's more fortunate than most. Look where he came from.'

'We don't know where he came from,' she points out. I see that she's holding her temper in. 'He don't belong to us, nor Hallett. He could be anybody's child.'

'He's no one's child.'

There's a silence. She watches me. 'That's the pity of it, Joe,' she says. 'Don't you see? Can't you understand it? Let him be somebody now. Raise him out of London somewhere quiet. Get him a tutor. He'd pass for white and he's clever. He could have a future.'

'He's got a future now.'

'I mean a respectable future.'

'Are you saying we're not respectable?'

She slaps one hand on the table, sits sideways in her chair, and takes a breath. I think she's going to get up, but she doesn't. 'Give him what we never had. Send him to school.'

We stare at each other. 'This is too good a chance to pass up,' I say. 'You know that.'

'I don't know it.'

'You don't *want* to know it.'

'All right, I don't want to know it. I don't want folk laughing at him. Pointing at him in the street. Trying to paw at him to see if he's real. I don't want to hand out pamphlets with his picture on, poor mite. Don't you know how much you scare him?'

'I do not.'

'No? Then you're not looking.'

'He'll thank us for it.'

'What for? For being frightened out of his wits? He won't thank *me* for it, for I'll have no part in it. Not this Galleon Theatre parade, nor watching you force him to it.'

'You've always thought my ideas were good,' I mutter.

'Aye, and followed you. Through hell and high water.'

'Yes, you have.'

'Like a pet,' she says. Now she stands. 'But there's one thing you don't see, Joe. I'm not a fuckin' beast. I've got my own ideas.'

I see the change sweep over her face. Anger and pity. And a kind of longing.

'Like what? Better than making money?'

Her face flushes. 'I just told you how to make money. But you don't want it. You want to carry on with your... your flourishes. Your look-at-me. The show ain't for the boy, and the show ain't never been for the beasts. Not to be admired, like. Just to make you look clever. The keeper of Behemoth and Pompey the lion and all the rest, look at Mr Eliot! But think how you got here, Joe.'

'Bloody hard work.'

'No. You got here because of Sophia. Used her. Used me, the both of us. Carried us along with you. Made your name. Learned to speak proper gentrified. And then what happened? You dropped Sophia and never looked back.'

I'm shocked at the accusation. I've never considered it. I start to laugh, then abruptly stop. 'I didn't mean anything to her much,' I pointed out. 'And you know why. I was just her entertainment. She dropped me because I had no title, Becca. No fancy carriage.'

She is shaking her head. 'Ah, men are all blind,' she mutters.

'Blind? I'm certainly not that.'

'Yes, Joe, you are,' she says. 'Don't you think she cared for you? Not even a little?'

'A little, perhaps...'

'A lot, perhaps,' she retorts. 'Though you never bothered to ask.'

'She made her living. I couldn't prevent her.'

'Could have married her.'

'What, a whore?'

'Why not? What are you but a street boy?'

'I'm better than that.'

'You think so, don't you? Making yourself all fancy. I know what I am, and I don't care who knows it. I'm proud of what I am. Proud to make a living that ain't Sophia's.' She takes a shuddering breath. 'And proud of you. But I shan't be proud if you ill-treat this boy and make a mockery of him.'

'You've had too much ale tonight.'

'Oh, is that so?' She stifles a half-laugh, but there's no humour in it. 'I told you my ideas. But you don't care for 'em, do you? Don't care to wonder what I want or what the boy wants.'

'You don't know what he wants. Not any more than I do. You're guessing at what he wants.'

'House in the country. Quiet life. The three of us. No more tramping in all weathers. A servant or two maybe. The good carriage you never gave yourself. Nice little country house with a park to walk in. Like what Hunter's got at Earl's Court. Who wouldn't want that?'

'No, Becca. No.'

She puts both hands on the table, leans on them and brings

herself to within a few inches of my face. Her mouth trembles and her skin is flushed dark. 'Would you sell him?'

'Who?'

'The boy.'

'No.'

'No?' she echoes. 'What if someone offered you a thousand pounds?'

'No.' But for a second, I hesitate. And she sees it.

She sits back, arms crossed. I sit and wonder at her. I wonder at her anger. And I see what I have not seen in many years. There are tears at the corner of her eyes; they collect swiftly, and they run across her puckered flesh.

It's a pitiful sight to see, the tears going this way and that across her skin. There is a corner to her mouth that is drawn very far down because of the fire; it is as if the heat melted her, and it makes her always wear an expression of disdain. The grief, or perhaps the frustration with me, runs down now into that melted corner of flesh. But she doesn't seem to feel the tears. She doesn't put up a hand to wipe her face.

'Lord Somebody-or-Other, say,' she insists. Voice raised and hard like flint. 'I'll paint you a picture. Buys the lad from you. Wants him for an ornament, like they want black boys for ornaments. Until they're growed. Then they get chucked out. You've seen 'em, wandering. So have I. Poor stricken lads, thin as a lath, dancing a bit for a penny thrown. Lady Somebody-or-Other maybe likes him too much when he gets big, got to be a handsome man. Husband takes him out of the big house and gets the carter or the groom to push him off a waggon somewhere. We've seen ones like that tramping the highway.'

I know her to be right. There are twenty thousand blacks in London, and these mostly are men.

It's all very well to say, as Mr Johnson did, that no man by nature is the property of another. Or that fine upstanding gentleman William Pitt, who claimed that black slaves from the plantations become free as soon as they set foot on this happy island. Very fine words indeed, but it can be a strange kind of freedom. Blacks are sometimes put ashore and then they must find their way, and sometimes the way is to sell themselves as if they were still owned. I saw a sale of gentleman's effects in Belgrave Square, and a boy who had been his ornament – and who knows what else – was sold for thirty-two pounds. That was only ten years ago. Some call the blackamoors savages, but they're not savage. The savages are the ones who own them, trade them and make money out of their misery.

And I suddenly think of all the animals that I've caged and the wretched ape-beast taken from Dodds, and my part in it all. Cold guilt comes raging up through me.

Still, I'm unable to acknowledge it to Becca. 'Well, what of it?'

'All right,' she says. 'Suppose this. Suppose Lord Somebody-or-Other or some big menagerie owner – bigger 'un than Hallett, menagerie keeper at the Tower, maybe – hears the boy is half tyger. Maybe even believes it. You sell the boy to him. Seems a decent sort even if he is Lord Whatshisname or menagerie keeper to the Tower. Puts him in a cage. Keeps him on a leash. Then the boy gets growed up, gets a fondling from Her Ladyship or a beating from the menagerie man, whatever. Twenty years old then, and what is he? He's dancing for pennies. Or he's dead on the street. Or in line for Tyburn with a rope round his neck for stealing bread.'

'None of that would happen.'

'Why not? You'd refuse a lord, refuse the money they'll pay you, him or someone else?'

I can't answer. She sees it. And she says it.

'You can't answer.'

'I can't answer because I don't know, Becca. That's the truth. I haven't had a chance to think about it.'

She looks hard at me, draws her shawl tightly around her.

'Oh my God,' she whispers. 'My God. It's a fucking wonder you've never shown me as a monster. Or sold me.'

She goes out of the room and I hear her climbing to the place in the eaves where she's made a bed for the boy.

I listen to her footsteps until I can hear them no more.

## 17

BOY TYGER

Storm coming.

Becca sits next to me and holds my hand.

Misery travels, like rain. High-coloured pictures in her head. Memories. Sitting at the side of a stage called Paradise. The Garden of Eden, like the Bible. Palm trees and women dressed as angels and a boa serpent and the big armour-scaled beast. There night after night, sewing, carrying, bullying. Keeping men back, pushing girls on. Seeing beyond the stage the open-mouthed faces at the near-naked Adam and Eve. A girl she knew once dressed in her angel wings who had nothing in her head at all, a vacancy washed with music and she rolling her eyes and happy, not more than twelve.

I rest my head on this hand.

'He won't do it,' she says.

But he will do it.

Money and smoke in his mind. Giving money to her, her open palm waiting, and there's no money to give. Men like hounds at his door. Fury and fear. Joe lies awake trying to think of something better, or something else. Goes away in safer memories. High days on Essex marshes in winter. Being seventeen, salt-slicked hair, struggling with iron cages so cold that his skin stuck to them. Fires of all kinds. A woman with hair piled high, and his fingers on her warm wet body, candles snuffed, world hid away. Walking head down against the hail. Against hot sun. Small hand in his and this woman, a child, skipping in front of him picking crab apples off the road, scaling and walking along walls and catching and falling, falling and catching. This woman, sewn into his blood. He wakes with a jolt wondering how to feed her, frightened of the future.

And for her, nowhere to go. She's thinking that now. She's thinking of us on the street, like they were before, and she doesn't want it. She doesn't want it for me.

Storm comes in, rain on the roof, lightning across the city. Feel it washing towards the river where the filth swills out into the place where a thousand ships are moored, one up against the other, and the bell tolls on the bridge for tide turning.

The sound unlocks the horror in my head, things buried because it was no good to see and no good to remember.


It was the time of short days, wind whipping across the long green parkland, sleet rain hitting the glass of the window, the house below filtering sound up the long staircases, and carriages coming and going in the cobbled yard far below. We watch. Watch horses stabled, sweat on their backs, footmen huddled against the cold holding open the carriage doors. There's no women. Only men staggering down the steps, some travel sick, others drunk and weaving in circles and met with more drink, hot wine on trays in the rain, and him below us in a greatcoat. Their noise slaps the house in waves. Night comes on and a maid brings us food and is distracted and she leaves the door.

She was afraid on nights like these, waiting for him to come in throwing the door back, laughing at who knows what, eyeing her as she stood like a statue, waiting for the worst. Sometimes I wasn't quick and got a blow to the head. He called me lice and vermin. I learned to crawl fast. Often the last I would see was his hand to her throat. But he don't come that winter night. No footsteps on the stair.

I watch my mother sleep, and I edge out of her grasp, and go to the door. It opens easy, no lock. I look at the brass of the handle, waiting for a sound, but all I hear is the thunder of voices below. I've not seen this corridor, bare floorboards, limewash walls, a pinprick of light that I creep towards. More stairs, and on the third set is stone and not board, and on the fourth set there are soft things underfoot and the stairs get very big and the floor at the bottom is black and white and streaked with mud. Dogs lie in the dirt and a man lies slumped over on a wood bench, fine clothes but not stirring and there comes a screech of sound which still don't wake him at all, and out of the door to one side comes him, all fired like his face held to a flame, red like a devil, and he tows a lad behind him by the wrist and the lad has fallen and blood comes from his nose like a river.

'You *dare*,' says him. Low like a threat.

The candles are burning dimly. The blood looks black.

He sees the man on the wood bench and he grabs hold of the boy tighter and strides on, all the while the boy begging, dragged now by his hair, feet squealing on the floor, his footman yellow breeches yellow no longer but smeared with muck. He looks up, a second only and he sees me and says *help me* and the man says *there's no help this side of hell* but I'm following for I think I might help the boy even so.

There's a side room, not lit but something like I've seen on the island, with a cross, a chapel of sorts, and the cross sits on an altar very plain, a plain cross, a plain altar. At his back I catch his fury, it comes full flood, a writhing red tide, a beast. The sword is drawn, it's all over with one slash, the boy dies quiet and he stands over the body fighting with the beast that drew the sword, his own foul body and soul that always gnaws at his heart. A heart that's got out of its cage, as much a cage as any in the 'Change, as much a cage that keeps Joe's heart in chains, and this beast has broken out and strangled this man's senses.

He pants in the darkness like a dog.

For a minute or more.

Then he straightens all of a sudden, and turns, and looks right at me.

He's on me in three strides, and he takes hold of my arm. He brings the blade up to my face.

'You say any word, *any word*, and though you be blood of my blood, I swear I'll cut you down the same.' I feel myself shaking. 'You hear me?'

I can only nod. He looks me over close as if trying to feel inside my head and find what I'm thinking.

'If it weren't for her,' he mutters.

As he pulls me back up the long flights of stairs, he tells me of the devils that will come to seek me out if I open my mouth.


I cry now, and Becca pulls me even closer.

'There now,' she says. 'No tears.'

'He killed the lad.'

She turns my face to hers. 'Killed?' she repeats. 'What lad?'

'He killed him with his sword.'

'Who did?' she asks. 'What sword?'

But I can't say. I can't.

Frowning, she lays me down, covers me, and sits with me.

'Sleep,' she says. 'Sleep.'

# 18

## REBECCA

It rained all that following week after my disagreement with Joe. The boy and I kept indoors and I tried to show him his letters, some of which he seemed to know. I asked him what he thought his name was and I explained mine. I would be leaving, and wanted at least to know what to call him. Perhaps he saw that in me; I'd be surprised if he didn't. He would lace his fingers with mine and look at me in such a way.

'What can I give you?' I said to him one day when he held me too tightly. 'All the money's in his name at the bank. I can't draw on it. I can't take you anywhere. You must do as he tells you.'

It broke my heart to say so, but what's a heart? I began to think Joe would sell us both if he could. I'd thought I knew him, but you don't know nobody until their back's against the wall and they're fighting for their little bit of themselves, whatever they think they've got left. When we was first alone together it was like two starving dogs on the street, begging and pinching what we could. But he started to get these high ideas after Sophia and after going to The Yellow House and knowing Henry and seeing how the gentry lived at their parties and the

Pantheon, and he wanted that. And I was like fading weather, days that had passed. I started to get invisible. I'd done too much. He took me for granted as much as he took for granted that the sun would come up in the morning. He'd go on with me or without me. And all the hope I had was that this boy would get his affection some way. Someway that I couldn't see, and had failed at.

The boy and I were sitting in the kitchen when I talked about names. I was so desperate to have something to call him, at least in my own head. Something that I could take away with me when I left.

I told him that Rebecca came from the Bible, that she was the mother of two sons, and her name meant a noose or a binding, because all men that saw her were bound by her beauty. They used to say in the workhouse that I was a bit pretty. I remember sitting on some woman's lap and her combing my hair. I remember because there were cats that walked along the wall outside and I wanted to go and get them.

There were probably seven or eight summers like that before the fire. We'd get to spend just a few hours outside. Sometimes seeing the hay being cut and the men passing down the lane with the scythes on their shoulders. And the circus coming in the autumn, of course. Winter was long, although there was a better meal at Christmas – meat, and boiled potatoes, and greens – and people sometimes came and sang songs for us. Every now and then, not often, not often at all, a man or a woman or both would come and take their children back because they had got better times. They would hold them and more often than not cry while they were holding them, and I was always puzzled why they cried or how anyone could feel that way, so much that they got on their knees and held their child and hugged them, and afterwards carried them or held their hands. And I always wanted to go out of that gate with them and see what the world was made of.

When I tell the boy that my name means beauty, I smile.

'Not now,' I say.

He lifts his hand and touches my face. He's done that before. And there we sat, two cast-offs, wondering at each other, trying to figure another way out.

'Perhaps you were given a Bible name too,' I said. 'John or Matthew?'

He just stares.

'Perhaps you are Jacob,' I whispered. 'Rebecca's son.'

And he smiled, God bless him.

I wanted to ask him about the sword, but dare not for fear of setting him crying.

After the storms of that week were gone, Joseph came and took the boy. He went to Mrs Peppard's in the city and he got him clothes and shoes. They came back with Joe looking mighty pleased with himself and the boy walking like dogs do if you ever put anything on their feet, lifting each leg and looking down and frowning.

'What did she say?' I asked him.

'Who?'

'Peppard!'

'What about?'

'About *him*, Joe, for Lord's sake.'

'Ah.' He touched the side of his nose. 'Sworn to secrecy. Although...' He smiled to himself. 'If she spreads the rumour that the boy is extraordinary, what harm?'

He took him out and they walked the city. Joseph said he must get used to crowds and noise. He said he told him about the rivers, because the boy seemed drawn to water as if he knew it. And said he asked him but the lad still said nothing. He said that he told him how all London is fed by water pipes made from elm trees and that they go underground and the water to Long Acre is brought by them, coming up from the water-wheels at London Bridge. And he even took him to the bridge and let him see how fast the river runs. They sat in one of the stone alcoves and Joseph said there used to be houses all along it, and that they had all been taken away after six hundred years, and that ships came and went from here to wonderful far-off places. But nothing seemed to move the boy except the story of the water being pumped up and through the city, because he kept looking down at every road and street, and once the boy laid himself flat and put his ear to the ground.

Joseph complained of it when he came home.

'Perhaps he's not right in the head,' he said, gazing at the lad as he picked his way through the plate I set in front of him. 'Look how he eats.'

'He probably hasn't seen a proper plate,' I reminded him. 'And he won't eat meat.'

Joseph pointed with his knife. 'That's what I mean.'

'He's sensitive,' I said. 'He hears things that I'm sure we can't hear. Maybe he could hear the water under the streets.'

Joseph leaned across the table and pushed the boy's plate with his hand. 'We'll get you beefed up and eating a whole horse,' he said. 'And you'll be a big, roaring boy, won't you?'

I grabbed hold of Joe's arm and fairly pulled him off his seat. 'Listen to me,' I hissed at him. 'You're dabbling in God knows what.'

He smiled. 'Ah, Rebecca.' And he shook his head.

'Don't you talk to me as if I know nothing,' I said. 'Don't give me that look.'

'What look?'

'Like you know everything. We don't, Joe. We don't know where he came from. We don't know what he is, or has been.'

He spread his hands. 'We got him out of Hallett's clutches. And now he's ours. More fool Hallett.'

I despaired of him then. That was the moment, the last straw. 'He's not the fool,' I told him.

It was as if he hadn't heard me at all.


I leave during the night, and go to Sophia's.

As I walk through the streets I think of the boy, heart aching. I wish I was a lady, I wish I had money, I wish I had a little house of my own with a fireside and a hand to hold in the dark. I wish for a dozen things that I'd never have. I stop at the Garden, just on a side alley, seeing the place lit up and watching the drunks pulled into Hargreaves Folly, where the lowest go, where women stand on polished trays and lift their skirts for the money that's thrown, and where I've seen young lords tumbled for whatever money they've still got in hand, and where the whoremongers tie a girl to their wrist with a fine handkerchief and deposit her at each address and stand on the thresholds counting their money. We're a cold world and a cold gutter it is when either man or woman lands in it. I thought it was a fine game when I was a little girl to sit on the street and wash my feet in the summer rain and the swill off the market. Joe saved me from worse, or else I'd be up on those polished trays or else hanging out of the windows with false flowers in my hair. Or in St Bede's churchyard long ago, as many are. It was Joe that kept me out of there and out of the alehouses.

And now I don't know that Joe cares any more if I be in his house or some other's. As long as he has hands on the boy.

I wander for a long time until I see that Sophia's is near, and I climb the few steps and I knock on her door.

A gentleman is there, sitting with Sophia in her room, his feet against the fire fender, comfortable-like. A hearty-looking man who looks as if he came out of the country, very plain, a jug of port in his fist. When I come in the door his face falls as he takes sight of me, but he rearranges it.

Sophia is in an armchair opposite him. The bed is made. It doesn't look as if she'd plied her trade that night. Perhaps they were old friends, got long past expecting a tumble and glad instead just for each other's company. Sophia wears no rouge, and her hair is in a plait to one side.

'Rebecca,' she says, surprised.

'I'm sorry to come so late.'

'Is something wrong?'

I look at the man. Glancing between the two of us, he gets up, coughs a little and says he must be going, and thanks Sophia in a polite way – a way no bloody aristocrat would bother to – and takes up his hat from the table. When he's gone, I take his place by the side of the fire.

She looks at me closely. 'Becca, you've been crying.'

'I have not.' I rub my hand over my face. 'Smoke at night smarts my eyes.'

She shakes her head. 'Have it your own way.'

I tell Sophia everything: the child, Joseph and the way he is. I tell her about the trek backwards and forwards to the Fields, and the cost of the beasts, and the fate of poor Molly, being used now to trundle at a snail's pace through the 'Change, sunk so low that even children could be put on her back. Sophia says nothing. She looks sunk low herself, and even has nothing to remark on Clement. She looks weary and keeps putting her hand to her throat.

At last, as the fire dies out and we're all in shadow, she says, 'There is no use loving him, you know. He is just for himself. He has a kindness to him, but he forgets.'

'I don't love him.'

'Ah,' she says, wagging her finger at me. 'Don't tell me lies, Rebecca. I had your sickness once, and here is where it's led me.'

It's another month before the show.

Sophia comes in and tells me about it, wearing that same exhausted smile like she's had enough of the world. Clement is as bad as Joseph, she says. Puffed up with himself, pleased that the town is talking about this curious child. She says he and Joe were grinning together all the time, and the boy was always there looking as miserable as sin as she puts it (though I don't know as she ever found sin miserable).

The scenery is all made and delivered and there are the palm trees, and I know they cost a fortune out of ships coming from the Indies, stacked below deck with sugar and molasses and no doubt smelling of that same oily stickiness as they did before, as if the leaves got coated in it. And Joe has bought the monkeys and they live in a cage in the wings and they screech and the boy puts his hands over his ears. And they had got not just the tightrope walker from the Fields but her brother, and a boy dancer from the Grimaldis, and that their costumes is all made and look real.

She says she's been to the 'Change with Clement. I told her about Shaw. Hallett was griping about the tyger and would only loan it for twenty guineas a night – *twenty guineas!* – and that all the cost of waggoning was to Clement because Hallett wouldn't deal with Joe and grumbled even though the tyger had made him money and Molly too.

I don't know how it has all become one to me. I can't summon up a feeling. I sit in the back kitchen with Sophia's cook as I used to years ago. Although the woman is different, the situation is the same: I'm sitting passing the hours while Joseph is having a fine old time somewhere else, although this time it isn't with Sophia. I feel drenched with sadness, wet through with it, folded in on myself like second-hand clothes. An old coat with a piece torn out of it, worn thin but familiar, like a skin of cloth. Pulling apart at the seams, weak and unfastened.

I wonder about the boy all the time and think of the ways that I could thieve him away and take off by ourselves, until I remember that old problem. Money. Sophia says I must speak to Joe and come to an arrangement. She says that the business is rightly half mine. We both know this is all just froth. It matters not. Women have no money of their own, except the bawds who run the houses in Covent Garden, and even then only a handful manage it by paying some oaf or other to beat her oppressors out of the door. It all comes down to men. Marriage is no way out, either. Worse, if anything. Then he can do what he wants. He can have a hundred mistresses and still be allowed to take your children away. It's a lucky woman who has a good husband.

A week before the show, Sophia looks at me and says I must have a dress.

'I don't need a dress,' I tell her.

'Oh yes,' she tells me, determined like. 'To go to the theatre with me on opening night.'

'I'm not going.'

'You are,' she says in the same kind of voice, smiling now. And she opens the armoire. She takes out a blue gown and holds it up against me. 'You're smaller than me,' she says critically. 'Let me see how much smaller.'

She wants me to take off my clothes, and it's no use arguing with her. She is fiercely opinionated when she wants to be. She hands me out of the skirts I'm wearing and draws in her breath at the state of my wool stockings. She takes off the outer petticoat and looks at the cloth pockets in it, peering in. 'What in God's name have you kept in here?'

'Feed. Money. Tickets. Food.'

She makes a disgusted noise, and throws the petticoat on the floor. By the time she's finished, I'm sitting wrapped in one of her robes on the side of her bed. Nothing I have, she says, is any good at all.

'We have to borrow finery,' she tells me. 'I can rent it. We have to at least have lace about the shoulders, and a good hat with feather and ribbon. Not too gaudy. And not white. White is for titles.' She's into her stride now. I can see she's plotting to net a man with more money than Clement. Hedging her bets. Although she might well stay with him if the show is a success. 'Shoes,' she's saying to herself. She tries her own shoes on me but there's no way I can fit in them. 'Shoes cost money,' she tells me, as if accusing me of deliberately having bigger feet than her so as to cost her. 'You'll go as my companion, so they don't have to be good,' she decides. 'Just not... them.' And she kicks the wooden pattens that I've had for years and that are perfectly good for keeping feet out of mud.

She gets in a dressmaker. The blue dress is taken in at the waist and taken up at the hem. Both women exclaim at me when I say I have no stays, no bodice. I've had a red jacket for years, and a black one. They keep me covered. But now I'm told that I have to be laced into these things that mean I can't breathe properly. I'm all right at the front though. 'A good bosom,' the dressmaker says, and Sophia looks at me speculatively. 'No rump to speak of,' she remarks. And a gruesome article is made, cork covered in linen with two straps, and I have to tie it around my waist under the skirt to make it look as if I have as much arse as breast.

When the night comes we set out in a carriage that Clement has sent, and for a half hour I am the queen, looking out onto the streets where I always walk. It makes you feel better but also worse. Higher than most but stuck in one place. Looking upon but also looked at. We can't get to the theatre steps, though. The street is blocked.

Sophia makes an almighty show of being outraged. She calls a man to come hand her down, and she pays him a penny to walk ahead. The crowds part a little at the sight of us, but not much. The poor with tickets for the pit part to let us pass, but there's plenty of quality standing on the steps and complaining as much as Sophia at the indignity of waiting.

It's a hot day, and waiting makes it worse. Sophia has a fan, but I'm left to swelter, feeling an unscratchable itch where the rump hangs, and a worse one still under the stays. My breast feels and looks like two half-moons at the neckline. I've never shown so much, but the ladies are all the same. One or two gentlemen look at me behind their wives' backs and smile. I keep my face lowered, it's covered with a lace veil to the chin falling from the brim of the hat, which weighs heavier with every moment. Why we have to have these enormous brims God only knows, but in my case it suits the purpose.

Sophia looks neither left nor right. A whisper is continually circling her. Hisses of disapproval. Murmurs of delighted scandal. She has got herself up very well. You wouldn't know that she's thirty-six. Her hair is done up so tight under the wig of curls that it's taken ten years off her. She smells very strong of geranium water. She's wearing a gown that Clement at last agreed to buy: very pretty it is. All embroidered with flowers and a little bell-shaped with no pannier in the front. It's all the rage, she's told me, proud. Maybe Clement has bought himself a few more months of attention.

When we get in at last, we have a box. That causes more hissing and conversation, but Sophia says she told Clement he would suffer something dreadful for his manhood if she wasn't given a box, so here we are, looking down at the crowd, looking across at the gentry. We're being inspected though no one acknowledges us.

'Hypocrites,' Sophia breathes. 'See the fourth box? Lady Worsley come from Pall Mall. See the rogue next to her? Captain Bisset.'

I look, but it makes no odds to me. Lady Worsley looks triumphant in a fraught, high-coloured way.

'And next to them that young blue-eyed devil Leveson-Gower.'

I see nothing but a group of men masquerading as peacocks.

The heat is overpowering. There's some sort of minor operetta onstage, in front of the curtain. I pity the performers. They can hardly be heard. I can't follow the storyline, and it seems not to matter. Worse is to come for the actor spouting Shakespeare: the crowd is impatient and getting rowdy. There is a smell of sweat and candle smoke. Of a sudden, there is a roar like a wave. It travels from one side of the theatre to the other.

'Fanny Abington,' Sophia tells me. 'And Lord Shelbourne. They have no shame.'

Abington is an actress, but she's dressed like royalty.

The crowd begins to cheer. She bows, and laughs. She looks across at Sophia and me, and waves.

'Ah, you strumpet,' Sophia whispers. But she nods back.

It's past six o'clock. There's been nothing on the stage for a half hour. Even those with seats are beginning to complain. And then, silence.

By God. It is the queen.

She glitters with diamonds in the candlelight. The crowd are still, the gentlemen standing.

'His fortune is made,' Sophia says.

'Clement?' I ask softly.

'Joseph,' she replies.

19

JOSEPH

For twenty years I've wanted to confound this city.

Not only to amuse or scandalise, but to hear that absolute silence, that intake of breath, those seconds of fear and amazement. The kind of silence that I've heard in Hunter's dissection rooms as the students peer down on the body of a hanged man.

A crowd can yell, it can turn on you and hiss, it can politely applaud. But a silent crowd, a crowd whose heart has been wrung – that is something I've longed for. The paradises at Drury Lane had a hush sometimes, particularly from those seeing Molly for the first time, but they never stayed silent for long. And it was not real silence, not absolute silence despite there being many examples.

I heard once of the boy at Bartholomew Fair who had one head and two bodies – it was years ago when the old king was on the throne – and there was a boy without legs who was brought from Austria to be shown at the Eagle and Child in Fleet Street, and it's no doubt that a child excites pity that will still a crowd for a second, and then make it buzz with intrigue. Perhaps they experienced such silences, but I doubt it. Not at the noisy freak shows and fairs where they were exhibited. I've shown such oddities myself, not because they have much appeal to me but because their parents begged me to. There's no other way to make money. A woman has a child that she hopes will keep her in old age, and to give birth to a monster wipes out that hope. But she can show it to ward off the debtors' prison. One little girl I knew when I was first here – and before I knew Sophia – had no arms but could beat a drum and embroider with her feet. Blakestone paid her to ride a horse up and down Cheapside.

Such perversions and oddities are everywhere. But that long pause when all the world stops and remains still through many heartbeats – ah, that is something new. Something that means a fortune. And we heard it tonight.

The curtain rose to the jungle scene – not so hard to conjure since the *Edens* – and on the left-hand side Pompey laid in his cage that's been made to look like a cave, his head on his paws. Despite starving him for two days he is merely sleepy. He is old – God knows how old, I have had him for eleven years and he was slow then. The audience has no reaction to him, which I expected since a lion is a regular sight at the Tower. They say the first came five hundred years ago, a gift for the long-lived King Henry, and that the keepers were given money to keep them in chains. But Pompey doesn't need a chain. He's used to noise since being in the Fields, and doesn't stir except to lift his head for a brief moment.

Above him, the acrobats squatted until the music started. Then they progressed along the tightrope that had been made to look like a branch. They were better than I hoped, acting up as monkeys and pretending to fall. It raised only a ripple of laughter, though. Up in the boxes I could see the silk fans fluttering – a sign of interest elsewhere. Supposedly there's a language with the fluttering. Messages to lovers that are sitting nearby. I wouldn't know, but it irritated me that the quality might not be paying attention.

Then came Molly, trundling in her usual way, but still raising a rolling sigh of surprise. That was better. Hemp was with her, sitting in the wings with a long rope and his hands wound round it with a look of determination on his face, since he has been threatened with a beating if he can't control her. My blessed Molly, so immense and so placid and so drunk. She made straight for the stream – a waterfall that was not only water.

In the wings, Hemp and Clement and I made noises – we roared, we chattered, we whined. Then from the cave top, we let the serpent hang, held by one of the acrobats. She was paid a shilling to do that. Not that she had any fear at all; it was her father who claimed that she was afraid to get more money out of us. The suspension makes the fifteen-foot python writhe and the girl pulls her up and drapes her about her shoulders. Unlike Pompey, the snake has been fed, and she has no poison in her bite. We made quite sure of that.

The music started. We dropped a dark sheet at the back of the stage to indicate darkness. We began the thunder – Clement has a man who rolls a cannonball in a wooden box – he goes around London for Shakespeare plays, for *The Tempest* and for others – and it makes a good noise. And then from the back, we produced the boy. He did as he was told. He ran on looking frightened – he clutched his throat, he whimpered, he looked at Pompey and took a step back. Then he looked forward, into the great gulf of the stalls and boxes, and up to the ceiling where everything was gilded and painted in Clement's colours, red and black.

We'd rehearsed, of course. He had done what he was shown. It was explained to him. He had taken it all with a listless apathy. Tonight he had to be shoved on by me, but he still looked like he's running out of fear, and he went through the motions. But it's the sight of the audience that unnerved him. He walked forward and he stared. We had told him what to expect – that there would be hundreds of people – but he looked as if he hadn't grasped it. I saw him shaking.

What we hadn't told him – because of the way he was, and because we wanted the best reaction – was that we would employ firecrackers for effect. Molly had heard them before and Pompey too in the *Edens*. Thunder and lightning. That was the story of this panorama – a child caught by the storm and changed by the tyger. I had told the child a dozen times that the tyger would be there, sheathed up to this point in a cage covered in leaves and vines, all sewn to marvellous effect by the wardrobe women and looking real – but I don't think he had ever listened to me.

At the first crack of the firecracker and roll of thunder, the covering dropped away and the tyger was revealed, and in the same instant prodded through the bars – prodded hard until he let out a roar. I'd lost sleep thinking that the tyger wouldn't roar, but he did a marvellous part for us. He not only roared but he clawed at the bars of the cage. The audience yelped, actually yelped. The man-eating tyger from the 'Change, there in all his glory, a beast to better all beasts, and looking straight at the boy.

The child dropped to his knees. This wasn't the plan. He was supposed to run off the stage shouting in terror. I called him above the thunder-rolling, but he didn't move.

Clement swore alongside me, but he showed remarkable presence of mind. He called to the male acrobat, who dropped from the height and scooped the child up, chattering as the best kind of chimpanzee. We blew red smoke across the stage – that was always planned, though it gives off an unholy stink from the resin in the candle flame it was always necessary – and bless that savage great beast, it kept on roaring and the child at last reached out its arms as he was dragged past, as if he and the captive had made a connection. The music raised up very high, almost deafening, and I caught hold of the boy as he was handed offstage, and I took off the tattered garment – peeled it off, it was thick with sweat – and pushed him back to the front of the stage.

I have never heard the like of that tyger's roar. I don't know if we could ever do it again – if the beast would stand for it, if Hallet would stand for it in case it was damaged – but I doubt we would need to do so again. We cut the sound, we cut the music and we left the boy there in the half-light, shuddering, looking at the tyger, his markings very plain to see. The child looked like a mottled ghost: the white face and hands, the muddy pattern on his chest, and then the perfect stripes over his stomach and across his shoulders and down his legs and feet. And there came that eerie silence over the whole crowd – that moment of stunned astonishment. We had said in the flyers that his markings were real, but there was no precedent for the actual sight. It was plain that it was no paint. He turned right around – bless the child! – and a kind of murmur rolled over the audience. Soft, it was. Puzzled, or pitying, or delighted, who knows? I do not.

But then he surprised me. Astonished me. He did what I had not taught him to do – he dropped to all fours, and he looked at the audience, he looked straight up to the boxes and the upper galleries – and he let out such a cry, a cry half human, half creature – such a perfect cry as if he had indeed been transformed into something that had never been seen before on this earth.


We have been swamped in this last half hour.

All the crowd wants to do is touch the boy. I keep him apart from the rabble and take him up to the boxes. To Lord Shrivington, to be exact. He and his wife asked to see the child – a footman came down and made a demand – and since Shrivington is an equerry to the king we could hardly refuse. We carry the boy up the stairs, Hemp forcing others out of the way, and we're admitted to the box where Shrivington and his wife are waiting.

'Why,' says the lady. 'It is a real boy.'

'Did my Lady not think so?' asks Clement.

She reaches forward and takes the child's arm by the wrist. 'Are you a real boy?' she asks, and laughs. She looks up at us. 'I said to Shrivington,' she explains, 'that it must be one of those little people. A dwarf, you know. One sees them occasionally. Lady Missenden has one.' She considers the boy a while, watches him shake. 'Is he ill?'

'Not at all, ma'am. Very tired, and taken aback by all the shouting. But not ill.'

She touches his legs. 'How very curious.' She wets her finger and rubs it on the skin of the boy's thigh. 'Not painted on. How strange.' Then she examines her finger. 'Is he infectious?'

'No, ma'am. He was born with the condition. It is the same skin as you or I.' She frowns at this, wiping her finger on a handkerchief. Not annoyed at the news, I suspect, but at the implication that she and I share a similarity of flesh. I can read her thoughts from the expression on her face – *you and I are not of the same constitution.*

'Where did you get him?' asks Shrivington. He is shifting from foot to foot with an odd look in his eye.

'Mr Hallett of the Exchange, M'Lord.'

'That so?' Shrivington seems less assured than his wife, an heiress ten years older than him and dressed twenty years too young for her age. 'Surprised he don't show the boy himself.'

'He had no inclination.'

Shrivington gives both Clement and I a calculating look. 'Have you ever been to Kew House?' he asks, naming the king's residence.

'Yes, sir,' I tell him.

'Deliverin' golden pheasant?'

'Yes.' I am surprised he knows that. I try to remember if he had been there that day. Their Majesties have a wonderful aviary in the Chinese style, and the queen has her own cottage in their own menagerie. Every animal trader in London wants to supply that house and garden. It's all for the children – the princes and princesses, who have cows and hogs and waterfowl – there is a zebu, a wonderful cow-like beast with a huge collar of flesh, and there are gold fish in the ponds. The Prince of Wales has three leopards, which are kept at the Tower; no doubt he has a hankering to bring them to Kew.

Shrivington is looking at me while tapping his cane very gently on the floor. 'You had a helper as I recall, a lady.'

'Yes, sir.' It was the only time I had ever seen Becca nervous. She said she wouldn't go at first, of course. But her curiosity overcame her. She wanted to see the place that the king and queen referred to as Buckingham House, and the children too.

'I remember the king took rather a shine to her.'

Did he? I didn't notice. Becca never said a word. I spoke to Her Majesty and we walked the birds to the aviary, Hemp and I following the ladies. When I got back Becca was standing by the new trees – the pagoda tree and the black locust and the rest – and the king was nowhere to be seen. It must be eight years ago or nine. A hot summer's day. A walk afterwards by the river.

'It was a great honour,' I murmur, puzzled.

'Oh yes,' Shrivington tells me. 'A shine no less. He talks of her sometimes still: "the lady with the face".' He looks troubled and uneasy, and keeps staring at the boy. There is a redness in his face under the fashionable white coating of lead, and he works his mouth, chewing at his lip. 'Of course, the king talks of a great many things.'

I have heard. The whole kingdom has heard.

Shrivington takes a pace towards the boy, and leans down to him. 'I expect you would like to meet the king and queen, eh?' His hand is trembling.

Since coming through the door the child hasn't said a word, nor has he moved. His hand in mine feels frozen. Perhaps he thinks he knows something about Shrivington. I've no idea where he gets these ideas, for ideas they are, phantoms that come out of his mouth. Things he could hardly know. And yet he does know.

Shrivington's breath smells bad. The boy stiffens and tilts his head to one side. Then he smiles. Not in the way that one could expect of a child, but rather the cynical smile of an old man. The lopsided smile of a rake. And Shrivington is such a one, or used to be. A bloody young lunatic who gambled his way out of his father's fortune and had to marry another. They say that he keeps the king occupied at whist, His Majesty's obsession. But you'll never erase a man's past from his face. It shows, sooner or later.

Seeing the smile, Shrivington removes his hand. His eyes widen for a moment as the boy grins back at him, that awful lopsided apelike grin that shows his teeth.

'Well, well, we shall see,' Shrivington murmurs.


We come out of the door to the street, the back door that empties out from the stage to the ginnel. Just as we take the last step of the stair, the boy stops dead and vomits. He clings to the wall, shaking.

I wipe his face. 'Too much, eh?' I say. 'Too much for one evening. We'll go home.'

Clement has built a low crude barn in the corner of the yard, much like the one that we have at Long Acre. The stagehands are employed to push the cages into it, which they do with much cursing, and meat is given to the beasts. We can hear the crowds still massed at the entrance – shouts and the rumble of carriages. The tightrope walkers stand in the cool night air of the yard, costumes pulled to their waists, mopping sweat. I see now that the girl is no girl at all, but a boy with his hair left long. In the Fields he wears pretty little ballerina dresses. I'm too tired to fathom it and I stand by the tyger's cage and watch the animal.

Of a sudden, the boy catches hold of the bars.

'No, no,' I tell him. 'Enough.'

'Let him do what he wants,' a woman's voice says.

I turn to see Sophia in all her gaudy and flowery glory, looking better than usual, grasping Clement's arm. At her side is a younger woman, very well made, stylish in blue silk. It takes all of ten seconds before I realise it's Becca done up beautifully. It's only when she lifts the veil.

The boy wrenches out of my grasp and runs over to her. She holds out her arms and he flings himself in them and I hear him speak – a whole torrent of words – and she crouches down and smiles at him. Her own lopsided smile that I haven't seen for weeks. She listens intently to him, frowning, and strokes his back.

I walk up to them. 'Good heavens above. Lady Talland.'

She glances at me, then bows her head. 'Mr Eliot.'

Sophia begins to laugh. 'You see what a jewel you discarded.'

'I've discarded no one.'

But I do feel it. I feel all of her rushing past me, quick as a tide. All of her, the temper and the work and the fearlessness – like a boat rushes out on a current and is soon out of sight – and

I see that her hands have gone soft, softer at least. I've felt her absence even in the thickening of my own hands and the ache in my own shoulders and the silence of the house and the fire dead every night in the grate. I think of how she always stood in the yard looking up at the clouds in the day and at the stars in the night and would never say what she was looking at, wanting something she couldn't reach to grasp. I miss her standing next to me, my right arm.

She stands. 'Did you change your mind?' she asks.

'About what?'

'Selling up and leaving the city.'

'What, now? After tonight?'

The boy whimpers.

'Come,' I say to him. And I have to prise his hands from hers. 'We're going home.'

I walk to the gate of the yard and as I pass Sophia, she touches my shoulder. 'What happened to you, Joe?' she says quietly. 'You never used to be a fool.'

20

JOSEPH

It's expensive to hire a carriage, but I am now a man of means.

Ten days on the stage. The tyger, the lion, the tightrope walkers, the boy. Money. A great wealth of money, thank God. The pain in my chest, the tightening through worry, has eased. I can breathe again.

We're watching the river, the child and I, as the road nears the Thames on a bright, windy day. For once, he shows an interest, leaning with his hands on the edges of the landau. It is midday. I can hear the church bells ringing in the city. The light is blinding from the water. As we pass over the bridge, the boy stands up. For a horrible moment I think he means to throw himself down, but he sways a little and then sits again almost at once. He makes a gesture with both of his hands as if scooping the water to wash over his face, and he actually smiles.

'Would you like to sail on the river?'

He nods. 'River.'

'That's right. River to the sea. To the whole world. Perhaps we'll go down to Rotherhithe. Or to Essex marshes. I used to have winters there once.' I have to bite my lip as he watches and makes the gesture again, water to his face. I am nervous. Their

Majesties want to see the child and no one refuses a royal command. I only had a day to find clothes for the boy, a court suit. He showed no surprise when it came, and let himself be dressed.

We have moved into The Yellow House. I've ordered furniture. The boy has his own room overlooking the square, and is wonderfully obedient, though he speaks hardly at all. I was lost on that first morning we moved there. It was the lack of Rebecca. Henry was waiting on the doorstep to hand me the keys and made no mention at all of her, but asked me if I wanted to retain his housekeeper. I said yes. I hadn't thought of it, the theatre has so occupied me.

So we live, us three – such a different three. It's very strange to not know exactly in which rooms I'm supposed to show myself. On that first day, the housekeeper gave me to understand that she would not expect to see me in the kitchen. A brisk, surly woman, though she knows her work well. I sit in the parlour of an evening when I come from the theatre and think of Becca giving me food at any hour. I have bought the boy a small dog, since he likes to be with animals and seems to understand them. He keeps it in his room and so even that kind of company is denied me. But it is good... Yes, it is good. It's what I wanted, after all. I wanted the parlour and the library and the dining room and, I suppose, the housekeeper. I am a gentleman. I am not supposed to be lonely. I look around me now at the landau that I have rented and I think I shall buy one exactly the same, and the matched pair of greys too. People come to my door now: ships' captains bring their stock to me. Only yesterday a fellow offered me that thing I've longed for so much – the kangaroo. There is one in Paris. I have told Hunter, and he has asked to see it when it arrives.

I look at the boy now and take hold of his hand, but it lies like a cold fish in mine, motionless. I let him go. And then I find myself babbling to him as we get nearer to Kew.

'I will take you to places,' I promise him. 'We can take a boat downstream from Chelsea Stairs, and we can see Westminster Hall. We can walk St James's Park to Buckingham House. But Kew is very pretty, all red brick, very small for a palace. The queen is sweet-natured. You've no need to be afraid. She loves beasts, and has playthings for her daughters. She is a botanist. She has created gardens...'

But it's not the boy who's afraid. It's me. I am afraid that the queen might take him from me, and as I look at him, quiet now, watching the houses here with their great frontages and rails and wide windows, and as the road curves towards the gates to the park, I know that he must stay with me. And not for money. No, not for money. But for him to look at me one day and talk to me as he talks to Becca. To have him travel like this with me, and be taught what I've never learned. To see him as a man. And to have what other men can never have. This curious tyger-striped boy.

We go under the great trees and we see the red-brick house with its Dutch gables and the thought charges at me, *a son, a son.*

*And Becca.*

The carriage stops and there are two footmen waiting to meet it and to my surprise the queen herself is coming down the path to us. It is informal here – their little paradise in the country – but still. The queen. Queen Charlotte of Mecklenburg-Strelitz. Married to a man who seems to be getting ill in his mind.

I've taught the boy that he must bow to royalty, but he does not. I push him in the back, but still he doesn't move. I feel the hairs prickle at the back of my neck in terror.

The queen laughs, God bless her.

Behind her come the children. The boys are not here, but the girls form something like a gauzy train behind their mother. She keeps them very close, it's said. When I was last here, it seemed to me that she did not like her children at all, even though she has fifteen of them. Or rather, thirteen. Octavius and Alfred died two years ago.

She speaks softly, her German accent distorting her words.

'Mr Eliot,' she says. 'Our golden pheasant man.'

'Yes, Your Highness.'

'And you have brought me your boy.'

'Yes, ma'am.'

She turns to her daughters. 'This is the boy who is supposedly half beast,' she tells them, then looks back at him, her eyes narrowed. 'Though he seems very human to me.'

The girls all peer at him, especially the princess royal. She is a young woman now and though people say she is plain, she is clever. She can recite poetry at a whim and did so when we toured the gardens, and she is not shy like her younger sister, although Augusta – well, Augusta was always a very pretty child. She looks at the boy now, head drooped much as his and she asks me what we call him.

'George, ma'am.'

'George,' says Augusta, and steps forward, 'are you a tyger?'

By God and all the angels, he smiles very broadly.

'Oh, I see,' she says. 'It's a game.'

'A game?' the queen echoes.

Augusta turns and holds her sister Charlotte's hand, but she is still looking at the boy. 'We all play games,' she says. 'Have you any brothers and sisters?'

'Don't torment the child,' the queen says, and the girls fall silent.

She then beckons to me. 'Walk with me,' she commands. 'Both of you.' We reach the end of the garden before she speaks again. The girls hang back obediently, a cloud of pretty flowers. 'Now, Mr Eliot,' she says, 'we shall walk to my cottage, and you shall show me the boy properly, and not as the theatre-goers see him.'

'You did us a great honour, ma'am, coming to the Galleon.'

She waves her hand carelessly, as if it's not of any importance, though it was all too important for us. It increased our takings tenfold. We are halfway along the path – it's a mile or more and nothing else has been said – when she stops and turns to me. 'Where is the lady who was with you last?'

'Rebecca, ma'am.'

'Yes. I expect the king will want to know.'

Just as Shrivington said. 'I'm sorry she is not here.'

'Is she ill?'

'No, ma'am. She's living elsewhere.'

She frowns. 'Are you not married?'

'No, ma'am.'

'But she always accompanied you.'

'She was my helpmeet in the business, ma'am.'

'And is no longer?'

'No, ma'am.'

She is looking at me with a great deal of curiosity. 'I had always supposed that you were married. I approve of marriage. The king approves of marriage.' She purses her lips but says not another word until we reach the cottage. But we're not destined to go in. Around the back is a pasture and a Chinese pavilion that I've not seen before. 'Here are our pets,' the queen murmurs. She looks at the boy. 'Do you like birds?'

'He likes all living creatures,' I say.

She is considering him. 'I've lost my youngest boys,' she tells me. 'Through inoculation, Mr Eliot. Is your boy inoculated?'

'I doubt it, ma'am. He was living in the 'Change on the Strand until we took him home with us.'

But she seems not to be listening. 'I don't know why it failed the boys as it did,' she is whispering to herself. 'That is what puzzles me. All the children of the king's father received variolation.'

All I can do is nod. There's not a single thing that I know about the practice except that it is a protection against smallpox. Nearly every person I meet has some sort of scar or other, but neither Becca nor I have ever suffered. I know what a terror it is, though. We had a bruiser for the Fields who went down with it, and his wife. They both died. They had taken themselves out in the open for fear of passing it to anyone else, God rest them. They were both used to his injuries after the matches – I can see her still wiping his face and binding his hands in the firelight of the Fields – but the smallpox destroyed their faces, producing an unholy mass of corruption. I found them myself in the little woodland two miles from the Fields. The local priest would not bury them. There's such a terrible fear of it. A more kindly young man came all the way from Harrow and gave them a decent interment at his own church. On the boundaries of the churchyard, of course. Even his own congregation were hard pressed to be kinder than that.

And so I understand Her Majesty's dedication to the practice. But to have her two boys die within months of each other is very sad. They don't lie in the corner of a country churchyard, though; they were taken in state to Westminster Abbey.

As I watch the queen, I've hardly noticed the boy edging closer and now, to my horror, he takes the queen's hand. He looks up at her with a level, almost adult, gaze. I snatch him away as quickly as I can. No one touches the monarch. No one. But to my amazement the queen smiles indulgently and bends down. 'My boy was only a baby,' she says. 'How old are you?'

'I don't know,' he says. As firm and loud as you like.

'I think you must be seven or eight,' she says. 'The same age as Adolphus. Perhaps a little younger.' She's smiling. 'May I see how like a tyger you are?'

His pantaloons are nankeen – yellow stuff, buttoned to above the knee. He obediently undresses himself and shows his calves.

'My goodness,' the queen murmurs. 'Does it hurt you?'

'No,' he says.

'Is your mother from the West Indies?' she asks. 'Is she a slave?' It seems that the queen might have heard of Hunter's portrait too, his little Sabah from Guyana. She considers him for some moments, her head on one side. 'Is she alive?' she asks.

'My mother lived in a house like this,' he says. I'm astounded. He has never said so. But then I've never asked him. Did Becca ask? I just don't know.

'Like this house?' the queen says, pointing to the cottage.

'No,' he tells her. 'Like that.'

And he turns and points at Kew House.

The queen looks up at me. 'Is this so?'

'I'm afraid I don't know, ma'am.'

'A big house like mine?' she asks the child again.

'Bigger,' he tells us.

# 21

## REBECCA

I stand on the opposite side of the road and look at Clement's theatre.

They've built new bars across it, fancy iron gates with brass fittings. No one can get in during the day. A sign of the success of the show, I suppose. It's been two weeks now. I hear that all the other theatre managers hate Clement and Joe – that they'd cut their throats for half their success. I listen to the stories of how Joe has taken a carriage and goes to and fro in it from The Yellow House. He's now all that he ever wanted to be: a gentleman. Although in reality he is no such thing. I know what he keeps inside – that small child who wanted to see the world. He has settled for show, for a little glorifying, but he is an imposter to himself. He'd like to take a trading vessel tomorrow and see wherever the ship's sails took them. I feel a heavy weight thinking about it. I wonder if he ever recalls me or how I looked on his opening night. Nobody looks at me today like they looked at me then, and all the clothes have been sent back.

Yesterday Sophia asked me for money.

'Money?' I said. We were breakfasting at the little table in her bedroom.

'Your bed and board,' she told me.

I suppose it had to come, but not in the way she suggested now. 'You cut a fine figure at the theatre,' she said. She was looking at me with her head tilted to one side. 'More than one gentleman has asked after you.'

'They've not asked me.'

'No,' she replied, and laughed. 'Nobody would ask if they saw you now. But fussed up and dressed… you would pass.'

I thought she meant for me to accompany her about town, like a servant. 'I'm not lady enough,' I said.

She nodded. 'You certainly are no lady, Becca. I often wonder why. You and Joseph made money when you were together. You could get money off him now, I shouldn't wonder. Why do you go about looking like a fishwife?'

'I like to be plain,' I said. 'Because I am plain.'

She waved her hand as if to dismiss it. 'Do you think all the toasts of the town are pretty?' she said. 'Mrs Harrington looks like a pig if you get close up. They say Eliza Harvey has lost her hair completely. Don't you think, if you showed yourself without clothes and let down your hair you might make money? Your hair is very beautiful. Such a nice colour, and all real.'

'Without *clothes*?' I said. 'Without *clothes*?' And it dawned on me all at once what she meant. She meant her own trade. I stood up. 'I'm not selling myself,' I told her.

She gave a little shrug. 'If you came with me today, you'd have five guineas in your pocket by midnight. Perhaps ten.'

I couldn't speak.

'We might set up our own little enterprise somewhere quiet,' she said. She'd obviously been thinking hard about it. 'Not in the Garden or anywhere near it. I've seen pretty little houses at the back of Sudbury Yard. You'd be surprised what a charming residence we might have. No madam to instruct us.

We could go about in the day as ladies. We might have a little barouche sometimes and go to the park in the morning. There's business to be done from an open carriage. A smile, a word, an address given.'

'I'm not doing that,' I said. 'I'd be laughed at. If you want me out of here, I'll go.' I started to clear away the tea things.

She got up and walked towards me, and got hold of my arm and turned me round. 'Don't you like men, Becca?'

'Not particularly.'

'Oh, I see,' she replied thoughtfully. 'I see. That's why you and Joe... I see. Well, that's not a problem. It might well be an attraction. You'd be surprised. There's many a place for ladies and their friends.'

'There's no such thing.'

'Of course there is,' she told me.

'That's ungodly.'

She burst out laughing. 'Ungodly! Why, Becca, don't tell me there's a righteous little church-going mouse inside that curious face.' She patted my cheek. 'Ungodly indeed. Don't you think we have our share of the clergy? Bishops and archbishops and everyone down to the lowliest verger come up to town as a break from his poor little parish in God knows where? You really don't think so? How naïve you are. And you've spent all this time in London.'

'I don't want to know about it. I see it at the Fields and I saw you getting trade in the first years. The wardrobe room and the alley before you got Melbourne on your tail.'

She smiled. 'Aye, that was my turning point.'

'That and Joe.'

'Yes,' she admitted. 'And who wouldn't have him after being pawed by Melbourne?' She looked me up and down. 'But I'm serious, Becca. It need not be a bagnio at all. Not in the common way. Just a quiet little practice for the discerning gentleman and his friends.'

'No.'

She pouted in that old, old way she'd never cured herself of. Only it didn't look so charming now, on a woman half a mile from old age. It looked grotesque, like the faces that our monkeys pull. That horrible half grin. 'I can't keep feeding you and keeping you,' she told me. 'Not when you could earn money.'

I could see she'd been thinking about this for a while. Probably since opening night after shoving me into that tight dress. 'I'll find a place of my own, then.'

'How?' she demanded.

'Hemp has a woman who's got a house off Strand Square. So he says. I've never laid eyes on her. But he says there's a top floor.'

'Some infested attic? Rent free?'

I bit my lip. 'I can go back to Joe.'

'Oh, really?' she said. 'Don't you know he's thrown you over? He went visiting the queen this week at Kew. You used to go with him, but he didn't invite you, did he? You're not good enough for him now, Becca. I saw him at the theatre last night and he never spoke a word of you. It was all "what the queen said".'

I'd been up at the Fields last night, looking after the business that Joe never has time for now. Mucking out the bloody animals and keeping the gates open all day and arguing with meat suppliers. And all the time he was making small talk with Their Majesties. Sodding, *sodding* man.

'He took the boy too,' Sophia said, triumphant.

I glanced out at the street. All the world coming and going. Waggons dragging backwards and forwards, horses sweating, sunlight pouring on the dusty road and the barely swept walkway and flies settling on the window glass. I looked back at her.

'It's Clement, isn't it?' I said. 'He won't put you up somewhere better than here. He's a stingy bloody sod with you, is that it? So you're going to branch out on your own and you'll take me with you.'

'I don't know where you get the idea that you're better than me,' she retorted. 'You've always looked at me with that sad sack face of yours. As if you're not a kept woman as much as me.'

'I'm not kept. I work.'

'And stink as a result,' she said. 'Don't you think that you stink? And why should you be content with that? You could smell like a rose all day, Becca. Get up at noon and have a maid. A maid for both of us. I know women who'd housekeep for us and be glad of it, just to look after our house and not have to earn a living on their backs. Nice women too, cheap girls. Keep a fine clean place with flowers in your room. No mud, no filth. No walking through the rain. Fine wines in our cellar for the gentlemen. No bawdy shows. Refinement. You've got a fine body, not a mark on it. Good legs, a small waist. Think of it. I've known a man pay a year's wages for the sight of ankles. Old men will pay anything and they like a house to seem proper and decent. Makes it more worth it, see? And besides the legs you've got that bosom. Wish I had one like it. We could lead men a dance seeming like two maids and having fine times when the doors were shut. No reputation, see? Nothing but *special* care.' She laughed a little to herself. 'And we could retire after another ten years. By the sea, perhaps. Don't tell me you wouldn't like that.'

'No. I won't.'

She threw her hands in the air. 'Can't you see this for what it is? It's a step up, Becca. You think you're too good for it? Don't you know what happens to nicer girls than you when they come up from the country like you did? They're no sooner off the coach than they're on Harris's list. You were lucky. Joe defended you. But no man will forever, and now he's got hold of that boy he doesn't need you.'

'That's not true. I'm running the Fields.'

'The Fields?' she said. 'He's no interest in the Fields any more. As long as he keeps that boy near him, he's a gentleman made.'

I looked away from her. I knew in my heart it was true. I'd not seen him or heard from him since opening night. The arguments this morning with the suppliers were because he'd not paid them. He hadn't even asked for the gate money. He didn't care.

'The show took four hundred guineas last night, Becca. How much money did the Fields take?' She stood with her hands on her hips, staring at me. 'Two, three? Or maybe it was just shillings. Or pence. Joe is taking a thousand guineas a week after he's split it with Clements and paid the crew.'

I sat down again and crossed my arms over myself.

She leaned down next to me and whispered, 'And he's got that boy, hasn't he? You like that lad, don't you? Like mother and son you were when I see'd you together. Regular holding of hands. And he talks to you, doesn't he? He never talks to Joe. I've heard him say so. But he's going to keep that child close and never let him near you, because that boy's the money-maker. That's how much he cares about you.'

She stood up, walked back to the bed, ran her hand over the tea table. I saw her imagining the things she could have if she set up her own house and had enough clients.

'He owes you half that money,' she said. 'Money we could use.'

'Half? No.'

'Is that the only word you know, God help you?' she cried.

'Why not? It was you that noticed the boy in the first place. By rights he's yours. By Christ, you're blind when it comes to him. And here's me offering you safe harbour and you won't take it.' She stamped her foot. Then all at once, she gasped. She put her hand to her mouth, and then she started to laugh. 'Oh my Lord in heaven.'

She ran across to me and pulled me up. 'That's why you won't go into business with me,' she said. 'It's because you won't let go of Joseph Eliot. You're thinking he won't let you down. It's only ever been Joe. And you stick to him like a fly in a web – like the flies out there in the street stuck to horseshit, drawn to it, whatever muck it puts you in. It's him and no other. Always has been.'

She then held me at arm's length, looked me up and down, and started laughing all over again. 'You won't take my idea of business because you can't, can you? Because you've never had a man. Never in your life! Never! Because you're waiting for him. Him that never sees you, him that's forgotten you!' And she took herself back to the bed and threw herself down on it, still laughing, and put her hands up to her head.

'Oh, Becca,' she said between sighs. 'You poor bloody wench.'


I'd gone out straight after. Left Sophia stewing.

I wanted to see Hemp and guessed he was at the Fields, but fury at Joseph kept me walking in another direction. Let the gates stay closed out there this morning. Like Sophia said, it was only a matter of pence anyway.

Seeing the Galleon closed, I went to the Strand. I wanted to see Molly. I shouldered my way past the oaf on the door, but he caught my arm. 'Brought money, have you?'

'What money?'

'Ask Hallett.'

Sure enough, Hallett was standing centre between the cages. He was talking to a fine couple, and excused himself from them. He asked the same question, and even held out his hand.

'I haven't any money,' I told him.

'You two owe me for the tyger.'

'I haven't seen Joseph Eliot in two weeks, and he don't see me.'

Hallett raised an eyebrow. 'That so?'

'That's so,' I told him. 'I've come to look at Molly.'

He followed me as I went out back to the yard and the stable. Molly was laid down. Her eyes were closed and she was heaving with each breath. Hallet was right behind me, leaning on the gate. He watched me as I kneeled beside her.

'How long has she been like this?' I asked him.

'I sent Eliot a letter. He told me to send Molly for the show. I told him she couldn't come on account of this malady, whatever it is.' His voice lowered to a threatening tone. 'He's got my tyger and he don't send a penny. I've been up there at night and they won't let me backstage. Been up there in the day and the door is barred.'

'I know. I've seen it.'

'Well, what are you going to do about it? If he won't pay, I'll have the tyger back.'

I put my hand on Molly's neck. She was more dead than alive. I looked up at him. 'She's dying.'

'Well, what do I care?' he said. 'Can't show her, can't get her on her feet, and can't get paid for housing her. It'll be a load off my back.'

I pressed my face to Molly's hide. Both of us were being cast off. It hurt my heart to think of it, and the way people once clamoured to see her. Poor beast.

I stood up. 'I'll try to see him.'

'Aye,' he said. 'You'd better.'

As we walked back out into the yard he gave a great sigh, his anger cooling. 'I don't know why I took on this business. Nothing but trouble.' He glanced in my direction. 'How is the boy?'

'Your guess is as good as mine.'

'I never knew about the skin on him. Shaw took him in.'

I stopped. 'Did he? When?'

'I'm not rightly sure. Two years. Three.'

'Where did he find him?'

'None of your business.' He stopped, and the line of his mouth hardened. 'Making money for Mr Eliot and Mr Clement, eh? Making a lot of money, and you two took him off me. So tell Eliot that as well.'

I shook my head a little. Nothing really seemed to matter to this man but money. He had no feelings for the animals, took no part in caring for them, and resented their cost. He either didn't see suffering or it didn't get under his skin. He strutted about like he owned the ground he walked on, a Huguenot whose family came here out of need three generations ago and took over Spitalfields, and hoarded money between themselves and got rich. I saw that his clothes were silk. A very fancy coat, and a silver-topped cane. A hollow man, I thought. If you'd rap him, he'd echo inside.

As he walked away, back to his rich customers, I took a step to Shaw. 'You know where he came from,' I said.

'I don't.'

'You know where he came from and you took money for him, I'll warrant.'

He looked at me with that flat dead stare of his. 'Free labour for Mr Hallett. No questions asked.'

'But someone paid you to take him away.'

'Not a penny piece.'

You could feel the lie. It was a substantial thing hanging in the air, a solid thing made of wickedness.

'You didn't find him in the Garden,' I said. 'Somebody brought him here. Not a whore, not a brothel keeper, not a man off the streets.'

'Oh,' he said, and he smirked. 'And you know that, do you?'

I saw him.

Joseph Eliot took me there.

Up in the candle smoke of the theatre, up high. That first night. Climbing back stairs and then a little space behind a door. A man and woman there and they told me it was Shrivington. I wished I had a knife, a blade. Or a rock in my hand. I thought of catching hold of him and taking him to the edge and pulling us both over to break his back on the seats below.

He smelled of something sweet, something he'd put on himself. I remember he used to smell like that when he came to my mother and me at night. Sweet oil masking a smell of meat and drink. High up then, too, up back stairs like these, high up and out in the far wing of the house behind a locked door. Lots of locked doors, and he had the keys. He kept things. Living things and dead ones. Two boys, fed well. Kept them together in a bedroom. You could hear them cry in the daytime and scream at night. They said that the house had forty bedrooms.

And when he came to us, whenever he came to us in that spring and early summer after I saw that lad lying on the chapel floor, I think he knew what was in my head because sometimes he would look guilty. Just for a second. Guilty and then angry. When he saw me in the theatre box I heard his heart thundering away; I saw that same look of guilt. And something else: fear.

My mother had dark skin, very soft. Been brought from the West Indies across the seas. From the sugar plantation that belonged to him. She was a secret. Was his in the Indies – his servant and slave – his little toy that he would make a display of because she was clever, he told her. She would dance about in a skirt and bodice and have a woman who did her hair, and she could recite any poem he told her and people came to the house and watched her and petted her like a toy. That was her child life. She never knew her mother or father but she was happy enough, she told me. Worked in the house and made him laugh. He was younger then, but he got himself into trouble, lost his fortune when the hurricane came and had to leave. She came with him. Older, not a child any more. Kept separate on the ship, and brought to the house one night as a girl, not knowing why. Not understanding what was waiting for her.

She was gentle. Lovely and frightened. She sang songs. She could sew and she could read and she could draw, and he gave her books out of his own library and he would tell her that his wife never read a book. She taught me to read and she taught me to see and listen. Listen to the house. The trees. Birds outside. Land itself. All who'd lived there. All the breathing of the world. Light and dark. The way the sun laid on a floor. The voices in things. The weave of a carpet. The tree inside the panelling. She made me see what others can't. She had that in her.

I can see them as if from far off, her and the books and the way she looked up at him knowing there was a price to be paid for the reading. One day he told her not to sing any more because his wife had heard it. I don't think that was true, for we were a very long way from wherever the wife lived. I think it was just that the songs were sad. And I remember that he would turn his face away as she dressed me. Wouldn't touch me when I got bigger. I made him afraid. I could feel that.

I remember the keys because she was always looking to see where he carried them. He was careful. He put them on top of the door's lintel when he came in. She used to follow those keys with her eyes and then she put me in the dressing room. A cubbyhole more like. Wash basin and jug. A narrow window with a view out onto the park. There was a little bed for me in there. It had a pillow that I could put over my head so as not to hear the noise. A pillow with an edge of flowers. A coverlet of the same. Trace my finger along the pretty vine.

Dark night, nothing stirring, the door come softly open. She was in the doorway with her finger pressed to her lips. *Shhh.* Half asleep, thinking I was dreaming it, she picked me up and wrapped a shawl around us. Stepped back into the room. *Shhh.*

I thought she'd killed him. But closer and you could see his mouth open and hear him snoring like a pig in a pen. She passed him and we went to the door, and out of the waistband of her dress, she took the key.

By then I'd heard a lot about that house. The room maid would tell us bits and pieces, trembling. Warning my mother not to move. Not to even think of running away. She and my mother were close, heads together, whispering. There was all sorts of stories about that house. There was supposed to have been a maid walled up in a room, and a baby thrown onto a fire. It wasn't true – I would have felt it – but Shaw liked to hiss those things when he got me in his grip and tell me to be thankful I wasn't there any more. Tell me to be grateful to him. He said things about Shrivington, how it was rumoured that he'd had a slave woman and a child by her and how they'd run away and how Shrivington had looked all over but never guessed she'd got as far as London. But *he* guessed. He thought he knew, and he'd stare at me closely in the face when he talked of a slave woman dying in the Garden and her body been thrown into a pauper's grave, and he'd watch me to see if there was sadness in my face. I never gave him that.

He'd say that Shrivington was the devil, how he was friends with other great men who had a club where they were the devil's disciples, and he knew that because the girls at the Garden told him. And Shaw would put his hand over my mouth and tell me that Shrivington would come and get me if I spoke out. Him or one of his men. One of his devil's disciples, he said, and they would find me and slit my throat. Them that were outside the law, too high up to be held to account. And of all the things he told me and tried to make me afraid, I knew that that much was true of Shrivington. He had a darkness inside him. But being in the Exchange meant that I was dead to Shrivington because I was of no consequence at all. Because I was no longer living. I'd vanished like I had never been born. My mother died in the Garden of some pestilence, he said, and now I was one of the animals. That give me protection. 'I give you protection, boy,' he'd say. *Protection.* And his spit would be on my face and his hands groping.

'You is just an animal, boy. Don't forget I saved you from him, so shut yer mouth.'

Better not to speak.

Be nothing.

Be nobody. Just something slung on the shore of the city, like wreckage. My mother lived in me when I saw the dead – those girls walking through the 'Change at night. That man running. And the animals. Animals who kept their little flames burning.

Oh, she did not deserve her death. We got to London truly starved, eating peel and cabbage leaves and oats meant for the horses – aye, even their mash of a morning in the tavern stables of the Garden. We were lashed out of there a dozen times, but hunger doesn't care. To be hungry is a terrible thing. And I saw my mother start to cough blood and I saw her take men at the back of the inns. For pennies, mind you. Only pennies. And I saw the light of the islands go right out of her, snuffed out as silent as a candle, until it wasn't she who dragged her body about or took my hand but a picture of what she'd been. She died next to me one night, gone cold in the dark, and it was Shaw who stumbled up against us, falling over and then righting himself, and coming back to stare at us and pick up my mother's hand and drop it just as quickly, and haul me to my feet. Afterwards there was rumour that one of the king's men was looking for a woman and a boy. He must have been tempted to take me straight to the man, but his filthy hands had too much enjoyment. I didn't care at all by then. I shut my mouth. I shut up my memories and tied them tight.

When we had run away from the big house that night – walking quick, barefoot on cold flagstones when we got to the kitchens, past the cook's room and the housekeepers', past the footmen's rooms, past the deep in the bottom of the house then, deep in the oldest where it ran damp, deep past storerooms, past the washhouses, past woodstacks, past the cold houses where meat was hung – that was where standing in the half-lit gloom was the maid that brought us food and she had a key, too, and she opened an iron gate. My mother and her clung to each other and my mother cried and said *Come with us*, and all I remember was her face fading as she closed the gate, a pale sliver of moon of a face before it vanished and we was running.

I don't know how old I was. I don't know now. Old enough to run, though. Down the flower bed paths, through a walled garden. I thought a gardener's boy saw us running. He was up and stoking a fire for the hothouses in a little lean-to, and he shot us a look and then looked quickly away. Perhaps his soul come running after us for a while, for nobody wanted to stay there. We got to the woodland, great oaks and beeches. We ran, but it was easier. We could make a sound. You could hear our breath echoing.

We never stopped. When the light come up, we still walked and come to the edge of the trees where you could see a great vale. In it was a white line going along by the fields.

'Look,' she told me. 'The road to London.'


I don't know how many years it is since we ran through the house and the gardens and the woods, or got to that thin white line that got wider with every mile we walked. And in all the years I've tried never to think of Shrivington. But Shrivington's come back to me. Joseph Eliot's brought me to the man that Shaw said would kill me. I've been waiting every day since for the disciples that will slit my throat. Wait for them every night in those big crowds, that sea of faces. The faces that made me scream when I saw them beyond the lights of the stage. I thought they'd all come to find me, and when Joseph Eliot took me up the theatre stairs and showed me who was waiting, I got ready to kill my father before he killed me.

But Shrivington didn't move. He stared at me like I was a thing out of his nightmares. He leaned down once to look in my eyes, and he stood back while his wife prodded me and asked if I was carrying a disease. Said nothing. Thoughts ran across his face: I felt his disbelieving guilt. Yes, felt him like I feel everything else: a finger stirring my gut. I don't know who was more afraid or angrier standing there, staring at each other.

I'm in the yard at the theatre now. I stand and let the sun warm me up. I feel cold so much. I wish Becca would live with us. I wish I didn't hear all Joseph Eliot's thoughts and see the pictures in his head. Becca's misshapen mouth. The claws of

Pompey faded and yellow. The wash of the river. Sailing boats. Cages. So many cages. An elephant walking at night through the docks. The stench of a skin.

The acrobat boy passes me in the yard and ruffles my hair. 'What you doing, little tyger?' he says. 'Dreaming?'

A dream, yes. Coming out of the cage.

Poor creature. Man-eater. Got when a cub. We're made from the same cloth. The tyger thinks of free air, half forgotten. Grasses. Heat. I go over and sit by her and she looks at me, all of it flickering in that eye. Tormented by smells, all the meat walking around on its hind legs, human creatures, the taste of blood. But more than that. She wants to run. Only run, stretch out her body and feel its power. Flexes her feet thinking about it. She can scent the horses, and beyond the horses, and grime and sweat, and she can feel the river. She is a big cat. She can swim. Wants to. Thinks of a rush of cool water. Oh, the pleasure. Oh, the pain of the scent. Too much longing. We roar together at night on the stage because we're calling. Two of us alone in the heaving dark.

Run, run, run.

I know how the cages open.

The world fell apart today.

I'm at the theatre with Clement when Hemp comes slamming through from the yard, first there after hearing the acrobats scream. Everyone out there comes bundling back inside, falling over each other. I hear them say something about the boy, the tyger boy, and the hair on the back of my neck stands up and I fight my way past them all as they scramble to get out of the way.

I grab hold of Hemp. 'What in God's name is it?'

'Tyger,' he says. That's all he says. 'Tyger.'

Clement is at my back and I hear him whisper, 'Jesus Christ.'

The door is still half open and I see the cage in the far corner. Pompey is up. That's what astonishes me first, because Pompey never bothers to stand except when food is coming. And then, in the strong midday sun I see the tyger walking past the door. Walking as if out for a stroll. Looking about itself. It glances towards the door and stops. Nobody makes a sound, not even to close the door. We're struck dumb, everyone holding their breath. Once or twice I've felt scared as I've handled beasts but I've never felt fear like in this moment when the animal looked at me. Sizing me up and thinking.

Then, 'Close the fucking door,' Clement breathes.

'You can't leave the boy out there,' the acrobat says.

Oh God.

The boy.

Hemp shuts the door and fumbles with the bolt. I wrestle with him, take his hands off it. The acrobat says, 'He let it out.'

I look back at him. 'He what?'

'Let the beast out. *He let the beast out,*' he repeats, eyes wide. 'He was stood by the cage and then he undid the bolts. He opened the door.'

I hear what he's saying, but I can't believe it.

'And the woman was in the yard.'

'What woman?'

'Your woman. Becca.'

Clement groans. 'She did it.'

I turn on him. 'What are you talking about? She wouldn't open the cage.'

'You think that child had the strength to open those bolts? They've done it together.'

'They wouldn't!'

'They did,' he insists.

'There's no...' I can't spit out the words. 'There's no... reason...'

A scream outside. A man's scream.

I open the door.

'No, no!' A jumble of voices behind me.

And there is Becca on the far side of the yard by the open gate. There is a crash. Becca looks toward the noise, down the alley that leads to the road, and she's saying something, calling out. Between her and the tyger is the boy.

He's standing quite still, not afraid, watching the beast and he has a smile on his face. I'm not imagining it. *A smile.* He opens his hands as if to say *look what I did* and then he laughs. *Laughs.* The tyger looks at him.

'Be quiet,' I whisper. 'Don't laugh, and don't speak.'

Beyond the boy, Becca holds out her hands and calls him. He glances at her and says something I can't catch. She inclines her head. She looks at the tyger and I can see she's shaking, her hands are trembling as she holds them out, but she doesn't move. She doesn't run. She's talking softly to the boy. I can hear their conversation. I can hear that Becca's voice is wavering. But still she doesn't run. My own words are choked in my throat now, shut up inside me by sheer fear. This beast tears men apart. It should have been shot. But Hallett's greed for a good taking at the 'Change and my own for showing it here mean that it's walking around in broad daylight, walking the yard as if measuring it. Swinging its great head from side to side and then lifting it, scenting the air. It walks past the boy and *in Jesus name oh holy Christ!* the boy puts out his hand and lays it on the tyger's back then he walks with it toward the gate and Becca.

'Why doesn't she run?' Hemp breathes behind me. 'Run, run.'

I step out into the yard. I don't know what I'm going to do. I don't even know that I'm really walking at all until I come out of the shadow of the theatre and the sun strikes me and I feel the heat coming up from the ground. I shade my eyes against the light. Only then can I see the source of the crash beyond the yard gate. A waggon is being towed from side to side in a narrow alley because the driver has gone – he must have been the man who screamed – and the horses are trying to wrench free of the tack and the reins, pushing each other in their frantic attempts, rearing up and plunging down again. The boy and the tyger get to the gate. Now they're alongside Becca. Her mouth is open slightly. The tyger comes within six feet, five feet. It comes slowly, padding, swaying a little, flicking its tail and the boy is still walking along by its side and he still has a hand on the tyger's back.

'Eliot,' Clement says.

I look back. 'What?'

'Do we have anything? Do we have rope?'

'What are you going to do with a fucking rope,' I mutter, and look back.

Maybe the beast will stop for the horses. We keep him hungry, and they must smell like a vast plate of food to him. They've pranced about so much that the waggon is now sideways on, stuck in the alley. In a moment I see it teeter and then fall on its side, and the horses are still pulling and managing to drag it. I can hear screams down the street, crowds coming to see what the noise is and then falling back. The tyger still walks. So calm. So slow. And the boy still has his hand on the rippling back. I think I must be dreaming when I hear his childish treble raised in a song. *Singing*. Becca looks as if she might fall. She could run away now, run to the theatre. They've passed her. But she doesn't. She looks at me and then she follows the boy.

'Becca!' I shout. 'Becca!'

By now Hemp has half a dozen theatre hands following him like a pack of inquisitive dogs. He is out of breath, having run right through the theatre from front to back calling for help. Though I'm damn sure these men don't want to help him much. They hang behind him and among them are two little girls that sometimes sell flowers in the foyer, not more than five or six and each of them round-eyed and gnawing on their fists and then wringing their hands by rote. I notice – as if it matters, but it's strange what you do see and it sticks in your mind for no reason at all – that both children are barefoot and I wonder why I've never noticed that before.

'Where is it?' Hemp says.

I point at the alley. Both horses give an unearthly cry – nothing like any sound I've heard before from horses – and Hemp grips my arm.

'Don't go, sir,' he tells me.

'I can't let a tyger run into the street,' I say. 'Go back through the ground floor and out to the front steps and see if you can see where he goes.'

Although that's a stupid instruction. We can already hear where it's gone by the sound of mayhem from the main street. Crashes. Shouts. Screams.

Clement is still at my back. 'They'll call the militia to it,' he says.

He's right. The barracks are only four streets away. A half mile, no more. And they've dispatched beasts before. Some years back an elephant was killed at Fentimans – a poor show the other side of the city. Killed by muskets. Or, more accurately, injured by muskets. The beast had started behaving very oddly, started pulling at its chains, and had thrown a keeper and trampled a woman who came too close and tried to pet it. But when it was lying on the ground it was still alive, and a captain drew his sabre and delivered the final blow. Hunter looked at the body afterward and announced that there had been an abscess on the tusk and that the thrashing about was caused by toothache. Only toothache. It made the city sad. It was buried – buried, all that enormous carcase – out at Earl's Court.

I run to the yard gate and there's no sign of the tyger, no sign of the boy, and no sign of Becca. What there is, by some miracle, is the waggon on its side and the two horses alive, standing, shaking, sweat showing in white patches on their hides, and their eyes wide.

*Where are you where are you where are you?*

We run. Clement, Hemp, and I.

People are flat against the sides of yards and houses. I can feel sweat running down my neck. Someone shouts from the crowd all of a sudden, 'Witchcraft!' I look about, and some old wretch is doing the screaming and waving her fist at me. 'The tyger boy! The witch woman!' And I see that the nearest believe her instantly. A few yards further on, hands are pointing – a forest of hands – towards the river.

The main thoroughfare has halted. Carriages and carts stock-still, men and women and children clambering all over them for safety. They all point in the very same direction. I grab a man who is half on and half off a cart and he squeals like a pig.

'Where did they go? Which way?'

He gives me a mad grin, bloody lunatic that he is. 'Dancin' to the water.'

'It will kill us all,' a little girl keens. 'Kill us, kill us!'

The streets begin to slope. Everywhere mayhem. You can smell the river before you see it. Every kind of filth goes into it.

'There!' a man shouts from an upstairs window. 'They cut back from Durham Yard when they see Ivybridge is blocked, and they went out at Salisbury Stairs.'

'Where's the boy?' I call up to him.

'With it!'

'And the woman?'

'With the boy!'

And he flings his arms about in a show of astonishment.

Behind us, braver folk have followed. I can hear the words *tyger boy tyger boy* being repeated.

'Water,' Clement says in a high-pitched croak. For all his walking, he's lost his breath. 'A tyger won't go to water.'

I want to slap his face or, better still, knock his head off his body. 'Don't you know that big cats can swim?' I tell him. 'Ask Hunter! Ask the ships' captains. A tyger will leap. It will swim.'

He glares back at me. 'Does the boy swim?' he demands. 'Does your woman? What the hell are the pair of them doing?' He slumps where he stands and leans against Hemp. 'The Devil's work,' he moans. 'I'm going no further.'

'Curse you for a coward,' I tell him. 'Do what you like.'

I start to run. I'm running against the crowd – people running away from the river. One man grabs my arm and tries to tow me backwards. The flow up from the river collides with the fearful, fatefully curious crowd coming the other way and I hear them murmuring and yelling and crying behind me as I reach the edge of the water.

The Thames is a rolling, murky tide. Ships crowd the docks. I come to one of the wherries, the stone steps that lead down into the river, and see the watermen and their boats and sculls pushing out from the shore as if all part of one machine. 'Tyger!' one shouts, and points to the east of me.

There's a wharf here, and warehouses behind, all the narrow gateways and doors and alleys forming a haphazard rash. I hang on to the top stair and try to see what the man below me on the water is seeing. I step back and look up the wharf. A mile downstream they are rebuilding Somerset House for the city – making fine government offices. It's looked derelict for years, but it is said that what will rise from the ground will be magnificent. But for the moment it is a jumble of wood structures and piles of stone, and hard up against the river wall is a great barge loaded with sand. I see men scrambling from it and up onto the wall by a ramp, all gesticulating in our direction.

I walk slowly along the side of a yard, my heart in my mouth, expecting at any moment to feel the huge weight of the tyger in my back, or see its face fixed on mine and its body ready to spring. I see that there's a small ship right alongside on the wharf. It's hard to distinguish what they're unloading, but I hear the shouts and I see the panic to get back on the boat. And in another few steps, they come full into view. The beast and the boy.

I can't see Becca. And in that moment of terror I am again sixteen years old, holding out my arms to a lighted window, and I see her flying with arms outstretched and her hair a halo of flames. Her pathetically thin shawl alight and her face looking at me, such a small and terrified face, so pretty, her arms stick-thin, her dress ballooned by the air, and I catch her by one arm and somehow she miraculously climbs up me like one of the circus monkeys, and her weight flings me back against the beech. Smoke all around us, ash in her hair, her face scorched, blackened. I put my jacket over her head to quench the fire and she clings to me so fiercely that her fingers dig into my ribs. We get down this way, slithering down the tree, her small frame welded to me. At the bottom, on the ground, we run, although God knows how she runs at all, her lungs full of soot. Over the narrow lane and into the field. Along the field path for half a mile until a footbridge. We run along the other side then through wheat, Becca gasping for breath but not saying a word, until we charge unawares into a stream and I make Becca put her face in the water, and we lie there, each of our gazes fixed on the distant orange glow of the burning building.

'Becca,' I told her. 'I can't carry you.'

But I did. Half walked, half carried, reaching Oxford on the eighth day and begging in the streets until a doctor saw Becca's face and took us into his rooms. That hot summer day long ago was the very first time I heard Hunter's name. The old man in his Oxford College was a scientist. 'No oil except spirits of wine and a little oil combined,' he said to himself. He had Hunter's treatise open on the desk, and read it as he looked at Becca's face. He peeled away the dirty linen that some woman had put on it in one of the villages we had passed through. Becca cried a little. The first tears I'd seen since the fire. 'Fresh air is best for healing,' the old man told us. 'And a soap made with limewater, and vinegar as the days go on.' Much later, Hunter himself would smile when he told him how Becca's face had been treated. He tutted at the scarring, but he found her interesting, just as syphilis chancres were interesting to him, and wounds of waggoners whose hands had been torn, and noblemen who had been thrown from their hunting horses. It was all grist to the same mill to him.

I can't see her now, but I see the boy and he stands away from the tyger whose feet balance on the very edge of the dock. Some idiot or other is throwing things from the deck of the ship as they haul up the gangplank. Ships' stores rain down and split open on the ground: boxes of spice, a roll of fabric, a box of books. They all miss. Suddenly, the boy looks back at me and I try to beckon him. He has a sorrowful expression and puts his hands to his head and pulls at his hair as if he's faced with an insurmountable problem.

He steps forward.

And suddenly the tyger is gone. The child runs to the edge of the river and screams. A cry goes up on the ship and, at the back of me, from the watermen and their barges and rowboats. The tyger is in the river.

I charge to the boy and hold him at arm's length, searching him for a sign of injury. There is none. I stare into his face and see how insanely calm he is, although I can also see the marks of tears on his face. He actually smells like the beast. I hold him to me, and he stiffens as he always does. 'You're all right,' I tell him. 'You're all right.'

I can't ask him what I want to ask him. If the acrobat was telling us right when she said that he opened the cage. I can't fathom it, I can't imagine why he would, except that he is such a strange soul, so untroubled at times of chaos, so seemingly despairing when I can see nothing wrong.

'Where is Becca?' I ask him. 'Is she hurt?'

He draws back from me and looks out at the river beyond the boat. I think I see – but I cannot surely see, it is all a dream, highly coloured and unreal – the tyger coming strongly against the current, unhurried almost, moving through the water without effort, a yellow dart; its eyes fixed not on us, but upon some distant point. It swims past, half under the boat, lithe and fluid and quick as mercury, then a rapidly fading shadow racing across the tide, first dark and then light and then becoming part of the rippling as it gets closer to the bridge and the weirs; and then disappearing altogether.

There is a fearful thunder of feet behind us. People crowd to the edge of the wharf, and the ships' hands call out to them. Curses, telling them to leave the stores alone – some are already picking up and making off with the boxes – and then slamming down the gangplank again and finding a captive crowd willing to hear what the tyger did, all their stupid mouths agape, grinning, and already telling themselves their own stories of fictitious courage.

Hemp comes blundering through them all.

'You were a great help, you bloody oaf,' I tell him.

'Where is it, the beast?'

'Gone in the river.'

'By Christ. Mr Clement ain't goin' to like that. Nor Hallett neither.'

It hadn't occurred to me until now, but he's right.

He looks at the child. 'And the boy here?'

'Unhurt.'

'A miracle,' he says, and pauses. 'But, Mr Eliot, of Becca...'

'Where is she?'

'Some women got hold of her. Caught her and wouldn't let go. I seen them argue with her, she's trying to follow the boy and for a start off I think they're saving her but it's not so.'

'How is it not so?'

'Because...' He looks at his feet, then back at me. 'I'm right glad the boy is well, sir,' he says.

I take him by his coat and start to shake him. 'Where is she? Where?'

'They took her back into the city,' he says, very quiet. 'They took her to Bow Street.'

Bow Street is Fielding's own court, run by his half-blind brother, and only two minutes from our old home. 'What the devil have they done that for?'

'On account of her letting the tyger out,' he tells me.

24

JOSEPH

Midnight in Leicester Square.

I enter Hunter's house through the back, using the entrance the corpses come in. Hunter himself opens the door and I follow him down a candlelit passage, the lecture theatre and the dissection rooms are in shadow, until we reach the stairs. There, he turns to me and I clasp his hand in both of mine.

'I'm obliged to you,' I tell him. 'For his life.'

He smiles. We go into his study. There is a fire still lit. He gives me a glass of gin. I'm perfectly fine until it scalds my throat, and then the day seems to fall on me. He helps me to a chair, and sits himself, pulling on his unkempt beard as he looks at me.

'There's a waggon in St Martin's Lane. Everybody knows my driver. He'll come to the back door shortly. Nobody will ask what's under the sailcloth,' he says. 'They're too afraid of the answer.'

'Thank you,' I tell him. 'Thank you.'

'The boy will go to Earl's Court. My housekeeper never questions. She's seen too much.'

'I don't know why he would do such a thing,' I murmur.

'You don't? Truly?'

'No, sir.'

'How long have you had him with you now?'

'Six weeks.'

'And you mean to tell me that you don't know of his peculiar affiliation with animals?'

'Yes, I... I know that they stir themselves around him.'

'And that he speaks to them.'

'I have heard nothing like.'

Hunter sighs. He finishes his drink and pours another. 'Then you've not been listening nor looking,' he says. 'I suppose Rebecca did all the caring while you bought and sold and showed him.'

I can't deny it. I find myself gripping the arms of the chair to keep my body steady. 'Becca has been living with Sophia Baddeley.'

'And she left you because she knew you might sell the boy to the highest bidder.' He smiles at my discomfort. 'London is a small city. Populous, but small nevertheless. News travels.'

'Yes.'

'And would you still sell the boy?'

'No, sir.'

'And why is that?'

'Becca would not forgive me.'

'Ah,' he says, and tilts his head to one side, surveying me as if he has discovered some new thread in my character. But the thought of Becca is too much. I lean forward and put my head in my hands. Hunter drinks. 'A small light has dawned at last,' he mutters. 'A small light illuminating that woman's worth to you. A worth beyond money.'

'Becca is in Newgate,' I tell him. 'The crowd took her. Bow Street condemned her for affray and have set a fine.'

'She's lucky it's not thirty years ago,' Hunter replies. 'Or she'd be dead in the morning, or set in the stocks, which is a slower execution with the same result.'

'I know that, sir.' I do know it. I've seen men and women both pelted to death. The sodomites fare worse. Molly houses net a fine catch. A drummer's boy and a guardsman were hanged a month ago. Their fellows were put to the stocks to be pelted by ten thousand fools of a drunken crowd. It lasted the whole day. But many suffer simply for cheating at cards, or stealing a chicken or filching a handkerchief. Or they ship them to the other side of the world if they don't die first in the fetid hulks on the Thames.

'Aye,' Hunter muses. 'Lucky to be in Newgate. How high did they set the fine?'

'Ten thousand guineas.'

'Ten– what!' The old man leaps to his feet. 'Ten *thousand?*'

I spread my hands in the same disbelief.

'Good God!' he splutters. 'A ransom indeed.' He stares at me, agitated, rocking back and forth on his feet. Then he stops suddenly. 'Do you know a man called Shrivington?'

'Lord Shrivington?'

'The same.'

'Only that he came to the theatre to see the boy.'

Hunter nods. 'And you know Mr Hallett, of course.'

'Yes.'

'And are you aware that they know each other, these two?'

'No, sir.'

'And what you may not know – for why should you know – is that Shrivington has been my patient for some years.'

'No, I didn't know, sir.'

'Of course not. But patient he is. A man like so many who will not take my advice, or at least only takes it until some other young lady catches his eye, and cannot keep himself away from his mistresses.'

'I don't know him.'

'But he knows you.'

This surprises me. 'How so?'

Hunter leans forward, elbows on knees, copying my own gesture. 'Joseph, can you pay this fine?'

'Ten thousand guineas! No.'

'Then what will happen to Rebecca?'

'Sometimes such sentences are repealed.'

'On what grounds?'

'That it isn't true. On her innocence.'

'Oh, I see.' He nods. 'And how do you prove that?'

'By her character.'

He nods again. I have a feeling that he's playing with me, as a fisherman plays with a fish flailing on the line.

'Joseph,' he says. 'Forgive me. But though we know her to be virtuous, she lives with a common prostitute. Though we know her to be industrious, her industry is all in the Fields, which is hardly polite society. Though we know her to be kindly, her face says otherwise.' He pauses. 'You needn't look at me like that. She looks as if something's befallen her or that someone has attacked her because she mixes with thieves or drunks or, at best, theatre folk whose reputations are never spotless. It isn't the truth, of course, but it's a conclusion that might be drawn. On top of all this, she looks poor. She looks needy. In short, she looks to be of doubtful character. One who might open a tyger's cage if she were paid to do so. That being so, all her tears before Fielding count for nothing.'

The news that Becca has cried in court absolutely wrenches my heart. 'She would never open the cage,' I whisper.

'You know that and I know that,' he replies. 'But Bow Street does not, and Newgate does not. And besides... someone did.'

'The boy.'

'Precisely. The boy.' His eyes stray upwards, to the room on the upper floor where his own wife and Hemp are sitting with the child. 'And because of the boy, Hallett and Clement want recompense. Especially Mr Hallett.'

'I can pay him for the tyger.'

'Ah, but it's not the tyger. Or shall I say, not only the tyger. Hallett wants recompense for you stealing the child.'

'What!'

He sits back and sighs. 'What a puzzle the boy brings with him. Do you know anything of his history?'

'Other than he was in the 'Change, no.' I feel angry. 'Hallett never cared for the child, he hardly knew that he was there. It was that filthy rogue Shaw who looked after him, if you can call starving the boy to death that. And beating and using him.'

'Ah, but times change,' Hunter says. 'Hallett now says that he adopted the boy, saved him from the Garden.'

'Covent Garden? When?'

Hunter clasps his hands across his stomach and stares at the fire for a moment. 'Some time ago, perhaps two or three years.'

'I don't believe a word of it. Hallett has never said so.'

'Until now.'

'It's a lie.'

'Perhaps half a lie. Perhaps Shaw got him from there.'

'More likely. But...' Exhaustion is gripping me, affecting my reasoning. 'Why would Shrivington come with Hallett, other than knowing you as a patient? Why come to you at all?'

'Because they know of our association. It's been no secret, has it? You're well known for delivering dead animals and I'm well known for dissecting them. And so if someone needs to find you, they may well come to me.'

'They don't know for certain that he is here?'

'They do not.'

Well, there's that at least. And soon he'll be out of here, and safe.

'Joseph,' Hunter continues. His words are slow now. Slow and exact. 'Have you ever been to Shrivington House?'

'Why would I? No.'

'Marvellously large, it is. Huntingdonshire. Three thousand acres of park. Shrivington's ancestors ran Jamaica, you know.'

'Ran it?'

'A rod of iron. There in the beginning, when the Crown gave ex-Naval men land on the island. Shrivington's grandfather was no military man, but got his through bribery. Made a plantation bigger than his neighbours. Bought slaves and traded sugar.' He shakes his head sorrowfully as he looks into the fire. 'Shrivington's grandfather was the devil incarnate. Beheaded a judge that he didn't agree with, if you can credit it. Lawless place entirely. Fathered a whole generation of mulatto children. Shrivington was always a weakling and fled the island after one of the hurricanes almost took down his own house. It's said – a rumour, mind you, but I hear with perhaps more than a grain of truth – that he brought a slave woman with him.'

I sit forward in the chair. 'To his own house?'

'Kept secret from the wife. Not hard. Lady Shrivington is a puff of air. No brain at all.' He laughs a little. 'But, Joseph, there was a child to this woman. A boy.'

'A child? How do you know that?'

'I don't know it. I'm telling you the rumour.'

'Go on.'

'And that woman and child were kept in the house, but escaped.'

'Who told you all this?'

'No one at all. But servants speak to servants. The coachman sits in our kitchen and talks to the cook. The cook talks to the housekeeper. The housekeeper talks to my wife.'

'I see.'

He leans towards me and points a finger. 'Pure rumour, Eliot.'

I smile. 'Of course.'

'And one day Shrivington House is in uproar. Not from the wife. She is visiting her sisters. Shrivington himself comes down to the servants' quarters and rampages about. He won't exactly say why. He claims that an item of value is missing. The maids are all called to account. No one has anything to say.'

'You mean the mother and child?'

'Rumour, Eliot.'

I let out a sigh, and fall back into the chair. 'You're saying that our boy is Shrivington's son.'

Neither of us speak for some time. The fire cracks in the grate and the logs begin to fall to ashes. I hear the bells of St Martin's toll one o'clock, followed by distant echoes of other churches across the city.

'He wants his son,' I murmur. 'But not to have him live.'

'He doesn't say that, of course,' Hunter says. 'He comes here tonight purely to help Mr Hallett secure the child, as a friend.'

'How can Shrivington know a tradesman, let alone be his friend? And a Huguenot at that.'

Hunter shrugs. 'Who can say what relationship two men have?'

'I can guess this one.'

'Shrivington says his wife bought a bird from Hallett. A macaw.'

'And did he see the boy then, and recognise him?'

'I doubt it. He only recognised the child at the theatre, I should think.'

My God. Oh God. The boy was shivering, slick with cold sweat. I took him up there through the mass of crowds, people pawing at him, women exclaiming, through that press of palms and bodies, hauled him off his feet because he was limp, almost dead with fright, and I took him into the theatre box and I showed him to his murderous father. And afterwards we came out of that box and made the same route down and I had to carry him, and when we got outside and were waiting for a carriage, the boy was sick in the gutter. An irritation to me then, and a shame to me now. I put my hands over my face.

'What have I done,' I whisper.

'You were not to know,' Hunter says. 'And remember. This is all supposition.'

'A supposition that makes sense.' I raise my eyes to him. 'What did you tell them tonight?'

'That I had heard of the tyger's escape.'

'And the boy?'

'They told me that the boy had let the tyger out.'

'They knew this?'

'They had heard so.'

'And they wanted the boy back now because...?'

'To protect him.'

I can't help laughing. 'Hallett wants him to show. Shrivington wants him to hide, or worse.'

'Shrivington, of course, may have a fatherly interest in the child.'

'You really think that?'

'No, I don't. I'm simply putting the case as devil's advocate. But I've known Shrivington for fifteen years. He never speaks of his children. He has a daughter and four sons and has never cared for them. Two boys are in the army, one's a curate in the West Country. One is drinking himself to death at the house. The daughter was lately married and he did not give her away. He was too busy. Other rumours come my way too.' His expression darkened. 'That he is murderous. He has dispatched men.'

'Then I'm right. He doesn't want to raise the child at all.'

The truth sits between us, real and solid, a pressing weight.

'Joseph,' Hunter says. 'This ten thousand guineas. You must raise it. You must get Rebecca out of that hellhole.'

He doesn't have to tell me that. Newgate is a sink, a sewer. To think of Becca in there – even for a moment, even for an hour – makes my heart race. 'This is Shrivington's doing,' I realise. 'He's spoken to Fielding. He has some hold over him.'

'Perhaps.'

'It's not Hallett that wants recompense. It's Shrivington. They don't think I have the money. It's to force me to release the child.'

'Perhaps.'

'If I release the boy, Becca will be released.'

'I really can't say,' Hunter tells me. 'They didn't speak of Rebecca at all.'

'They didn't need to.'

Hunter is holding my gaze. His face betrays no emotion.

'Will the boy be safe at Earl's Court?' I ask. 'Truly safe?'

'He will.'

'If Shrivington found out, what would happen to you?'

'Nothing will happen to me. I am the king's surgeon.'

I look at the dying embers and see my own disintegration in them.

'I'll find the money,' I say. 'And keep the boy.' I stand up at last. 'And damnation to them all.'

25

REBECCA

The gaoler's wife is standing over me.

She has my clothes.

It's past midnight. But Newgate is mostly awake. Awake with those who are sick and have no physic. Awake for the children who hardly know why they're here. Awake for those whose time will come when it gets light. I know only too well that people come in this terrible place and they never come out. Or they only come out to be hauled up to the gallows that stand right outside.

I can't pay the garnish. They want money, the payment made by all prisoners when they come here. But I have no money. Only a shilling or two. It's not enough. They don't like me arguing about it, either. I've stopped shouting and screaming. It isn't because I'm not angry but because the fear's got bigger than me. I try to breathe. My blood's knocking hard. They've brought me here from the Strand, delivering me up to Bow Street where Fielding looked at me as if he'd already decided what he was going to do. No use saying that I didn't know about the tyger. No use saying that a man called Shaw was driving a waggon right outside the theatre gates. I stood in the dock and couldn't figure it any more. Shaw looking aghast, seeing the tyger, dropping the reins and running off like the rat that he is.

'Two shilling's not enough,' the woman tells me.

'Give me my clothes.'

'Going deaf? Two shilling's not enough.'

'I don't have it.'

'That's a pity,' she says. She has a clay pipe between her teeth and the smoke curls over her head and stays there, a miasma. 'Witch like you should magic some up.'

'I'm no witch.'

She leans down and stares for a long time at my face. 'You surely look like one,' she decides. She's eyeing my scars with interest. Just like you'd look at a mangy dog. Half pity, half disgust. And then, with a down-turned mouth, a face of disdain, she lifts up one hand of mine and turns it over, back and forth. And then she looks down at me, how the rest of me is unmarked, and she smiles.

If you can't pay the garnish to the gaoler, they take your belongings. They take every stitch on you, and they give you a gaol dress to wear, and you're freezing, even in summer, because the place is built over the dead. You can feel it. St Sepulchre is just across the road. Full of burials, and another burying ground behind Newgate, and down the road a little way is Fleet prison, built over the Fleet, a rotting ditch.

And if you can't pay, then you get nothing. You don't get fed, and you don't get a cell, and you're shackled and treated like a wild animal. Treated worse than any show beast. The prison draws you inside. Whatever you have will be stolen unless you can pay. Even the prison dress. I see it. I see women naked, men naked. Things I've never laid eyes on before. The flagstone floor is littered with complaining, whining bodies.

I hold the threadbare dress against me tight. 'I'll wait,' I tell her.

'Oh? Wait for who?'

'My friend will come and get me.'

'You've got a friend with ten thousand guineas?' She laughs and walks away, taking my clothes with her.

I keep thinking of Fielding. Fielding once bought a pair of Norwegian ponies from us, strong little beasts they were, very pretty to look at. He bought them for his children. I thought he would remember, but if he did, he said nothing. He looked more down at the desk than he did at me, and his eyes kept flickering toward the door of the court where crowds were pressing. They started pounding on the great barred door out to Old Bailey Street. And the justice's eyes flickered from me to the noise, and back again to me, and he wiped the plate he was eating from with a piece of bread.

A mob is a marvellous persuasive article. It grows and multiplies and barrels along, and nobody cares any more what the trouble is about. A mob has a mind of its own, and it's not sane. I've seen a mob go into a brothel – one that was supposed to have cheated its customers – and tear every piece of furniture out of the place, and throw the girls into the street, and pull the clothes off them, and roll them in tar, and all because some cheat wants his money back because a frightened little girl of nine didn't pleasure him enough. I've seen a London mob pull a shop to pieces that sold bad meat. I've seen a mob of forty thousand watching a hanging. A singular thing is a mob.

All I can think of is, where is the boy?

This morning I'd come to the theatre yard to find Joe, and see the child if I could. I got my chance when the gates opened because the fools that Clement employs thought that Shaw and his waggon were the feed men. Shaw was done up well, I'll give him that. Looked like a grain merchant's man, dusty and with a cloth wrapped round his face and sacks of what looked like grain but evidently wasn't – they rolled off the waggon light as feathers, probably stuffed with straw – and in that second, I knew what he had come for. Not Joe nor Clement, nor beast. He'd come for the boy. Even though Hallett had argued with me over the tyger. I knew it by the look on Shaw's face. He was going to get his whipping boy back. That slathered look in his eye. He took the cloth off his mouth when he saw me, and he grinned.

I'd have stood between that man and the devil himself before he got the child. I'd have fastened my hands round his dirty neck first. But then I saw the grin slide off his face as he stared at the yard behind me. And I looked back too. And there was the tyger and there was my boy.

I close my eyes. Try to think I'm outside in the summer night. Imagine the house in Long Acre and the stars in the sky. Wonder what's happening at the Fields and the theatre. When I open them again, I see a boy a little older than our child, and he's come very close.

'I've got nothing to steal,' I tell him.

He sits down on the floor in front of me. 'You was with the tyger.'

'Yes, I was.'

'I heard it.'

I sit up a little. 'When?'

'Today. I was in Cecil Court and heard the noise.'

I know it well. Strange little place is Cecil Court, very old. Barbers and bookshops. Women washing the steps of the buildings looming overhead. Narrow alley that's kept clean. A bootmaker. A coffee seller brewing by a hole in the wall. A man coloured like coffee selling it. Chocolate too, and a barred gate with a padlock to stop thieves coming in and getting it. Coffee and chocolate lingers like a walk through river gardens, lingers just as sweet.

'What was you doing there?' I ask him.

'Dipping.'

Picking pockets.

'And somebody caught you.'

He shrugs. 'Got me pocket full. Handkerchiefs and two five-pound notes.'

'And they brought you here?'

'I knocked a man down and he broke his head.'

'Did he? Proper broke?'

'Proper broke. They carried him off and they took me to Bow Street and then come here. They was putting me under the Keeper's House but then they brung me here.'

I look at him closely. 'How old are you?'

'Don't know.'

I think about fourteen. Maybe less. Living on the streets makes old men of young boys. But fourteen or twelve, it doesn't matter. He'll still get the force of the law.

'What did they tell you?' I ask him.

He wipes his nose on the sleeve of his shirt so that I can't hear what he says next. But I think it was 'to swing'. To hang. That's why they were taking him to the Keeper's House, but they changed their minds. Perhaps for his age. A grain of compassion.

'Condemned men aren't kept here,' I say. He brightens a bit.

'I can't pay nothing for food nor drink,' he says. 'They took the money.'

'Maybe they'll transport you. You'll be all right,' I say, trying to make the lie seem cheerful.

'I wish I see'd that tyger,' he whispers.

We sit in silence for a long time. The dark is more than dark in here. It's blackness, like being buried. Black as Thames silt by the old bridges. There's only a faint light from a window high up on the wall at the end of the room, and the fear makes it blacker still, a fear so thick it settles on us all like another skin.

Eventually the boy shuffles close and I put my arm around him. He asks me if the tyger really killed a man and I tell him that it did, and that no one knows where the beast is now.

'Maybe it got in the river and swimmed away.'

'Maybe.'

'All the way to Africa it could swim.'

Somewhere in the middle of the night there's a clanging of the gates, and the boy jumps up, wide-eyed. The gaoler with a lantern comes down the block and looks in at us all sitting on the floor of the public cell. A man behind him steps forward.

'Rebecca Talland,' he says. 'Come here.'

26

JOSEPH

It's dawn when we leave Newgate.

Becca doesn't speak. We walk the empty streets side by side.

I hardly know where we're going until we find ourselves on Ludgate Hill. We look out to the river and the whole city lies still, too early for the smoke that always settles as the day goes on. There used to be a gate here, one of the gates of the city that was only lately demolished.

'Do you recall the gate?' I ask her.

'Not much.'

'They took it down soon after we got here.'

'I remember a lot of pushing and shoving,' she says. 'It was narrow all along here.'

We look at where it used to be, and the church that was alongside it and now stands alone. As we watch, the first light touches the steeple. In the quiet you can feel how old it is, how the roots go down past the old Saxon kings and crawl through the Roman armies and their altars that they say were under St Paul's and go straight down into earth that once never saw a human being and bears it all now – the churches and the streets and the people – on its back, or on its belly, patient and uncomplaining.

I wonder how many thousands are buried here. How many sons and daughters, mothers and fathers. I feel it coming up through the soles of my feet where we have stopped. I wish I could go forward and see what becomes of it. I wish I could go back and see what it was. I wish I could go out in the river and farther out in the waters of the world and I wish I was also rid of it. The city and the things I've never grasped. I wish the quiet could go on forever.

'We came here with Molly,' Becca is saying. 'We walked her up here and we grazed her, and the priest ran out, red in the face and furious, and he was gulping when he was speaking, he was trying to get his words out but he was scared to death.'

She's right. The memory makes me smile. 'We were like Moses parting the Red Sea,' I say. 'We stayed there and took money and the same man read to us from the Bible about making trade in the temple of the Lord.'

'We walked her to Tottenham.'

'Aye, we did.'

Becca looks up at me. 'It was after Sophia first gave you money, and we went all over finding beasts. We were deranged, Joe.'

'Deranged, yes. Nothing touched us. Nothing could.'

She walks away, turning left to avoid Fleet Street in all its iniquity, and we wander by ourselves past shuttered houses, those overhanging and those with gardens, until we stop at the top of Cheapside and look down on the market where all the stalls are clattering open. Thousands of candles light this place at night and now in the daylight you can see all the stubs ground into the street and feel the wax under your shoes.

We've come to Bow Churchyard and we glance at each other. I take her hand and she doesn't object and she doesn't pull away or hide her face. She looks at me directly and her mouth is pulled in a straight line, the kind of look that she has when she's trying not to laugh or cry. We sit down among the graves.

'Where did you get ten thousand guineas, Joe?' she asks.

'It doesn't matter, Becca.'

'Yes, it matters.'

'I sold Pompey.'

Old Pompey, poor lad. Clement insisted. I thought that I might wake him when I called at the theatre after seeing Hunter, but he was not asleep. He was awake and sullen. Furious. Wanting Pompey was the first thing he said. Wanted the lion left where he was in the theatre yard so that he could make money from showing him at the gate. People wanted to see where the tyger had been. They had all come back after the tyger disappeared in the Thames, and he had had trouble fending them off. The show was cancelled: no tyger, no child.

'I have to have the boy,' he had told me. 'Or there's no show.'

I lied to him. I said I didn't know where he was.

Clement's face had darkened. He was still in the theatre and he was drinking. He went to his office and he brought out a paper and drew up a contract, there in the theatre stalls lit by two-foot lights. He wanted a lot. More than Pompey. He wanted all the animals in the Fields. He wanted the lease of the Fields. And then at four o'clock, Hallett appeared. He had been looking for me at The Yellow House and Long Acre and he was white in the face. 'Give me the boy,' was all he said.

'He hasn't got him,' Clement said.

I looked from one to the other, two men that were strangers. Or so I had thought.

'Give me the boy and I'll see to it that your woman is released,' Hallett said.

So there it was, exactly as Hunter had supposed only three hours before.

I couldn't persuade Clement. I tried to tell him the show was something we'd gone into together, that we had joint losses. I could sue him for opening the gates, and he retorted by saying it was my boy who had opened the cage and my woman who had been arrested for helping him. He stood up and looked as if he would hit me.

'And I might sue you both for taking the child and making money out of him,' Hallett said.

At this, Clement sat back down in his seat with a thump. He seemed frightened. I gazed at Hallett. The man I'd known – that lazy, disaffected man in his silk breeches and silk coats and claimed to despise the 'Change but never sold it – was being driven by something other than his losses. Because, I saw at last, they were not his losses at all. They belonged to Shrivington and this was all a game to retrieve the child. Clement was merely sweeping up behind, seeing that I could be ruined and escaping with what he could while he could.

'Clement...' I began.

'I've had to close the theatre,' he muttered. 'I want recompense.'

Hallett smirked. 'And I the boy,' he repeated. No doubt the delivery of the child would let him off some hook or other by which Shrivington had him suspended. Something rooted in the stews of the Garden.

'I'll get you the boy,' I told him. 'I'll bring him to you at midday. But you must order the release of Rebecca Talland first.'

'You forget there's a fine to pay.'

'I'll pay it with the boy.'

'The boy and five thousand.'

I agreed.

I tell Becca all of this, and I see her hands grip tightly in her lap.

'Is everything gone?' she asks.

'All the animals and birds. The lease of the Fields... and Long Acre.'

'Oh.' Just that small helpless sound. Then, still looking away from me, 'You shouldn't have done that, Joe. Not to retrieve me. Not given everything.'

We hear the church doors open. They're preparing for the day. A woman comes out to sweep the steps, and glances over at us. She stands with her hands on her hips for a while, and then goes back inside. In the trees, a blackbird is singing. I can tell you this because every image will always be locked in my head.

'Becca,' I say. 'Please marry me.'

She turns her head. 'What?'

'Hunter has the boy,' I tell her. 'I saw him at midnight and I left a letter with him for Henry. I've asked him to buy back The Yellow House and everything in it. Or rent it for me and send us the money. Clement has my bond for the Fields and the animals.'

'You don't want to marry me,' she says. Colour has flushed her face and neck. 'You've got me out. I thank you. That's enough.'

This woman's bloody intransigence. 'For Christ's sake, Becca. No more of this. You've held me off enough.'

'Held you off?' she echoes. 'I have held *you* off?'

'What else would you call it? Going your own way, refusing me, living with Sophia...'

She holds up her hand. 'Wait,' she says. 'When did I refuse you?'

'When we first got Molly.'

She starts to laugh. 'You asked me once. Once, Joseph!'

'I don't take kindly to refusals. No man would.'

'Don't bring other men into it,' she tells me. 'But since you do, a man would pursue a woman he really wanted.'

'You've never said one word of affection.'

'No more have you!' She stands up, and then promptly sits down again. 'What do you think love is if it's not standing by you through all your bloody schemes?' she demands. 'What do you think it is if not watching you run after Sophia and still be there keeping your accounts and showing your great lumpin' bird at fucking dinners and cleaning your mess and every other animal's mess while you lie abed with her? What do you think it is keeping your house at Long Acre and making your food? I washed your clothes, God help me. Watched you walk out in them like a bloody prince, a cock of the walk you are, thinking yourself so fine. And that bed! I turned and beat that bed. I kept it free of bloody fleas!'

And at that she can't help laughing, and the sound of it makes me laugh with her. And I wonder where I would be now without her, she who has kept my life in order and been so faithful.

'I don't think myself fine, Becca.'

'Oh, you do,' she says quietly. 'By God you do! And you think all your ideas so fine when half of them are swill.'

'Swill! When?'

'That poor creature you took off the ship!'

'Well...'

'All to make a few extra shillings. That was cruel, Joe.'

'Plenty were cruel to her before me.'

'That's no excuse,' she says. 'You've got no heart.'

'You know that's not true, Becca. I've cried for beasts. Aye, and people.'

'You've no feeling for the boy.'

'I won't tolerate you saying so.'

'You put him on that stage. You've terrified him. And–' She

holds up her hand again to stop me speaking. 'Don't tell me how much he's benefitted from it.'

I nod my head. 'I know that.'

'He's different,' she says. 'Don't you know how different? How – here's your word, Joe – remarkable. The first really and truly remarkable creature that ever passed through our hands, and God knows we've caged many, may Christ forgive us. But you'll not put him in a cage like you've had me caged. You won't. Wherever you've spirited him away now–'

'Hunter has him at Earl's Court. I told you. He is quite safe.'

'I'll take him off you,' she warns me. 'He needs to be quiet... he needs to...'

'Go away and live out of the city.'

'Yes.'

'With us.'

She stops talking. She looks at me with such plaintive longing, and with anger. The two cross and re-cross her face and she finally sighs. 'I've been a fool for you all my life, Joe. Because you saved my life.'

'I won't have you marry me out of gratitude,' I tell her.

'I haven't said I *will* marry you,' she points out.

I pick up her hand and kiss it. I lean forward and kiss her mouth, and she doesn't resist. 'If there is any good in me, it's what you've made,' I say. 'Please marry me.'

We sit in silence, hands clasped. We listen for a while to this city that heaves and grinds and barrels its way through each day. There are voices now along the street.

'It's dangerous to be here,' I tell her. 'I promised Hallett the boy, and he's not going to get him. We haven't much time.'

'But where can we go?'

'There's an Edinburgh coach leaves at midday. It takes young elopers over the border and straight to Boyd's White

Horse Inn on Canongate. It has a room there for conducting marriage ceremonies.'

'Oh, is that so? You're very well informed.'

'It'll take us a week, but they'll never look for us there. And I've kept back a thousand out of the theatre receipts. I haven't put it in the bank.'

She gives the ghost of a smile. 'You never did bank money unless I stood over you.'

'With that we can marry and live quietly. In the Scottish Borders, perhaps. Or Westmorland. A pleasant little house just as you described it to me, Becca.'

She considers me in her old way. That straight, disarming look. 'The boy, Joe,' she says. 'The boy.'

'Hunter will send him to us.'

'At what expense?'

'Ah, that. I'll show you. An old friend is paying for us.' I stand up and hold out my hand. 'But you've given me no answer.'

'I'll make you wait for as long as you took to ask it.'

'Will you indeed, Mrs Eliot,' I reply. 'But we don't have the luxury of years.' I look up at the church clock. 'We have just to midday until Hallett and Shrivington come after us.'

## 27



It's no trouble to me to look like something used to the streets –
and after Newgate, I'm worse – but Joseph finds it hard to
choose a suit of plain cloth. But a disguise of some sort is needed
if we're to cross the city. On Cheapside he buys a leather bag
and boots, and a cloak for me that has a large hood. We go to the
back of the Dissenting Chapel in Old Jewry so that Joseph
might get out of his good clothes and into a working man's:
rough wool coat, breeches, and old leather boots that are cracked
at the heel. When he's finished, we look at each other. If I keep
the hood close to my face we might be anybody.

'Well,' he says. 'I shall miss my fine coat.'

'You'll miss the old life.'

He takes a step to me and holds me at arm's length. As I
start to pull up the hood of the cloak he stops me. He runs his
hand over my face, and he unwinds the scarf from my head. He
takes a strand of my hair and smooths it between his fingers. But
he says nothing at all.

We risk the Devil's Tavern on Fleet Street. A dive, but I
must wash Newgate off me. I can't sit in a carriage for hours and

smell as I do. We breakfast here and sitting beside him I'm suddenly swamped, like mortal drowning, just by looking at his hand on the table in front of us, his cutting of the mutton on the plate for me, his turning of the port glass towards me, and I rest my head on my hand and look at him.

'What is it?' he asks.

'I'm thinking of the birds in Prentiss's warehouse. You took me there.'

'He's long dead. He was dying then.' He stops eating and looks at me. 'What made you think of that?'

'You made me a cage for the songbird.'

'Marriage won't make you caged, Becca. I promise you.'

I say nothing else. Let him think me free now, and worry for the rest of his life that I'll leave him. That'll be a pleasant justice.

By a roundabout route we reach Hunter's. I only realise where we're going as we come off St Martin's Lane. When we pass by the church with its pretty steeple, I think for a second – only a second – that I'll be married in a room above an alehouse and that there'll be no fancy frock nor probably flowers, and I won't walk down an aisle like St Martin's. Will it matter? Will I care as I hear him say his vows while foot traffic and carriages and waggons and dogs yapping outside nearly drown out his voice? No, not at all.

Hunter's is another matter, though. 'We can't stop here,' I tell him.

'This is better than walking the streets or waiting by the coach. And there's something you have to see. A farewell that we both have to make.'

We go in by the back door, avoiding the square and its motley crowds. The patients come to this house from 9.30, and today Hunter is tending to some poor suffering soul who's sobbing quietly behind his door. I walk down the hallway with Clift and glance in at the lecture room door and there are perhaps forty young men there, waiting. On the table in front of them is something covered with a sheet, and from the room comes a godawful smell of cloves and formaldehyde. We walk on.

Clift stoops to a door that leads below stairs. 'We've stored her here.'

'Who is it?' I ask Joe, and he takes me by the arm.

There is a ramp. Both walls and ramp are slippery. As soon as my eyes are used to the shadows, I see a low waggon. On it lies Molly, quite dead.

'She came to us this morning,' says Clift. 'Your man Hemp brought her from the 'Change.'

'Hallet wanted her out,' Joe murmurs.

Clift is standing over her. 'Mr Hunter has yet to see her,' he says. 'She is like a prehistoric creation.' He's full of admiration.

I walk to her side and reach out my hand.

'There is some sort of fungus in the folds of her skin,' he warns me.

It doesn't matter. I put my head against her flank and close my eyes. 'Molly,' I whisper. 'Molly.' She don't smell like she used to. She smells of nothing at all. I stroke her softly, and even the skin feels different. Like it's been painted with something. It's supple and soft. I stand back, because the softness gives me a fright I can't explain.

'Do you know why she died?' Joe asks.

'A general decline,' Clift says. 'Age and smoke. Her lungs are probably full of soot. It's the curse of the age. We used to have wood fires and now every house uses coal and smoke hangs over the city by midday. You might have noticed the particles on your own skin. Mothers always say that teething has killed their child,' he went on, 'but it isn't the teeth, you see? D'you see? It's the fires.'

I stand up. 'What will happen to her?'

'Mr Hunter will add her to the collection upstairs.'

So she's going to Earl's Court to be boiled down to bones and remade.

Joe takes my hand. 'We must go.'

'Did Hunter pay you?' I ask.

'He paid Hallet. And then yes... a little for us.'

'Part of this arrangement? You agreed?'

'Did you want her left in the 'Change and have folk pay to watch her rot and then thrown in the river?'

I look back at her. 'No,' I tell him. 'I don't want that.'


We step out of the door into sunlight.

It takes a little while to adjust. To see what Joe sees, and why he has gripped my hand so tight.

At the bottom of the steps stands Hallett. He has a piece of paper in his hands. Alongside him is a man I've never seen before, but before long it's evident he's come from Lincoln's Inn. Slimy characters lawyers are, and this one looks slimier than most. Skinny hands gripping his coat like he owns the place. And behind them are militia: men in a uniform I don't recognise.

'Joseph Eliot,' the lawyer says. And he turns to another man behind him. I know this devil. It's one of Fielding's bailiffs. One of those who took me from the court only two days ago.

'Is this the man?' the bailiff asks Hallett.

'It's him.'

A little crowd starts to gather. Joe tells me to stay where I am, and he walks down to Hallett. 'What is it?' he asks.

The lawyer speaks up. 'You're accused of kidnapping and killing a child.'

'Killing?' Joe says. 'I've done no such thing.'

'Kidnapped from Exeter Exchange and taken to some place and disposed of.'

Joe turns to Hallett. 'I told you midday and it's not yet eleven.'

'Bring the child out, then.'

'He's not here.'

'Then take us to wherever you've put him.'

I feel sick. If Joe says where the boy is, Shrivington will get his hands on him. If he denies knowing, he'll be arrested. Kidnapping a child carries the death sentence, and no one is allowed to speak to defend themselves in the trial. Only the bastard prosecution can tell whatever lies they want.

Joe looks at all of them: the lawyer, Hallett, the bailiff, the men in their curious green colours who are carrying muskets. I see his shoulders slump.

'I don't know where he is,' he says.

'So much for an agreement,' Hallett mutters.

'You have my bond for payment.'

'The child,' the lawyer repeats. Faced with Joe's silence, he adds, 'Gone the way of the beast, I suppose.'

I run down the steps, but not before the bailiff has caught Joe by the arm.

'No, no!'

Hallett grabs my wrist. 'Not another word or you'll join him. You were a part of this.'

'She had nothing to do with it,' Joe says.

The lawyer smiles. 'An admission, then?'

It all happens so fast. They surrounded him. From out of the crowd behind us steps Hemp, looking as if he hasn't slept in a week, filthy, a bloody red mark on his face. I try to catch hold of Joe but the bailiff pushes me back. Joe is pulled into the militia, makes no effort to run, turns back to look at me once, and shakes his head. *Don't come after me.* I hold on to Hemp and we walk at a distance, swallowed up in the crowd until Hemp stops at the corner of the street.

'It's not safe for you, missus.'

'I want to see where they take him.'

'People will know you from the other day.' He towers over me. 'Be calling you a witch again. He'll go to court either today or tomorrow.'

I strain to see, but Joe has disappeared, with the remainder of the crowd trotting after him. 'Oh God,' I say. 'They'll kill him.'

'Maybe not.'

'Of course they bloody will,' I tell him. 'Shrivington is tied up in this. You don't understand. He'll have his way. Men like him always do. He knows Fielding and the justices.' I'm breathing so hard I choke on my own words. 'Joe won't give up the boy, and if Shrivington can't get the boy... he's like a piece of meat to him, a thing he owned and wants back and he'll do God knows with him, finish him like...'

I can't think of it. I can't. That child who's got so much love in him. Unless Shrivington wants to bring him up as his own. But that can't happen. Can't admit a bastard child, yet more a son. He already has sons. And can't admit the woman for fear of the truth coming out. Men take women, from royals down, and a woman's got no worth. Bastard children starve on the streets every day in London. Their mothers the same. Starve, or go on Sophia's game. Poor wretched things are women and I've kept away from men for fear of being one of them hawking their sad souls in town. And the wives and husbands go past and maybe he might see women he's had and maybe he don't even look.

I hold on to Hemp, thinking that Joe and I are nothing. We

weren't ever, even when we took little beasts and birds to their own homes. Not to the likes of them. Titles and lords and ladies. Them that sit in judgement but who are rotten from the inside. Them that own half the country and hang poachers. They don't see people. We're all just dross. Shrivington wouldn't know Joe now unless Hallett told him, pointed him out. Told him this was the man who had what belonged to him. And had the gall to make money out of his thing, his commodity, his belonging. Not allowed to do that. Not when you're a poor man or a working man. Not when you're in trade and do yourself up nice and try to be a gentleman.

Perhaps that was Joe's worst crime of all. Wanting. Wanting like he'd done all his life. Wanting to be more and better. Trying to climb that ladder. There's only one thing happens when you've got your hand on that ladder rung. Some rogue sitting at the top steps on your fingers.

I look closely at Hemp's face. 'What happened to you? Where have you been?'

'The Fields,' he says. 'Got woke up at three o'clock. Men come with torches, dogs, shouting their heads off, broke through the gate. Him was with them.'

'Who, Hallett?'

'Him and another. He's what you're talking about? Some title or other? Hallet said it was all his now. He said that Mr Joseph sold it him. And he wanted the boy.'

'They hit you?'

'Got men with them, lot of men. They searched everywhere. Even the hog yard. Even the shit heap.'

'This other... who was it?'

'I don't know, but he spoke gentleman-like. He was wrapped up, I couldn't hardly see his face.' He paused. 'Who is Shrivington?'

'One day I'll tell you.'

'You best go back to Mr Hunter's, ma'am.'

I know he's right but I don't want to. I can't move my feet. He manhandles me back to the steps, then up them, and I see Clift waiting in the doorway. He's holding out his hands to me.

'I'll go see what happens,' Hemp tells me.

'Come back and tell me.'

'I will.'

# 28

JOSEPH

Before dawn, a soft rain begins to fall.

They take me out of the door of the prison. Marcasite shows suddenly, a faint grey glitter, in the pennant slabs of the paving stones under my feet. Above me, a linnet in a cage hangs on a line between two houses. I watch it, momentarily black against a yellowing sky, as if thunder is coming.

It's not far to the court and there by the wall, wetted by the rain, lies a tuppence sheet song. We had songs written for us all the time for the panoramas and the paradises of the stage. I wonder if Clement has kept the tree ferns and will show Pompey and the birds, and I wonder what Becca is doing and I hope that she won't come to the court because one loss on top of another is too much. And they all rattle through my head, all the beasts, all the theatres, all the women, and the surprising silence that surrounded the boy and the way he took the queen's hand. I'm tangled up inside.

Inside, I listen to the court building coming awake. Down the hall from me sit poor wretches waiting for whatever the judge sees fit. Transportation for drinking a master's wine. Or breaking a fence or stealing milk. Death for counterfeiting.

Once they burned them for copying the king's coin. Now they just let them swing. There's women in the line: I can hear one weeping. A man asks the bailiff for a pot to be relieved. He does his business while chained to another man, and the pot passes down the line.

At seven o'clock, the stewards come in. I can smell lavender soaked in salt, briny smoke, a fumigant for the judge's chambers. There's beer warming too, somewhere, and bread. My stomach rolls but I'm not hungry. I guess no one in this damp corridor can eat today. The dew coats the flagstones with a greasy sheen and I can see my own breath. Somewhere under this building the River Fleet runs down to the Thames. At seven thirty there is a rattle and a murmur of conversation in the courtroom, sounding curiously like rolled pebbles in soft sand. At eight, the pebbles rise to a monstrous clatter. The crowds have been given entry.

They take me in.

I'm introduced to my counsel, a man recommended by Henry, which was a kindness by him, but one I wouldn't have chosen, judging by the counsel's youth. He seems cowed by Hallett's man – renowned in name and reputation. My heart sinks.

I'm placed in a panelled box alongside the jury, and the judge is on my left, muffled in his gown against the cold. He eyes me for some time, takes snuff, and wipes his face. I look up and see a sparrow flying near the roof, caught in the fog of old sweat and cold. I watch it, wondering if it will be successful. There are windows up there, but the rods to the skylight are pulled tight. While the court noise drowns the beating of its wings, it batters its body against the glass.

I think of the four thousand songbirds that Becca remembered yesterday, and of the kindness in her face. I saw the girl in her looking out at me, the girl who wanted to see the travelling circus lions under the red tents of the village field as much as I did. The girl who talked about elephants and asked where they came from, and I told her all kinds of fancy lies because I didn't know any more than she did. I recall her in the workhouse yard threading hemp with the other women on a summer's day long ago, her legs kicking at air because she was too small to put them on the ground. What was she then, five, six? Such a gulf between now and then. Time swallows us all and changes us, and the shutting of cage doors and the opening of them is chance. Only chance. Unless you hold the keys as I have done. Perhaps today is the price for holding those keys. I never thought of it as wrong.

The clerk has been speaking but I haven't heard him.

'The deposition,' the judge orders.

The clerk stands. 'The deposition placed before this court by the prosecution states the child was kidnapped for the purpose of exposing it to freakish exhibition to extort money from the general public, taken without permission from the place of its habitation at Exeter Exchange where it had been cared for for five years with the utmost consideration for its welfare, having been rescued from a state of starvation and destitution from the streets and from near death was nursed back to life and given gainful employment at Mr Benjamin Hallett's establishment. From this establishment the child was stolen by the showman Joseph Eliot of The Yellow House, Abercrombie Square, in the city of London, and put on show, exposing a medical condition which nature and humility decrees should be kept private, entirely without the permission or knowledge of Mr Hallett...'

'That's not true!' I cry. 'I paid Hallett. We had a business arrangement...'

The crowd hisses. Too late, I realise that a business arrangement is not what they want to hear when discussing a child. I look at the jurors – men like myself, men of a certain age and occupation, and I understand they are not disposed to trust this person who is set before them. I am a showman, and they recognise exactly what I recognise in myself, that I'm a spinner of stories and not many of them true. One, sitting closest, looks like a farmer brought in from Middlesex; such a man who might own the orchards south of the river. He looks as if he's never smiled.

In the body of the court, on the public benches, I see the gallants about town, who are a very different case altogether. They've come here for sport, and on their arms are one of two things: another gay blade like themselves, looking to patch the time between the gaming table and the whorehouse, or they have a lady on their arm, brought here for her entertainment. But even these lean forward now, waiting to hear what I have to say.

It's not hard to see why they don't trust me. They know what theatres and freak shows are. I've made scenes that are fiction, and claims that are fiction, all my life. That the lion is only young; that the tyger will not bite; that Molly was a hundred years old when I knew nothing of what her age might be. I have painted pictures and almost come to believe them myself: that the Hertfordshire hog truly was ten feet in girth, or that the monkeys were really little men. I claimed that anyone from Africa was a savage, because it was commonly said, and I profited by it, prodding the crowds to part with their money to see an elaborate lie. A scene, a theatre panorama, a story, a false witness. I have claimed that day was night and that night was day. I have produced paradises that were nothing more than paper and ink and candles, and angels whose wings were feathers and glue and whalebone.

'Be quiet,' the judge says, and slams his fist on the desk in front of him. 'Defendants may not speak.'

Nor do they hear the deposition before the trial. I clench my fists.

The clerk resumes.

'Moreover, Joseph Eliot took a dangerous beast from within the confines of the Exchange and presented it on stage to the terror of the child and at no time informed Mr Hallett of what his intentions were regarding the child. Nor did he inform him where the tyger was, when in fact it was housed at the theatre where the show took place and where the child was kept...'

'It's a lie!' a woman shouts.

I look to the upper gallery and see Becca leaning over the rail. Pointless, really, to suppose that she would have ever kept away.

'That boy was kept in filth and misery at the 'Change,' she cries. 'Beaten by the men given to look after him. He had no bed to sleep on, no food worth eating, he was skin and bone...'

'Remove that woman,' the judge says. We hear footsteps on the stairs; the gallery doors are opened. Becca is still shouting but then so are those around her. I see her hauled by both arms out of the gallery, and I can still hear her screaming as she's thrown into the street. There's a muffled wave of sound from the crowd outside who couldn't get into the court. I hope to God they've not set on her.

Hallett's counsel resumes.

'Moreover, it was against the wishes of Mr Hallett that the tyger should leave the Exchange and it was taken overnight, the reason being that the beast was a man-eater and very violent and Mr Hallett had been waiting upon the opportunity for the animal to be destroyed for the sake of the public–'

'I paid him! He knew right well where it was going. He took a fee!'

The clerk raises his voice. '...and that Mr Hallett was not paid either for the child or the beast and that all Mr Eliot's actions were conducted in secrecy to his own advantage, robbing Mr Hallett of a valuable property as well as the child, which he had severed from the familial bonds–'

'What familial bonds?' I shout. 'Who is his father?'

Bedlam drowns me out. The crowd like this turn of events. This is more like a scandal.

'...from the familial bonds of a fatherly figure and the good company of the Exchange–'

It's too much. 'Tell me the true father,' I shout.

The judge bellows across the raised voices. 'Silence, silence!'

The jurors look from me to the judge, and they pick out Hallett, who has suddenly stood and just as suddenly dropped back into his seat, and one or two lean forward to get a better look at the man making the accusation. A man who looks perfectly like a gentleman compared to my own rough clothes. I stare at him, and by God he smiles back at me. 'You are a liar,' I say. 'Who is paying you to do this? What does he have over you? I have done nothing to hurt that child! Nothing!'

And yet... and yet. I hear Becca's voice asking me if I would ever sell him. I hear her telling me that he knew us, knew our past. I hear her pleading for his comfort. And I see his face and feel his trembling, I feel him straighten in my grasp as I try to show him my books, and I see a kind of knowledge in his face, an understanding that places him above me. I knew all this when I put him on the stage. I knew it and ignored it.

I've ignored things before. Things I should have not allowed. In our first year of trading we had a little dancer. A woman not four feet tall. She was called Mari and had come from Ireland, and she was beautiful in the way that expensive dolls are beautiful. She had a father who made her dance, and showed her, and we came to an agreement, and Mari danced all that year at the Fields. When winter came she complained of tiredness, and I remember the way she looked between her father and myself. He was not a kind man. All he wanted was the money she made for him. He sold her to a captain in the army who married her. She died trying to give birth to a full-size child. Hunter has her in his anatomy class, I'm told. Mother and child in a grotesque tableaux. But it wasn't the husband nor the father nor Hunter who put her there. I put her there when I told her father that she could make him rich.

Hallett's barrister gets to his feet. 'Your Honour, the father is unknown,' he says. 'Mr Hallett has been the only father that the child has known and hence the reference to familial bonds. His wife too, a good upstanding lady, has treated the child like a son, and a brother to her own children.'

This is such a lie that it makes me gasp. Hallett's wife has never been near the Exchange. She wouldn't dirty her feet.

'Continue with the deposition,' the judge says.

'Moreover, all the while that the child was displayed at the Galleon Theatre,' the clerk continues, 'Mr Eliot made a considerable fortune from the exhibition, which was not lavished on the child at all but rather enabled him to buy a valuable property that he now claims as his residence.'

The crowd murmurs. A kind of low groan.

'No longer,' I mutter.

The judge points at me. 'Anything further and I'll have you removed much like your vociferous friend,' he tells me. 'I shan't say it again, sir. You may not speak. Your counsel may make a statement at the end of this proceeding.'

The room begins to swim around me, tilting gently. I haven't even heard these accusations against me until now. But that's the damned law. I grip the rail in front of me, fighting nausea.

I am guilty.

I am guilty of Mari and of taking the boy and of so much else. I never told Hallett what I was going to do and I never gave

Hallett any money from the show. I look at him now and he crosses his arms, and I wonder if the very same thought is going through his mind, and that this is the justification for his accusation as well as Shrivington's persuasion.

I am guilty.

They're calling a character witness. For a second I can't think who it is: an old man in a mildewed black coat with a chequered stock around his neck. He won't look at me. The prosecution asks him if he knows me.

'Aye, I do.'

'Through what circumstances?'

'He come to get a calf off me. One that was born a monster.'

A rippled runs through the court, a buzz of recognition.

'In what way, sir?'

'Born with two heads.' I see that he's clasped his hands so tight that the knuckles are white. 'He come to my place to buy it six month ago.'

'And did he?'

'He took it away right enough.'

The counsel turns to the judge. 'I believe London will know this animal, shown to great profit by Mr Eliot.' He turns back to the witness. 'And how much did he pay you?'

'He didn't pay me at all,' the man says. 'He took it and never give me nothing at all.'

'You mean he stole it from you?'

'Yes, sir.' But his reply can hardly be heard. Half the crowd look at me with triumphant delight.

'I paid you twenty guineas,' I say.

As this is the truth, I'm not surprised that he can't look at me.

But the judge does. He points a finger. *Keep quiet.*

Hallett is called to the stand. He makes a good impression standing there in his cutaway fancy coat, resting his left hand on a silver-topped cane. He answers his questions in a slightly accented voice, not French enough to raise suspicion, but careful enough to reveal his gentleman-like status.

He tells the court how the boy was found cowering under tables that had been set outside an inn, picking dropped food off the ground. He tells us how he carried him himself to the Exchange and laid him on a truckle bed in which he slept ever afterwards, and that he was fed and given light work to do around the animals, and that he was allowed out for walks and to play with Hallett's own children in the summer.

No one contradicts him, of course. I don't see Shaw here, and with good reason. Even cleaned up and dressed, Shaw would still look like a dog. No. Hallett's refined appearance speaks volumes. There are some sympathetic smiles in the court.

'Did you know where the child had gone, once he was missing?' the counsel asks.

'I was told that he was at the Galleon.'

'And who had taken him there?'

'Joseph Eliot.'

'For what purpose?'

'Profit.'

'Did you try to retrieve the child?'

'I asked Eliot to bring him back.'

'And did he?'

'No, sir. Gates were erected at the theatre, and the doors locked. And at times of performance the child was kept close, shown on the stage, and then spirited away.'

'Kept imprisoned, you mean?'

'Yes, kept imprisoned.'

'And the show consisted of what?'

'He was put on stage next to a man-eating tiger which I had planned to exterminate and which was also stolen from me.

Such was the danger that the boy was in. He was made to scream. Or he screamed of his own accord, and then was shown...' Hallet stops. He takes a handkerchief from his pocket and wipes his nose as if distressed. 'His condition was shown.'

I can't take any more. He's probably only ten feet from me, on the other side of the panelled gangway to the door. Out of the corner of my eye, I see the two bailiffs are lounging to one side of the judge, murmuring to each other. I stand up on the railing and jump down, and I grab Hallett by his fancy fucking waistcoat – birds on it, and flowers, bloody birds if you please, this fop who dabbles in dirt and is under some other man's control, a worse man than him who knows all about imprisoning this very same child with his stink of slaves and sugar – and I take hold of him to choke the air out of his body. But I can't. I drop my hands because they feel suddenly dirty. The bailiffs come.

'I am sorry,' I say. 'Sorry for the insult to this court. But you are a liar.'

I'm hauled back. The roar settles. Silence slowly descends while the judge does nothing. He has folded his arms. I can still hear the sparrow's fluttering wings. It's left the window and is somewhere along the crowd.

'And do you know where the child is now?' Hallett is asked.

He smooths down his coat as if he's wiping my touch off himself. He looks directly at the judge. 'I fear he must be dead.'

A groaning sigh goes up from the crowd.

'And what brings you to that conclusion?'

'He ran out with the tyger when it was let loose,' Hallett says. 'A travesty, a crime. The cage door opened and the child exposed to the viciousness of a beast well known to be a man-eater.' He pauses again to wipe his eyes. 'It was said that he ran through the city with the tyger chasing him and was seen at the edge of the river.'

'Perhaps you could explain to the court what happened to the beast,' his counsel prompts.

'That I cannot do,' he says. 'Some say that it went into the water. Accounts are that Mr Eliot was there at the time. He may have been instrumental in the animal falling into the river. In all honesty' – and here he directs a look at me, as if he alone is the possessor of the truth – 'in all honesty, I do not know. I can only guess. I am helpless to explain it. But I'm reliably informed that this animal, my possession, escaped the Galleon Theatre and that Mr Eliot, or a woman who is reputed to be his partner, and who now seems to have escaped Newgate' – there's a thrill of horror at this news – 'are to blame.'

'Oh my God,' I mutter. 'You lying blackguard.'

The crowd turn to me. I see a renewed prurient interest. Here and there an expression of contempt. The young gentlemen in their finery merely smile.

'And so you cannot say where the child is at all?' his counsel asks.

Hallett spreads his hands in a gesture of despair. 'He has not been seen since. How can he be alive?' he asks theatrically.

'I've spoken to you about him,' I shout. I can't help it. 'You've taken money for him. I've given you my business and my home in payment!'

The judge thumps his fist on the desk in front of him. 'One more word, Mr Eliot, one more word and you'll be taken from this court.'

Hallett shakes his head in sorrow. 'I have nothing,' he murmurs. 'No tyger, no child, no payment.' He pauses. 'Not that I should ever sell a child. You see what this man considers moral.'

I cling on to the rail in front of me, but I no longer hear what's being said. I feel I've fallen somehow. Fallen out of the decent world. Fallen into a pit of my own making. Minutes pass.

Words pass in a garbled thread. I sit down with my head in my hands, wondering only how Becca will fare alone. Henry must go to Coutts, take out the money and give it to her. Perhaps Hunter will let her take the boy somewhere. Somewhere far away. Even another country, to live quiet and unremarked and decent.

The prosecution is making a case – I don't know how long he has been talking. I study him now. The lawyer has a childlike smirk, and he thunders about child kidnapping, a recent case reported in a broadsheet that he now flourishes like a flag. The paper crackles in his hands. 'Is London to become another Dublin?' he is asking. 'Where the abduction of children is continued with impunity? Are we to become a nation of child procurers for the ships' captains, to enslave in the plantations, or for showmen to exhibit on a stage? Is the life of our children in London of little value? Are we, as we have from Ireland's *Morning Post*' – he flourishes the gazette again – 'to tolerate a child taken by strolling players such as Mr Eliot employs, only for the babe to be found in a ditch with its throat cut?'

A mounting roar of protest. Everyone has heard of this terrible case. He looks at me with flushed triumph, this squawking high-pitched purveyor of absurdities. And it seems now, having stoked his audience to boiling point, that he is done, and the outraged murmurs subside as quickly as they rose.

'Mr Eliot,' says the judge. 'You have entered a plea of innocence. Have you a statement to make to us?'

My counsel stands, but I wave him away.

'I don't deny taking the child. I took him to save him from the Exchange,' I tell him. Someone in the crowd makes an exclamation, and a woman says *shame on you, shame on you* very quietly. 'But Hallett was not at all fatherly. That is not true. The boy was not cared for at all. On the contrary, he was ill and abused. I have cared for him and clothed him and fed him.'

I'm about to say that he's alive. But of course, I can't say that. If I told them he was alive then his location might be found out, and if his location is found then Hunter himself might be brought before the court. Worse still, Shrivington would know. The boy would be returned to Hallett and I've no doubt he would then be sent to Shrivington. To say that I know where the child is would be to assign him a life of misery, if indeed he would be allowed to live at all.

In this moment, I see it is my life or his.

My counsel sits down heavily, and he makes a gesture that indicates he has given up on me. 'And, if the court still considers it important,' I say, 'I paid the man for that calf.'

One of the men in the jury exhales sharply, and then laughs.

I agree with him. An absurd thing to say.

But I can't think of anything else.

The room shrinks and expands in my sight. My whole body feels cold; my face drained of any blood. I must faint; the need laps at me.

The judge raises his hand for silence. 'Jury,' he says. 'Consider.'

They huddle together.

I've sat on a jury myself. There's never a need to leave the court. I've not heard any case capital; no death sentence rested on it. A woman who whipped her servant; two boys accused of stealing small change; a little girl who had supposedly stolen a book. We found the cattle thief guilty and he got seven years transportation. The woman was put to the stocks. The boys and the girl had no evidence to speak of against them, as the shopkeepers said that one child looked much like another in their layers of filth.

I wait, I wait. A direct stream of light pours down on the judge's bench: it is midday. I stare back at the twelve men who decide my fate. I wonder if my audacity is being revisited on me now.

And if there is such a thing as recompense in this life for one's sins.

They have reached a verdict. The foreman stands.

'What say you of the charge of kidnapping of a child?' the judge asks.

The man with the pinched face glares back at me.

'Guilty,' he says.

# 29

## REBECCA

I wait outside by the wall that runs along to Newgate. I sit on the pavement and cover my face, and just after noon Hemp comes out to find me.

'You're soaked through,' he says.

'Is there a verdict?'

'Guilty.' We look at each other. He takes my hand and we walk.

'Come to the place that I've got with Frances.'

I go, not thinking. Feeling nothing. Leicester Square is swarming. The sun is out now, but there are dark clouds gathering again in the north, and there is a pressure in the air, the kind that makes you feel as if your skull is shrinking. We pass Hunter's house and I see the door is shut and the blinds are down. 'Come, missus,' Hemp says quietly, pulling me along.

Their garret is in one of the old houses that people say are going to be pulled down, the ones that lean into the street as if they're trying to take off and run. We climb stairs. The whole place is dark, but when we reach Hemp's two floors, a woman meets us and takes us in. She is a nice sort, very wide, very cheerful. She takes off my cloak. The cloak that Joe bought me

"

to run away in. To board a coach and go to Edinburgh to be married. Only two days ago.

'Now then, let's be warm,' Frances says. She hands me hot tea that must have cost her a fortune. I try to drink it but can't. And to my shame, I start to cry.

'I've known people sprung from Newgate,' Hemp says. 'We might ask if it could be done.' He knows the prison well, of course. He's been in there, child-getting. But that was years ago.

I look up at him. 'Were you in the court?'

'No. Just by the door.'

'Did you hear what they said?'

He tells me.

'Have you seen the boy?' I ask.

'Last night, at Earl's Court. He's well. He wants to see you. He asked by name.'

'What did Mr Hunter say?'

'I didn't see him.'

All my life, all Joe's life, rests on that surgeon. It's too much to ask.

'I must do something,' I say. 'I must think of something.'

Hemp stands there, the great lump that he is, a poor man who has hung on our coattails for so long and now sees his own future blackened and wasted. He seems to read my mind. 'I won't go nowhere,' he tells me. 'I won't run. I'll do what you want.'

'Frances,' I say, turning to her, 'I want you two to go away. To go out of London and not be named as anything to do with us. Joseph is to hang and I'm no better for you.' Hemp has opened his mouth to speak, but I stop him. 'If I get the boy away, if Joseph...' The thought momentarily chokes me. 'But you mustn't be tarred by our brush. Tell the other men too. If I can get hold of money, I'll send it to you for all you've done.'

'I can't do that, missus. I been with you too long.'

'You must do that.' I nod toward Frances. 'You've got a lady of your own now. Think of her.'

We sit together a minute or two and look at the faint little flicker of fire that they have, with poor Hemp wearing a face like a doleful dog. And then I think of an idea. I take my wet cloak off the chair in front of the fire and start to put it on.

'Nay, missus,' Hemp says. 'Don't go out again.'

'I have to,' I tell him. 'I want Clift to write a letter for me.'

'A letter? Who to?'

'To someone who might be able to help,' I say.

'The judge?'

I smile at him. I take both their hands, and Frances clings to me a little. 'You'll catch your death if you go out again in the storm.'

'My life won't be worth living anyway if I don't,' I tell her.


If you mix with men who used to bring liquor to Tottenham Fields and who still supply others, and you know where men waste away their time on a weekday afternoon, secrets are soon secrets no longer.

And that is how I knew where they were.

The message was sent to the London address that I had for a man called Copeland. Ten years ago, when Hemp and I used to take little beasts and birds to the dinner parties of the good and the great, and the bawds and their lovers, and anyone else besides who would pay us, Lord Copeland was one of the better men. His wife, who used to love the coloured birds, the exotics, so much and had her own names for them as if they were her own pets, died after their fourth child was born and I still see him out and about sometimes, a gently smiling shadow of his old self. He had been there with the king and that bastard Shrivington the only time that I'd ever been to Kew.

I asked if he might come to the church on Queen Square, and though I don't know about God – I don't believe since the day I heard children crying in the fire, and every day since when I see them miserably lying on London streets at night (what God would allow that?), and since there are places like the Penitent Women Chapel run by a priest no less – for once, I did pray. I prayed that Copeland would come.

As I walk away from Hemp's, the sky grows darker. The pressure that shrinks your skull gets worse. It's the sort of strange quiet that used to make the beasts pace in their cages. A wind begins to blow, a salt wind off the distant marshes. It comes barrelling down the street so hard that I have to push against it.

I watch as carters take horses out of their reins and lead them to the side of the street because they're pulling at their shafts, and even then they pull their heads this way and that. A carriage passes me with the team frightened and pulling at the reins, and the woman inside looks out at me with her hands to her neck.

And of a sudden there is a strange stillness and there comes a thunderclap that I feel in my chest. They said afterwards that the thunderbolt went through Oxford Street, dancing from side to side until it buried itself in the ground by the corner of Soho Square, and it tore a great beech tree in two from crown to roots.

The sky turns black. The rain pours down. I thought of what a workhouse woman had said of a storm eighty-some years ago that tore windmills off their foundations and wrecked half the navy on Goodwin Sands. She said she'd seen something come across the fields like a great man walking, tearing up the ground as it went, and the priest ran out and prayed in the churchyard because the bell tower came crashing down. And that two thousand chimneys collapsed in London, and one man and his wife in bed went straight through three floors into the street and there was nothing left of the house but them and the bed. At least, Joseph told me that story. She told it to him.

At the thought of Joe, I start to run. I'm soaked to the skin for the second time that day, but this so much worse with my clothes clinging to me, wet wool and wet shawl and my hair plastered to my head and water coming in my boots.

The streets turn into rivers. At the corner of Oxford Street, close to where Joseph had his first menagerie, I sidestep floating lids and soup bowls and the cart that had served them, the brake dislodged and the great green-painted wheels turning fruitlessly in the current. And here comes a horse tethered to a waggon that has been swept right about, its hooves tangled in its reins. And there is a woman sitting, drunk, up to her waist in water, and two men trying to haul her to her feet, and all the slush and ferment of the city rolling past them and crashing up against them in a filthy shallow wave; and others huddle together sheltering under trees that soon are no shelter at all, leaking torrents from the sodden branches, weeping leaves onto them. And everything stops for a while and we're all just blurred by water, like the world has started crying and cannot stop.

I get up to Southampton Row somehow and out to Queen Square. I stand by the tavern and stare at where Conduit Fields once was, where you used to be able to see all the way to Hampstead. They've started building great townhouses there now, out where the cattle would be driven out evening and morning. Out where we once had a kind of ramshackle stable. I think we had it for six months until Joseph decided he didn't need the teams of horses anymore, because we weren't going anywhere much.

We were going to stay in London and make a lot of money instead. No more travelling the highways and byways. I remember I tried damned hard to look happy about it. But I always worried I'd lose him somewhere in this city. That he'd get too big, and come to know a lot of important people. That he'd mix with lords of the land like Sophia did with Melbourne.

And now it's me talking to lords and ladies.

I go into the church at the corner of the Square and it's peaceful in here, built up a way from any rivers and on dry ground. I look up into the roof space. Plain it is, like the rest of it. And down here in the main area of the church there are box pews, and each one with a name on it. I never sat in a box pew in my life, or in any pew. I don't go to church. I reckon that if there's a saviour he'll do what he has to do, save me or throw me away. I might find myself in the darkness with the soul of Molly. And that would suit me fine.

I see a man standing right at the front. He smiles and beckons me.

'Can you hear the rain?' he asks, glancing upwards as I've just done.

'Yes, sir.' Who could not?

'Will London be washed away, do you think?'

I don't answer this, and Copeland considers me, smiling. He's done up very smart: satin breeches and a blue tailcoat, and shoes on his feet with a diamond buckle each. He carries a cane with what looks like snakeskin coiled all around it. 'Rebecca, isn't it?' he asks.

'Thank you for coming, sir. And in this weather.'

'Well. We are only across the street.' He lowers his chin and winks at me. 'As you might know.'

'Yes, sir.'

He holds out his hand. A duke to a working woman. It ought to shock me, but it doesn't. Since court this morning, nothing can. I don't know if it ever will again. If I'm meant to curtsey, I don't. But I shake his hand. It's as soft as a down pillow. Softer. Though he is a duke, he don't say so. I suppose that he don't need to. You can see it all over him. He's one of the courtiers.

'You know too that the queen is nearby.'

'Yes, I thought so.'

'And the doctor who is tending the king.'

'I hear so. Yes, sir.'

He gives a crooked smile. 'Ah, I see that we are not as circumspect as we believed.' He points to one of the pews. 'Sit with me, please.'

Now, to my certain knowledge, the only time a duke sits with a commoner is if he has taken a fancy to one of his maids, or if he is visiting one of the houses around the Garden. But indeed, he does sit quiet, looking at the floor where many are buried. We both of us look at a gravestone, laid flat there among the paving stones, and I decipher the name *James* and the words *his wife*. 'Ah, mortality,' Copeland murmurs. He sits sideways on, then looks up at the altar and talks to me about the madness of the king as if he's addressing the cross on the altar table.

'His Majesty suffers greatly,' he says. 'He is being treated by Doctor Gillies in a house in the Square.' He glances back at the church door. 'As you know, not a hundred yards from here. He is not likely to stir from there unless he goes to Cheltenham for the waters.' The duke gives a great sigh. 'The queen is very troubled. Their Majesties don't care usually to leave their home at Kew.'

'No, I know.'

Again, he smiles at me as if I was a lady. 'The queen has remembered Mr Eliot,' he says. 'And you.'

'I'm very grateful for it.'

'You showed a cassowar, I believe. And various others.'

'Yes, sir. But the bird was a danger. We had to stop.'

'Some years ago now.'

'Yes, sir. She laid an egg.'

'She what?' And he laughs. 'That enormous savage thing?'

'We don't even know where it come from,' I tell him. 'At least – we know where it come from. It come from her.' I can feel myself blushing, and that's not usual for me. 'It just... come out. One morning.'

'Good Lord above. What did you do with it?'

'The men of the University in Oxford come and took it.'

'What, the bird?'

'No, sir. The egg. It wouldn't hatch.'

His laughing closes to a smile. Then, 'So you graduated to other things. Lions and elephants and the rhinoceros.'

'The behemoth has died this week.'

'Ah.' He nods. 'She caused a fire at Drury Lane.'

'It wasn't her fault.'

He smiles. 'Who's to say, I wonder?' I can't tell if he believes my half-lie or not. But he lets it go. 'I hear the child has a way with beasts. He let out the tyger that was lost in the Thames. And caused much distress in the meanwhile.'

'He did,' I tell him. 'I can't account for it, sir. He's a sweet-natured boy and I think the cages... I think if the beasts are upset, so is he.'

'You were there.'

'By accident, sir. I was at the gate when it was opened and I saw the child by the cage and I was as frighted as anyone. I couldn't move. But the boy...'

'The boy and the tyger walked away.'

'Right past me. Walked gently, sir. Never hurt anyone.'

'Extraordinary, extraordinary,' Copeland murmurs. 'That is something I should have liked to see.'

'Sir, the letter...'

'Yes, yes. I am coming to that.'

'What I said in it, sir. I took the child. I picked him out of the dirt in the Exchange and I carried him out. He was nothing but bone, sir. The head keeper used him very ill. Beat him and worse. They said the child was dumb but he spoke with us. We looked after him. Mr Eliot has cared for him...'

There is a silence. We can still hear the rain coursing down the church roof above us.

'Mistress Talland,' Copeland says. 'Do you know who the father to the child is?'

'I don't know.' After all, it's the truth. I don't know for certain. But looking in his face, I think he does.

'And does Mr Eliot know?'

'He's said nothing to me.'

Another silence. I can't tell what his mood is or what he thinks. I suppose that's how you get to be a courtier.

'Mr Eliot brought the boy to the queen, on her request.'

'Yes, sir.'

'Why did you not come with them?'

I don't want to say that Joe wanted to make money out of him. 'I had a fever,' I say.

'Ah, fevers, of course,' Copeland replies. 'You were much missed. It's not advised to disappoint the queen.'

'I'm very sorry for it.' People have been hanged for less. Beheaded, even. A picture of my head on a spike on London Bridge flashes into my mind, even though they don't do that now except for traitors.

Copeland is looking closely at me. 'So it was you who took the child, not Mr Eliot?'

'Yes, sir.'

'That might have made quite a different court case this morning.'

'Yes, it might. I tried to shout down, but they took me out.'

'But Eliot has protected you, has he, at the cost of his own life?'

I cross my arms across my wet dress. 'Yes, sir.'

He leans forward. 'His life for yours,' he repeats, as if I haven't heard him.

I look up at the cross on the altar and I think of what priests always say, that Christ gave his life for all of us, and as soon as I think it, I know this is blasphemy, and in a church too, and I must be damned for certain now, if I'm not damned already.

'He must love you a great deal,' Copeland tells me. 'As the boy does.'

I look back at him. 'You've seen the child?'

'I have.'

If there was any blood left in my body, it drains out of me now.

We are found out.

'Mr Hunter is the king's surgeon,' Copeland says, very quietly. 'And has seen His Majesty this morning.'

I don't know what to think. Knowing where the boy is, and not telling the court, that's an offence. It must be. Sheltering the boy himself, too. But Hunter's done it. He's said. He's told the king. He's spoke up for us.

'I beg you, sir–'

Copeland waves his hand. 'Nothing further.'

'If the king–'

He stands up and frowns. 'Nothing further, I said.'

I follow him down the aisle, seeing how my own wet footprints have marked the floor. I'm cold. Very cold.

Just as the duke and I get to the door, there's another almighty clap of thunder. We can feel the foundations of the church shake. I wonder if that pretty blue outfit of Copeland's will get ruined in the few paces it'll take to cross to His Majesty's dwelling house. And then I wonder if he'll care. He probably has another five or six just like it, and five or six servants too, waiting to receive him.

He puts a hand on my arm. 'You'll not go out in this storm?' he asks. 'Wait a while.'

'Thank you, sir,' I tell him. 'But the rain won't hurt me.'

And as I run out across the Square, for all that I'm a blasphemer, and for all that I've not been inside a church for so long, and for all that I've never asked God for nothing... for all that, I pray.


I get to the Fleet in another half hour.

It's still pouring, and the weather's taken its toll on the river. It's roaring under Fleet Bridge in a foaming torrent, and rolling about in it are all kinds of rubbish. The bodies of dead dogs that are always thrown in there, and all kinds else: weeds and rocks and boxes and rags, great clods of clay and torn-up bushes, and all the waste from Fleet Market – rotted food, straw, and all the usual filth floating in a dark scum on the surface. People are standing on the bridge looking at it, and up at the wood houses teetering on the edge of the river further up, towards the market, houses two centuries old with overhanging roofs that have always looked as if they're falling to pieces tile by tile. I can see lights burning on a top floor, and a woman hanging out of the window shouting down at a man going along Fleet Ditch path. I look over my shoulder at the drop to the Thames, where the Fleet comes out by Black Fryer's Stairs.

Suddenly there's a grinding sound, a groaning. I look back towards the houses and the edge of the path has vanished, and the houses – both of them – are toppling sideways, slow as you like, like gently falling leaves. Hard to believe what I'm looking at, and so horrible. The light in the top floor goes out – oil-wick lamp thrown from the windowsill, no doubt – and I see the woman throw up her arms and start screaming. And in the next instant the whole lot has gone, hitting the river with a whining, grating splash. The wood tears itself apart with a screeching sound like pigs a-slaughter, and for a second I think I see the woman come out of the water, and almost at once she's lost. The rain gets in my eyes, and the people next to me grab at me, 'Look, look there!', and we see in the river, in the rolling and the dirty churning foam, the hearth fire from one of the kitchens sitting on top of the water held up by something beneath it, turning about and about in the flood, alight in the gloom.

It goes under our feet, under the bridge, and the crowd rushes across the road to see where it comes out. But there on the other side there's nothing, no fire any more, only the debris, the splintered blackened wood, the roof tiles now spattered about and clashing up one against the other, and in the mess is everything that the houses were: chairs and tables, and pots and pans, and clothes, and a wispy piece of frayed curtain, and – I have to look twice – a cat. A cat, scrabbling wildly for its life, trying to climb up on the tabletop. And then, in a groaning crash, they're all gone: cat, furniture, clothes. The woman is nowhere to be seen. I look back up the Fleet Ditch path, and there on what's left of it, holding on to the next house that now looks in as much danger, is the man that the woman was calling to, tearing at his hair.

We all stand on the bridge, until someone says, 'The bridge will go.' And even though it's stone, it's the same age or thereabouts as those houses, and so we all move away, running left and right. When I come to my senses, I'm halfway up Ludgate.

I look around me, and there's no one about. They're all hiding in the shops, in the houses, in the doorways, staring out at me and at the rain. It's still falling like a thick curtain. I can feel it running down my neck, pouring over my face, over my arms. And I think I'll be struck by lightning. And I know I've got to move. I know I've got to put one foot in front of the other.

I close my eyes. I can't help what I'm thinking. I've done all I can. Where am I running to? There's nowhere to go. Joseph is surely lost, and without him I've got nothing. He paid for my freedom with everything we owned. Our world has crumbled and fallen down in the torrent.

I start to pant like a dog, and I think, I'm struck all right.

I'm struck with fear.

## 30

BOY TYGER

Rain drips from the eaves of Earl's Court house.

I've got a place to sit above the lawns.

I don't listen to the leopards. He keeps them in a den under the grassy mound. Instead, I like to watch the horses and the cattle and the mountain goats and buffaloes who all eat the grass together. Most days, children hang on the iron gates and walk up and down the road outside and try to climb the walls. Their mothers come and shoo them away.

The best thing is the bees.

He showed me them the first day.

I came here in a cart covered over with something that smelled of dead things. I thought I was going to hell because of the tyger. I kept thinking of its look with the river behind it. One last look. It knew where it was going, out into the ever after. Wanted to go. Needed to.

Like my mother's face as she kneeled next to me in dark woods beyond the house, the night we ran away, miles between us. 'We had to go,' she whispered. 'You understand, don't you? There was no good there. You remember?'

I looked up at the trees weaving against the wind above us,

singing their own secrets. She took hold of me tighter and pressed her lips to my hair. 'You'll find your voice again one day,' she promised. 'It'll come back now we're free.'

All sorts of dark were trying to find us.

I wish she was here now. I wish the woman, Rebecca, was here now.

The doctor came back to the house yesterday all hung down with worry. He looked at me and then he took my hand. I gave it, but I don't like his hands. They do good but they touch things that cling. They're not clean. Not clean.

He called for tea, and we sat in his study where it is all strewn about with paper and has piles of books and there are drawings. He explained each one, and he took down a big leather-bound book like Joe used to do to show me maps. He put the book on the table between us and there was land painted yellow and a great blue space.

'This is the Atlantic Ocean,' the doctor said quietly. 'And there' – he pointed at small pieces of land in the blue – 'that is the West Indies, where sugar comes from, and tobacco.'

'Sugar,' I said. I remember being in a carriage in the hot sunshine and the man standing up and telling my mother how much he owned, all the land of those tropic islands, those green and swaying islands all circled by a blue sea – and him saying he had title over all the people on it and I remember the yard and the garden with trees and hibiscus and fruit, and how sometimes it wasn't good to go in the garden, and I told the doctor this suddenly, and he looked at me.

'Not good to go in the garden?' he asked.

'Slaves brought there to be taught a lesson,' I whispered.

That's when my mother would sing most. Take me indoors and upstairs and shut the window of our little room and she would sing, but there were still screams below, outside.

'Do whatever he tells you,' she would murmur. She would rock back and forth with me in her arms.

The doctor frowned, but said nothing.

I told him it all then. About the man called Shrivington and my mother, and ship we sailed in, and the waves and storms, and being taken in a closed carriage with the little curtains drawn and the place being dark when we got there, a big stone house, a rattling cobblestone yard, and men and women who looked away from us as if they pretended not to see, and all we had in two bags dumped on the floor high up in the house, and it being cold with white ice on the windows, white ice like I'd never seen.

I saw nothing in the doctor's face. Perhaps he'd heard the story before, or perhaps he'd guessed it. All he did was close the book of maps with a sigh.

So I told him what I'd seen and heard. Blood on the floor, the chapel, crying, the silence after, and Shrivington looking at me with the sword still in his hands. And of my mother and me running in the dark for miles and miles and coming to London and being afraid of the noise and eating nothing and my mother's face hollowed out, hungry and cold and afraid.

The doctor listened for a long time. He nodded once or twice.

'I thought so,' he said. 'Yes.'

That was all.

And then we walked outside.

He showed me the glass houses, the hives.

'Have you ever listened to bees?' he asked. 'You see how industrious they are? A man might spend a worthwhile life studying them.'

I liked their company. I put my ear to the glass.

'They have different sounds,' he told me. 'When a bee is coming home loaded with a farina of honey, it has a soft and contented noise. When it's about to sting it's quite different.' He smiled at me. 'That is something worth knowing. One day someone will decide what it means. The bee with honey is making a sound like the lower notes of a pianoforte. A Lower A of the treble.'

He sats down and watched me and the hives. 'A life of study and contentment,' he said softly, 'would suit you very well.' He was tapping his fingers on the arm of the chair. 'But where to place you? Not a school. Public schools are nests of vice.' Tap, tap, tapping. 'A quiet home in the country, with resourceful parents.'

I turned and looked at him.

'Come here and sit with me,' he said. 'There is no need to be anxious. There is more than one kind of parent.'

I heard the bees go past me, singing their treble A.

# 31

## REBECCA

It's the day of the hanging.

Clift and Hunter stand opposite me. For two days I've been lying in the corner of Hemp and Frances's room, cold and hot, cold and hot. Frances wailed when she saw I'd been out in the storm. She took off my clothes and spread them on a line over the fire. They sent out for more coal. I don't have a farthing to give them.

I dreamed of Newgate. Newgate and the fire at Drury Lane and the small weeping eye of Molly. When I touched her in my sleep, she burst into flames. I dreamed of days in the city when we were younger and the business was doing well, and of joining in the dances on the Fields together and of all the blossom trees coming out in May by the Serpentine. I dreamed of touching Joseph's hair and of touching the paws of Pompey through the cage and how alike in texture they were. And how sometimes we'd go down to Hyde Park with the capuchins and let the people in the carriages pet them, and how we trained those cunning little creatures to take a money purse, or a handkerchief or a rose from a lady's hat and then hand it all back again with a little bow. I dreamed of the taste of chestnuts at Christmas and again of heat and so much fire and of it rolling over me and there being no way out at all. I dreamed I was standing at the window of the workhouse looking out at the chestnut tree but there was no Joseph there, no one to catch me. I dreamed that the fire, that white wall, rolled over me and the last thing I saw was the far lights of the tents in the field, and the last thing I heard was a little girl panting for breath at my side. I woke up in the dead of night crying.

A day, and night again. Frances brought a bowl of broth and put the spoon to my lips. They found a blanket somewhere. They sat up and watched me. In the early hours of this morning, I stopped dreaming of fire and looked out on to a clear and starry sky. I heard Hemp give a great sigh.

I don't know that I'm better. I don't know if I'll ever be better. I feel as if I may be dying little and by little and by little, but I had to come here today.

The first thing I asked was, how is the boy? and Hunter told me some strange oddity about the music of the world. I tried to look as if it mattered to me.

'Mr Clift here is going to come with us,' he says. 'Sit down a moment.'

I do as I'm told.

Hunter looks down at the piece of printed doggerel that he's taken from his desk. 'You see this?' he says. 'It's some years old.' I don't understand what he wants of me. I don't know what the paper means. A hot rush comes into my head and I shake until it passes. Hunter goes on as if he hasn't noticed.

The parchment is curled slightly at the edges, and creased from being stuffed into the drawer along with much else. Hunter lies it flat on the desk top, and smooths it flat with his hand. He reads the last lines to me.

*...whose power can raise the lifeless clay,*
*Drag the pale spectre into day,*
*And starve the hungry tomb!*

He sits behind his desk and smiles. 'Do you know who wrote that, Rebecca?'

'No.'

'A hack who liked me.' He starts to laugh to himself. 'Even those who admire me call me a grave robber.' He sits back in his chair, and links his hands over his stomach. 'The body can't be studied without looking at it, and how must a man look at a body without keeping it from its grave?'

I don't reply.

It's the day of the hanging.

The hanging. Hanging.

That's all I can think of.

Pale sunlight, the first of the day, creeps into the room.

'I was once asked to save the life of a man who had been hanged,' Hunter continues thoughtfully. 'A well-respected man, a priest. He hadn't done much, although he'd lived in a worldly way. He wasn't fit to be a man of religion, but then many aren't, and they don't die for it.'

'That's true enough,' I say.

'He'd forged a bond. A capital offence, like so many.' He sighs. 'The same penalty as murder. Money. As valuable, apparently, as another's life. It was the time of the Surinam eels – Joseph had an interest once, did he not? – every man in London had an interest; and it was thought that, once the reverend had been taken down from the scaffold, he might be revived if brought to me quickly enough. It was worth the experiment, at least.'

The great surgeon smiles at the memory. 'It was an irresistible challenge. Where does life reside, and when does it leave us? Might it be brought back to us? Is a man – or a woman, indeed – only a collection of nerves and vessels and fibres that might be rejuvenated? And if the soul has already been called to an afterlife – if such a thing exists – might it remain there? And, if so, can a human being live without a soul?'

I don't know any of the answers.

'You don't believe in souls,' he says. 'And I don't know that I do. My reverend did, but much good did it do him, all his prayers with the noose around his neck. Don't whisper that outside this room. My wife prefers to regard me as god-fearing.' He winks at me, in a good humour apparently despite the day. 'But I believe that every part of the blood has a life force. It is a wonderful subject. One day mankind will know, I suppose.'

'And you wanted me here because of... that priest?'

'Precisely. I've prepared everything just as I did for him. I will try to revive Joseph Eliot. I have a room near Newgate, in Fentamore Street.'

'Newgate?'

'A good fire has already been lit there,' he tells me.

I try to understand what he's talking about. I shiver despite the warm room. Clift comes up to me, takes up my wrist and measures my pulse. He raises an eyebrow and lets my hand drop.

'We have a pair of double bellows to stir the lungs,' Hunter is saying. 'I kept a dog breathing some years ago with such a contraption. We shall lie the body out and apply heat and oils. There is a Leyden jar such as that Mr Franklin recommends, and we might, I hope, successfully apply electricity to the heart if all else fails.' He stands up, and comes suddenly around his desk and takes my hand in his. 'Do you understand now?'

'You're going to try and bring Joseph back to life.'

'I have never seen you cry,' he murmurs.

I wipe my face. 'There's good reason for it today.'

'Are you afraid, Rebecca?'

'Yes, I'm afraid.'

'We are going to do great things today,' he says. 'We will starve the hungry tomb.'

He pats my arm. He looks as if he might hug me, but doesn't dare to. I feel as if I'm just like the Leyden jar, full up of tears and with a strange current, a recurring shock of sorts, running through me. Perhaps he feels it. Perhaps not. He's kind, anyway; has always been kind to me. But I know it isn't kindness alone that's made him try to set up an experiment to revive the dead from the scaffold. Not kindness. Science.

'We'll walk there together, shall we?' he asks. 'To Fentamore Street?'

I look at the clock. 'I'm not going to Fentamore Street, Mr Hunter. I'm going to see the execution.'

He looks mortally shocked. 'Ah, is that entirely wise?'

'I must see it. I owe that much.'

There is a silence. The pool of sun grows brighter. Eight o'clock.

Two hours to go.

'Then I'll ask Clift here to accompany you. You'll need someone alongside you, especially if you're recognised as being anything to do with the poor man.'

He holds my elbow to steady me as I stand.


It's a long walk: through Covent Garden, along Wych Street and Butcher Row, to Fleet Street and Fleet Market. Like all other days, the market's heaving. I pull the hood of the cloak over my face – nobody knows the gallows better than these. Clift, alongside me, thankfully says nothing at all.

They sell the food for the scaffold crowds here. Oysters on wet, ice dripping barrows, eased in two with a knife, sold with a pinch from the barrow boy and a slap on the rump and a feel unless you step away quick enough. Oranges and lemons from Spain, two halves held open and under your nose. Citrus peel under the feet, pith and skin, as I pass today. That smell is lovely.

I used to get oysters here and take them to Joseph with a half dozen lemons; and for a sweet aftertaste I'd make a mash of fruit and peel at the range and douse it all in rum. No such today; stalls go past – the gingerbread and furmity; the meat; the sack of grain. The pig heads staring at me at the last makes me want to keen in pity and grief. The eyes are all open. Sick, I wonder what's quickest: to cut the throat or strangle by a hangman's cord. Sun glitters on the road and the water, blood and sawdust scattered there. 'God help me,' I say to myself, picking my way over it all.

The noise gets much louder. We're at Newgate. Or rather, Clift and I are stuck at the entrance to Little Arbour Court, where Old Bailey Street and Hart Row meet. The crowds are packed solid. It's barely ten o'clock in the morning, but a choking heat steams off the crowd, and hangs, coloured by sunlight, between the people and the thin film of smoke that is level with the roofs. We push our way, getting cursed and trodden on. Someone's child sits on the road, bawling. No one takes any notice, and Clift lifts the scrap up and calls for its mother. Nobody answers. He puts the child on a windowsill and it drums its feet on the back of the man in front of it.

I force my hands between bodies and prise a path for Clift and I. Someone elbows me in the face and calls me a bitch. Further in, the road slithers with horse muck under us.

I close my eyes for a second. The noise in the crowd is rising. For a while, I'm lifted off my feet by the press of bodies around me; they surge forward in a wave. I don't know where Clift has gone, and when I open my eyes again, I'm much closer to the scaffold. It's as high as the first-floor window of the prison, built up so that they bring the condemned out through a window and straight on to the boards under the noose. The whole thing is hung with black curtains and I think, *It's a stage.*

While I stare, someone comes out, their hands tied behind their back. My stomach lurches, but it's not Joseph. It's a woman. The two men behind me, whose gin-drunk breath I can feel crawling on my face when I turn my head, discuss her.

'Tis the bitch who drowned her bastard child,' one says. 'Put him in the privy and then lied to her mistress about it.'

They agree between them that the poor screaming, shrinking sacrifice above us was bound for hell. She starts to pray so loudly that I can even hear her above the shrieks of the crowd. It goes silent, though, when she's pushed into eternity.

'Good riddance,' says the man at my shoulder.

I wait. I wait between worlds. That's what it is. Not in this one. Somewhere else: a bright, reeking, echoing space. I wait and watch as they bring out two other men. They're to die for stealing silver spoons and a gentleman's six handkerchiefs and bruising the man who owned them, and the futility of it makes me turned in the head. I start to laugh. I can't help myself. Silver spoons, from a house where they might not be missed for years. Silver spoons. A crack, a groan, a drumming of feet. Where is Joseph?

I don't know how many minutes pass. I grow faint; Clift holds me up. 'Come away,' he tells me.

'Not until I know.'

There's a ladder to one side of the scaffold. Awkward as it is, they lower the bodies down there and pile them on a cart. Some of them slither down when the men lose hold. I stop seeing the corpses as men and women, and I start to look at them as if they were puppets. They're bound for the dissecting rooms and the hospitals. Perhaps Hunter will put his hands on them later on. Perhaps tomorrow. A man comes out into the sunlight above me; I shade my eyes.

Joseph weaves a bit, as if he's had a drink. Swaying like a tree about to be felled. I can't breathe. All the strength drains out of me; I'm nothing more than paper gummed loosely together, a badly bound book; I'm ready to fall to pieces and be ground underfoot like the tuppence sheets. Last words of those who said nothing.

The hangman talks to the priest. The priest mutters to Joseph. Both men look at the sky, the priest for the succour of Christ, and Joseph for the sun.

Think of the summer, Joseph. Think of the first circus ring on the Fields and the way we used to let children ride on the back of the Herefordshire hog. Think of dancing. Think of walking all the way through Kent and the great houses where we showed Molly. Think of something astonishing. Let your mind race out to all the mysteries that you wanted answers to. Think that you'll know those answers. Imagine the eels racing each other's tails in the Surinam Sea, and the way you read out loud to me about coral reefs around Australis and said that you wanted to see them. Think of those colours while you look at the sun. You aren't here at all, Joseph. All of this is a dream. You're in the Southern Ocean, and maybe it's bright and shining there, and maybe it's a night sky with all the stars tipped upside-down.

'Look, Becca,' Clift says.

He's pointing at the scaffold. Joseph has gone.

I never heard him. I never heard the savage crack of the rope.

'Where is he?'

'Gone back inside.'

I grab Clift's arm. 'Gone back? Why?'

Clift is smiling at me. 'If you'd opened your eyes,' he says, 'you'd have seen them holding the paper up.'

I stare at him blankly.

'The paper, Rebecca.' He laughs. 'You did it. It was the king's reprieve.'

# 32

JOHN HUNTER

I have never travelled the west coast of England before.

It is a tedious journey beyond Liverpool, and one that has taken a day and a half to progress north from the great port. The time has given me an opportunity to reflect. It is spring, and I don't remember a lovelier season. The city gives little scope for beauty, and a man who has spent his life dissecting thousands and paid the resurrectionists and bartered at Tyburn for bodies, may never have the inclination for gazing on a blossom tree.

There are plenty here, however. Apple orchards and such. Cherry trees. We trundle along farm tracks and through villages that are merely a scrape in the fields and everywhere is green of the freshest colour. I am a long way from home and there is still further to go.

Gradually, the land begins to rise. I see the mountains ahead, but we are not going to the mountains despite how many poets may rhapsodise about them. We traverse instead a great shallow bay and almost turn back on ourselves until we run parallel to mud flats with the mountains at our back. The breeze blows sharp along the estuary. It is late afternoon.

The carriage stops when the lane ends. There is still a fair distance to walk. I am assured by the driver that the cottage is on the hillside and overlooks the bay, and although I am not necessarily pleased by the news that there is still farther to travel, I climb a path to my left.

The people I am going to meet have presented me with a great conundrum. I am not speaking about the boy, miraculous as he is. I am speaking of a principle for which science has no explanation at all.

When a body becomes excited, the eyes dilate, the heart beats faster, and the skin may become clammy. I have observed various fluctuations in the state, even observing that a pulse might be faintly detected after death if only for a few moments, perhaps driven by the terrifying prospect that had laid before the person who was to be executed. I have carried out amputations and found the subject to be quite alive at one moment and quite dead the next with the skin still warm and a flutter visible at the throat. Religious men say this is the moment of migration of the soul when it rises to heaven or is taken to the other place, but I have never once seen any evidence of movement outside the body.

A human being comprises of blood and bone and various humours, as surgeons were once pleased to call them. There is a brain, a complex instrument indeed, but it is only fibres and flesh like anything else. And so I can find no explanation at all for love. I can find no reason why a man might sacrifice himself for another, or a woman cling to her devotion with an extraordinary display of faith. These are things that have no place in the physical realm. There is no structure to be labelled.

Miracles do happen, however. Even in desperate circumstances the physical body may find a new route. With the permission of the king, I once operated on a stag at Richmond Park. I tied the carotid artery, which supplies blood to the antlers, and as expected the antlers soon grew cool to the touch.

And yet a week later when I visited the same animal, I found the antlers warm. The deer was killed and delivered to me, and upon excision I found the blood supply had bypassed the artery. Similarly, a human being may walk around with a broken back and seem not to feel the consequences. Nature will discover new paths despite every obstacle in some living creatures.

There is no doubt that the people I've come to see are such. Three years ago, the man suffered an apoplexy after being reprieved from the gallows. He endured for some time with a bad weakness in his left leg and hand, but to my surprise he recovered. I'm told that he is almost well now, and from a scientific point of view I'm intrigued to see it.

In the same fortnight, the woman hovered between life and death with a severe congestion of lungs and a high fever. The scientist within me claims a strength and inventiveness of the body such as that I witnessed in the stag. The fantasist in me tells me another story, however. Something beyond physicality made these two people live for each other.

As I walk, a small house becomes visible.

It is undoubtedly a picturesque place, in the finest meaning of the word. That is, it is framed in a way that painters like to copy. A garden before it, a kind of heathland or moorland behind. One long low building with no upper floor.

At the gate stands a man, but I don't recognise him at first. He is more stooped than I remember, and his hair has faded from its original fairness to a soft grey. Rather in my own fashion, he sports an unruly beard. Only when I get closer do I see the familiar expression of Joseph Eliot looking back at me, that inclination of interest that he always had even as a young man, a violent need to discover. Before I can reach him and shake his hand, a woman comes down the cottage path. She is smiling. There is no mistaking her identity because of the scars. She wears a yellow dress of sprigged muslin. Heavily advanced into her pregnancy, she is undoubtedly Rebecca Talland.

'A wonderful place,' I tell Eliot.

'The best on earth,' he replies.

Hard to believe that they are the same couple. Looking up at the house, I see a polished table in the hallway beyond the front door, a vase of flowers placed upon it. Curtains at the windows, and bright glass reflecting the sun. I see a carefully tended path and a copper beech hedge just beginning to come into leaf, and a wood store and stable all tidy and composed.

This is not the couple who led a great prehistoric beast across Kent, or slept on the ground, or ran a fair on Tottenham Fields and shovelled snow every winter. They are not the couple that forged great panoramas out of paint and candle grease and gunpowder resin. They are not the ones who dragged cages before crowds.

'No animals?' I ask.

'We used to have an aviary, but not for long,' Joseph tells me. 'Parakeets and macaws.'

'Not now?'

'No,' he murmurs. 'I neglected to lock the door one evening.' And he gives me a slow, confiding wink.

They have an orchard and a small rough field to one side, and from there we can hear a dog barking. The boy comes running, his two hands cupped in front of him. I see no physical deficiencies, no shade of his past. He is a robust boy, all smiles. I've learned a lot about him through his letters and particularly his drawings. Mr Clift started as he has done, drawing with chalk on the flagstone floor of his mother's kitchen in Cornwall and progressing to the fine anatomical artist that he has become. The boy will soon go to Hawkshead, because there is a good school there. It is a small place though, and still mercifully far from the world.

'Mr Hunter,' the lad says breathlessly. He holds out his hands, opens them, and presents me with a butterfly. A butterfly that doesn't stir from his palm but instead tries its wings in a leisurely fashion. He prods it gently with a fingertip.

'It's a fritillary,' he tells me.

'Very fine indeed.'

'And do you know what we have?' he asks, delighted. 'We have bees.'

Rebecca smiles. 'A man in the village has shown us how to keep beehives,' she says.

'No tygers?'

'No tygers.'

We turn, the four of us, and look out over the landscape.

A village church some way off tolls the hour. There's nothing else: no sound except a far distant murmuring that might belong to the changing of the sea tide as it rushes back along the bay and fills the view below with a dull pewter.

'And once we thought we had burned Eden,' Joseph says.

# ABOUT THE AUTHOR

Elizabeth Cooke is celebrating her fortieth year as a published author, with 18 novels, 2 non-fiction and 120 short stories. She also writes under the pen name E M Scott.

She lives on the Jurassic Coast in Dorset, UK.

# A NOTE FROM THE PUBLISHER

**Thank you for reading this book**. If you enjoyed it please do consider leaving a review on Amazon to help others find it too.

**We hate typos**. All of our books have been rigorously edited and proofread, but sometimes mistakes do slip through. If you have spotted a typo, please do let us know and we can get it amended within hours.

**info@bloodhoundbooks.com**

www.ingramcontent.com/pod-product-compliance
Lightning Source LLC
Chambersburg PA
CBHW050600190726
48283CB00007B/2222